**Praise for
LuAnn McLane**

Dark Roots and Cowboy Boots

"This kudzu-covered love story is as hot as Texas Pete, and more fun than a county fair."
—Karin Gillespie, author of *Dollar Daze*

"An endearing, sexy, romantic romp that sparkles with Southern charm!"
—Julia London, author of *Extreme Bachelor*

"Charmingly entertaining . . . a truly pleasurable read."
—*Romantic Times*

"A hoot! The pages fly in this sexy, hilarious romp."
—Romance Reviews Today

Wild Ride

"A collection of sensual, touching stories . . . *Wild Ride* is exactly that—a thrilling, exhilarating sensual ride. I implore you to jump right in and hold on tight!"
—A Romance Review

"Amusing, lighthearted contemporary romances starring likable protagonists."
—The Best Reviews

continued . . .

DANCING SHOES AND HONKY-TONK BLUES

LuAnn McLane

A SIGNET ECLIPSE BOOK

SIGNET ECLIPSE
Published by New American Library, a division of
Penguin Group (USA) Inc., 375 Hudson Street,
New York, New York 10014, USA
Penguin Group (Canada), 90 Eglinton Avenue East, Suite 700, Toronto,
Ontario M4P 2Y3, Canada (a division of Pearson Penguin Canada Inc.)
Penguin Books Ltd., 80 Strand, London WC2R 0RL, England
Penguin Ireland, 25 St. Stephen's Green, Dublin 2,
Ireland (a division of Penguin Books Ltd.)
Penguin Group (Australia), 250 Camberwell Road, Camberwell, Victoria 3124,
Australia (a division of Pearson Australia Group Pty. Ltd.)
Penguin Books India Pvt. Ltd., 11 Community Centre, Panchsheel Park,
New Delhi - 110 017, India
Penguin Group (NZ), 67 Apollo Bay, Mairangi Bay,
Auckland 1311, New Zealand (a division of Pearson New Zealand Ltd.)
Penguin Books (South Africa) (Pty.) Ltd., 24 Sturdee Avenue,
Rosebank, Johannesburg 2196, South Africa

Penguin Books Ltd., Registered Offices:
80 Strand, London WC2R 0RL, England

First published by Signet Eclipse, an imprint of New American Library,
a division of Penguin Group (USA) Inc.

First Printing, May 2007
10 9 8 7 6 5 4 3 2 1

This book is for my beautiful daughter Cara.
May you always have love and laughter in your life.

ACKNOWLEDGMENTS

I would like to thank the dedicated readers on the ScampsVampsandSpicyRomance Yahoo loop. Your cheerful posts mean so very much to me.

Thanks to the Ohio Valley and Kentucky Romance Writers of America chapters for your support and promotion of the romance genre.

I would like to extend a very special thanks to my editor, Anne Bohner, for making this book happen. I'm so lucky to have an editor who understands my quirky sense of humor.

As always, thank you to my agent, Jenny Bent. Your encouragement and knowledge is highly valued and appreciated.

1

Reality Check

"Oh, come on, Jesse, you're joking, right?" I pause in my task of filling saltshakers and glance across the counter at my brother, who's wiping down the speckled green Formica. Mama's already gone home and we're buttoning up the diner for the night. "Who in their right mind would bring a ballroom dance competition to Misty Creek, Kentucky?"

Jesse gives me a sheepish look. "Um . . . well . . . Comedy Corner, maybe?"

"You mean the cable channel that you watch all the time?" I sputter and he opens his mouth to answer but I just keep right on talking. "The one that has that disgusting cartoon that Mama said you couldn't watch?"

"Give me a break, Abby. I'm eighteen. I watch whatever I want to."

I ignore this and continue. "The station that makes fun of *midgets*?"

"Little people," he corrects, "and they don't exactly make fun—"

"The same station that defames *the president of the United States of America*?" I slam down the salt container and narrow my eyes at my little brother . . . Well, at six feet two he's hardly little, but I'm six years older, so that still trumps his height advantage.

"Yes, Abby, and it's called political satire. Comedy Corner does parodies . . . spoofs on pop culture. Most of their stuff is pure genius."

Okay, so he's taller *and* smarter. Jesse belongs in a big, fancy college but although the diner we own pays the bills we don't have that kind of money. "Whatever." I wave my hand like I know all about political satire and whatnot. "So, explain to me how and why Comedy Corner is coming to Misty Creek of all places to do a ballroom dance competition."

"Well . . ." His sheepish look gets more pronounced and all of a sudden I get it.

"To poke fun of us!" I sputter. "Gee, what are they gonna call it? 'Dancing with the Rednecks'?" I'm joking but red heat creeps up his neck and I have to gasp. "My Gawd, I'm *right*?"

"It's more of a spoof on reality TV, Abby, not rednecks. Where's your sense of humor? You laugh at Jeff Foxworthy and *he* makes fun of rednecks."

"He's one of us. That's different." I point at him. "Jesse William Harper, did *you* somehow have something to do with this?"

He runs his fingers through his dark blond hair that would be the same color as mine if I didn't get mine highlighted.

"Well?" I demand, nearly shouting. Jesse is such a hardworking, good kid that Mama and I rarely raise our voices to him, but I'm getting a prickly feeling running down my spine about this whole thing, so I want to know what's going on. "What's this ballroom dancing competition all about and just how are you involved?"

He takes a deep breath and jams his hands in his jeans

pockets. "Well, a few weeks ago I was surfing the Comedy Corner Web site and I read about the ballroom dance competition spoof that they were going to do. There was a place where you could type in an essay on why your hometown would be the best location for the show and, well . . ." He pauses and then finishes in a rush. "I suggested Misty Creek."

I put my hands to my chest. "How could you *do* such a thing? Why would you want them to come here and make fun of us?"

"Come on, Abby, think about it." Jesse slices his hand through the air in the direction of the big picture window overlooking Main Street. "Misty Creek has been like a ghost town lately. Business is suffering in all of the antique and craft shops. The inns are practically empty. Our traffic here has been off too, and you damned well know it."

"Watch your language!"

He rolls his eyes.

"This is the slow time of the year. Business will pick up when the weather gets warmer," I protest even though the lack of customers *has* been a real cause of concern lately.

Jesse shakes his head. "With the insane price of gas people aren't gonna take day trips like they used to. We need a reason for people to come here other than shoppin' and stayin' at bed-and-breakfast inns. Havin' this show filmed here could be the shot in the arm that Misty Creek needs."

I know he's right but I stubbornly remain silent and cross my arms over my chest.

"Abby, this show could put Misty Creek on the map. People will flock here if it's a hit and I think it will be."

"Yeah, but at our expense. I'm proud of this little town and I don't relish being laughed at," I tell Jesse in an uppity tone that's not like me at all. Being laughed at is something I'm no stranger to, so this is hitting close to home. As I start to screw the silver caps back onto the saltshakers I mutter, "Dancing with the rednecks . . . just who would even try out for such a thing?"

I glance up from my task and see guilt written all over his handsome face. Yes, Jesse is quite a hottie with his shaggy blond hair and deep blue eyes even though he has yet to realize it since he's such a nerd. Just this past year he's filled out from the tall and gangly proportions that had plagued him all of his life and let me tell ya, the girls have noticed. His tousled hair and chin stubble are from lack of caring rather than a concerted effort to sport the Keith Urban scruffy look. He just doesn't *get it* that the giggling girls who stop in the diner after school for Cherry Cokes and chili cheese fries are mostly here to see *him*.

I too grew up being all knees and elbows, hating my long legs that made me tower over boys like the Jolly Green Giant. But now those same boys are men and tend to give me the once-over every time they come in for the blue plate special. *Jackasses*. Where were they on prom night? But I digress. Right now all I want to know is why Jesse looks so damned guilty. "There's more to this story, isn't there?"

Jesse puts his palms up in a *whoa there* position and gives me a level look. "Now, just keep your cool and hear me out."

Of course that's the kind of statement that makes a woman immediately *lose* her cool but I take a deep breath and say as calmly as possible, which is not calm at all, "Tell me what the hell's goin' on here!"

"Well, after Comedy Corner showed interest in my essay, they e-mailed me this form that asked for names of potential contestants."

"Go on."

"See, they wanted six men and six women representing . . . *ah*, various walks of small-town life. I had to provide names of these certain individuals to help them narrow the field since they want to get this show on the air right away. For instance, they wanted a farmer and I suggested Travis Tucker."

"To ballroom dance?" I squeak. "No . . ."

Jesse nods. "And they wanted a truck driver. Mac Murphy came to mind."

I'm trying to picture three-hundred-pound Mac Murphy doing the tango and I have to chuckle. My mirth encourages Jesse and he smiles. "See, you're catching on to the concept. It'll be a riot. They wanted a high school lunch lady and I suggested Betty Cook."

"Olive Oyl?" We call her that because she looks just like the cartoon character. I try not to snicker. "Who else?"

He hesitates but then says, "Julia Mayer."

"Why *her*?" My good humor evaporates like rain on a summer sidewalk. Julia Mayer is one of the few people in Misty Creek that I don't like. She was Miss Popularity back in high school, homecoming queen and all that, and never gave me the time of day. Although . . . the thought of her being ridiculed by some snarky judge in front of millions of people does have a certain appeal. "Well?"

Jesse shrugs. "They needed a hairdresser. She may actually be kind of good."

I narrow my eyes at him. "Fat chance."

"Why do you hate her so much?"

I angle my head and tell him firmly, "I don't *hate* her. Although she did steal my boyfriend in high school."

"I don't remember you having a boyfriend."

Details, details. I feel heat creep into my cheeks. "Okay, *potential* boyfriend. I was making huge strides with Danny Becker when Julia up and snatched him away from me."

Jesse swallows and gives me a look that I don't like. "You mean Danny Becker the mechanic?"

I roll my eyes. "How many other Danny Beckers are there in Misty Creek? Of course I mean him. *Ohmigod*, is he part of the competition?"

When Jesse nods I have to snicker once more. Seeing Danny taken down a peg or two would suit me just fine, too. My major crush on him in high school went unnoticed because his sights were set on petite and perky Julia Mayer instead of tall and dorky me. Of course just last week I gave him a little bit of payback for snubbing me when I was a teenager. I had my Ford Ranger in at Becker's Garage for a lube job and when Danny was coming on to me like gangbusters I ignored his flirtatious comments even though I secretly wanted to flirt back. My mama tells me that I have a bad habit of cutting off my nose to spite my face. While I know that she's right it's hard to get over my hellacious high school years.

" 'Dancing with the Rednecks' might be fun after all," I admit and chuckle again. I expect Jesse to laugh with me since I'm coming over to his way of thinking, but he blinks for a second like he's trying to think of how to word something so that I won't freak. "You're fixin' to tell me something that I won't like, aren't you? Ohmigod, did you enter *Mama* into this farce?"

"No . . ." he says slowly but then clears his throat, which is a telltale sign for Jesse. He's chock-full of telltale signs, which is why I always beat him at poker.

"What, then?" I prod, but then it hits me like a ton of bricks. While shaking my head I point at Jesse. "No . . . *No*. Tell me you did *not* give them my name!"

"They needed a waitress, Abby!"

"I won't agree to do it! I refuse to humiliate myself on

national television! *Do you hear me?*" I'm on the balls of my feet shouting, so he doesn't have to answer that particular question. "No way! I won't, I won't, I *won't*. My God, you know I have two left feet. I would suck . . . *suck*! There's nothin' you could say to make me do this. Not one thing!"

"How about a fifty-thousand-dollar first prize?"

"Whoowee, shut my mouth!" I blink at him. "Except for maybe that." I continue to blink dollar signs at him while cha-chinging is ringing in my head. "Fifty. *Thousand*. Dollars?"

With raised eyebrows, Jesse nods. "Yeah."

"Wow." I'm still cha-chinging.

"I know." He's still nodding. "Think of what we could do with that kind of money."

"Yeah . . ." I respond breathlessly, placing my palms on the cool countertop. But then reality slaps me right upside the head. "I'm a horrible dancer, Jesse. There's no way I could win a ballroom dancing competition no matter how good my instructor might be."

"Come on, did you hear some of the names I threw out there? Besides, you're a hard worker and a quick learner, Abby. You can do this."

"Ah, so you think that I could be the best of the worst?" My voice is dripping with sarcasm.

"Something like that," he responds with a grin.

I'm not so sure but I don't want to burst his bubble. "Are these people really going to compete? Has Comedy Corner decided that Misty Creek will be the location? Where would all of the people stay? All we have are bed-and-breakfasts—"

Jesse puts up his hands again. "Whoa there, motor mouth. One question at a time."

"Okay, first tell me, is this a sure thing?"

"Not definitively until today."

Now, what teenager uses words like *definitively*? Jesse has been using fifty-cent words since he was a little kid. It occurs to me that winning this money could send him to a fine college that he deserves. "Why today?"

"Well . . ." He starts wiping down the already clean counter so as to avoid looking directly at me. Not a good sign . . .

"Jesse . . ." I say his name in a low-octave voice of warning that used to get his immediate attention. It has little to no effect now but I'm desperate.

"Well, I've sort of been showing a couple of big-shot producers from Comedy Corner around Misty Creek for the past week."

"What?" I squeak two octaves higher and a lot louder. "Why didn't you tell me about all of this?"

He shrugs. "I guess I didn't think it was really going to happen so I didn't want to get you all wound up for nothin'. Comedy Corner had to go through some red tape to get city permits to do the filming and take care of some other legal stuff."

"But it's a done deal?"

He nods. "Yep. They've rented out Rabbit Run Hunting Lodge. The whole doggone thing. Nothing is in season right now so it was just sitting there empty and there's plenty of room. The actual dance competition will be filmed live every Saturday night at the Bluegrass Dance Hall."

"Have all of your suggested contestants signed on to do the show?"

"Except for you. I asked them to wait to approach you since I thought it might take a bit of convincing. Are you willing, Abby?"

I look around the diner that could use some serious updating. I think of my mama, who has worked her fingers to the bone providing for us after my daddy died in a tragic farm-related accident twelve years ago. Without asking for a lick of help she sold the farm to get us out of debt and bought this diner. Yeah, I could send her to a fancy spa for some much-deserved pampering. I think of my old truck that coughs and sputters . . . man, how nice would it be to get a brand-spanking-new pickup with all the trimmings? But most of all I think of my little brother, who deserves the best education that money can buy and who has never asked for a damned thing.

"I'll do it."

"Woohoo!" He gives me a very un-Jesse-like whoop and a double knuckle-bump that nearly knocks me over. It's great to see my laid-back brother so revved up and I'm feeling pretty excited too; but in the back of my head I'm wondering what the hell I just got myself into. While my brain is still trying to wrap itself around this whole thing Jesse is already dialing up someone on his cell phone.

"Well?" I ask when he finally finishes his conversation and hangs up.

"Mitchell Banks, the head producer, wants to meet with you at nine o'clock tomorrow."

"That's during the breakfast shift, Jesse!"

"Yes, and he'll eat breakfast here," Jesse says patiently. "He just wants to meet you and probably have you sign some paperwork. No big deal, Abby. You can sit a spell with him. Mama won't mind."

All of a sudden another thought occurs to me. "What will happen when the show starts? Who will help Mama out?"

Jesse takes a step toward me and puts his hands on my shoulders. "Norma can come in early and I'll work extra hours."

"No! Not with your class schedule! School comes first, Jesse."

"I've got school under control," he assures me with a gentle squeeze. "My classes are easy. And if business picks up we'll hire another waitress. Don't worry, I won't let Mama overdo it in your absence."

I inhale a shaky breath but nod. "Okay. This is just all so unexpected, ya know?"

Jesse grins. "Yeah. It's about time we had some excitement here in Misty Creek. Things have been rather mundane lately."

I *think* mundane means ordinary, so I nod. "When are you gonna tell Mama? Tonight when you get home?"

He takes a step back. "I already have."

"And she was okay with it? I mean, what if—"

"Abby, stop!"

I'm so surprised by his outburst that I actually quit talking.

Jesse closes his eyes briefly and swallows before saying, "Listen, Mama and I both appreciate all of the time that you've put in here at the diner."

"Well, *yeah*, it's our livelihood." I'm not sure where he's going with this but it's making me feel uncomfortable. "Almost sounds like you're firing me," I tell him with a laugh.

"Well, you could certainly use a sabbatical."

This makes me frown at him.

"A break, Abby."

"I *know* what sabbatical means," I hotly assure him with a little head bop . . . and I *do*, in theory anyway. "So, you and Mama have been discussing the state of my *mundane* existence?" I cross my arms over my chest and tap my rubber-soled shoe on the floor.

"Ironically, yes, even before this competition was a reality. Let's face it, Abby. You've been in a rut. It's high time you shook things up a bit and this ballroom competition is the perfect solution."

"Tell me how you really feel, Jesse. Don't hold back." I say this in a joking manner but he doesn't laugh.

"You deserve a break."

"We all work hard."

He nods. "Yeah, but, Abby, you work too damned much. Listen, as much as I want you to win the money, promise me that you'll have fun with this. If you win, then *sweet*, but use this as an opportunity to chill . . . have a few laughs, okay? Don't obsess over winning."

"Right. . . ." I draw out the word with a shake of my head. "With fifty *thousand* dollars on the line I'll just kick back and chill."

He grins and gives my shoulder a gentle shove. "Okay, you can obsess a little."

I shove him right back and then tell him, "Go on home. I'll finish up here."

Jesse's grin fades and he gives me one of his usual serious expressions. "Do you have any idea how many times you've said that to me?"

My throat sort of closes up but I give him a casual shrug. "Go on . . . get outta here," I gruffly tell him and give him another shove. I watch him walk out the door all big and grown-up but still my baby brother. I would do anything for him, I think to myself as I grab the broom and begin sweeping, but then I stop in my tracks and lean against the handle. "Me, ballroom dancing on national television? Oh, Lord have mercy."

2

All Shook Up

I wake up the next morning in my little apartment above the diner at five thirty on the dot just like I normally do. After I pad across the cool hardwood floor to my bathroom, I attempt to wake myself up with a hot shower and strawberry-scented shampoo. I'm humming a Dierks Bentley tune and squishing my fingers through the warm suds in my hair when I suddenly remember that this *isn't* a normal day. My eyes and mouth pop open at the thought, causing some major blinking and sputtering . . . strawberry shampoo does *not* taste as good as it smells. Good God Almighty, in just a few hours the Comedy Corner guy is going to sign me up for the ballroom dancing show! I decide that I had better shave my legs and armpits even though they don't really need it and I manage to cut myself twice since my mind is preoccupied with nervous excitement.

Usually, I pull my hair back into a ponytail and apply a minimal amount of makeup for work but today I take some serious pains with my appearance. I go the whole nine yards with eyeliner and three shades of brown eye shadow. I even use the eyelash curler even though that contraption sort of scares me . . . always think I might squeeze too hard and chop off my eyelashes. Although I really want to do something nice with my hair I decide to go with the ponytail because of my waitress duties. People don't take too kindly to having hair in their food.

After taking a deep breath I frown at my reflection in the bathroom mirror looking for something to pluck or slick down, but I'm about as polished as I can get. Even though pretty soon I'll smell like a walking French fry I decide to splurge with a liberal spray of White Shoulders perfume but then I wrinkle my nose at my uniform wishing that I could wear something more flattering. It's the old-fashioned white button-up style with the hankie pointing up out of the top pocket. Mama likes to keep a retro look in the diner for the tourists and even though it's kind of dorky I usually don't mind. Besides, if they don't like it, well, they can kiss my grits!

"Oh, crap, it's getting late," I mutter after checking my watch. While the lunch and dinner crowd has been down due to lack of tourism, breakfast is still busy with locals. As I hurry down the back steps that lead to the kitchen I can hear Mama attempting to joke with Pete Jenkins, the crusty old cook who looks as old as dirt because of his two-pack-a-day habit. While Pete might be on the grumpy side, he bakes light-as-a-feather biscuits that melt in your mouth. His bacon is always crisp, his eggs fluffy, and his grits creamy so we put up with his sour disposition. Once in a blue moon Mama can coax him into a creaky, wheezing fit of laughter, but not often.

The heavenly scent of freshly perked coffee fills my nose, making me crave a cup. Starting the morning brew is my job and I hate being late for anything, especially work, so I feel a little guilty as I enter the kitchen. Pete's face is actually crinkled up in a smile from something my mama just said, but when they look up and see me they both straighten up and stop talking, meaning that I'm the topic of conversation. This has been happening a lot lately and I can't say that I like it.

Mama frowns at me. "Babycakes, why are you dressed like that?"

I glance down at my uniform expecting to see a ketchup stain or something. Mama won't tolerate anything but a pristine white uniform . . . not an easy task in my line of work, not to mention that I'm a bit on the clumsy side. "What do you mean?"

"You're in your uniform and that fancy television man is coming."

"Mama, I'm still gonna work."

"Well, I suppose." She purses lips that are lined and glossed a deep red and it strikes me how impeccably groomed Mama is even at this early hour of the morning. Her very big auburn hair is tamed into a classy French twist that's tight in the back but puffy on top. She looks as fresh as a daisy when most people are still rubbing sleep from their eyes. How she does it, I'll never know. She frowns at me and says, "I just wish we could dress y'all up a bit."

"I'm fine like this. After all, Jesse said that they wanted a waitress for the show and, well, here I am." With my palms up I do a little spin in a circle that ends in a wobble.

"Sure ain't no dancer," Pete points out with a little wheezing chuckle.

"I will have professional instruction," I remind him and would have given him an unladylike gesture if Mama hadn't been standing right there. *No*, I'm not giving him the finger . . . I'm too well raised for that! But I'm not above sticking out my tongue.

"We'll see about that," Mama tells Pete a bit sharply

while she arches one perfectly plucked eyebrow, shutting him right up.

Dang, I wish I were as put together as my mother. In a little while I'll be blowing loose locks of hair out of my face while waiting tables, but Mama will somehow remain stain-free, sweat-free, and with each and every strand of her hair swept back from her fine-boned face. Although Mama is soft-spoken and tiny she's a steel magnolia through and through, capable of both southern charm and intense intimidation. To put it simply: don't mess with my mama.

"You'll do just fine," Mama assures me as she slices open a box of coffee creamers with a razorblade knife. I was removed from this particular task after a couple of misfortunate mishaps requiring stitches. "With those long legs you're built to be a dancer, Abilene. Not only that but you're a hard worker and a quick learner. You just might surprise yourself." She gives me a warm smile and then turns around to get the small bowls for the creamers.

Pete snorts and since Mama has her back to me I resort to sticking out my tongue and he chuckles. Okay, so I'm not the most graceful of people. Jesse and I both inherited our daddy's height and I've always had longer arms and legs than I've known what to do with. The locals know this and hold on to their water glasses and coffee cups when I serve them. Mama's right, though, that I am a hard worker and a quick study. I just hope that my dance partner has a lot of patience . . . and a healthy sense of humor.

I'm taking the tray of saltshakers around to the tables when the first customers come in. Of course as luck would have it we're extra busy on the one and only day when I'm wishing for a lighter morning rush. When I see Mama pouring a steaming cup of coffee to a distinguished-looking man with slate-gray hair, tanned skin, and perfect teeth I gather that it's Mitchell Banks from Comedy Corner. He's wearing a soft-looking dark blue sweater with a starched collar peeking out of the neck, neatly pressed gray slacks, and shiny brown loafers with tassels, making him stand out from all of the truckers, construction workers, farmers, and a smattering of tourists. Quite frankly, I was expecting someone young and California hip, not some older gentleman who appears to be . . . *flirting with my mama* . . .

And she appears to be flirting right back! "Well, I'll be a monkey's uncle," I whisper. Clutched in one hand is her coffeepot and her other hand is waving in the air in an animated fashion while she chats. Now, don't get me wrong, my mother is a fine-looking woman and in my opinion doesn't look her age of forty-eight years. She gets hit on all the time, but in the twelve years since my daddy's passing I have never even seen her glance twice at another man . . . until now. One might think that she might be kissing up but my mother's not like that at all. When she turns and motions to me I realize that I'm standing in the middle of the diner gawking at them. Taking a deep breath, I walk over to the booth and paste a smile on my face.

"Abilene, I'd like you to meet Mitchell Banks from Comedy Corner."

I grasp his hand when he politely stands up. "How do you do?" His handshake is firm and he gives me a warm smile, making me relax a bit. His eyes are a gorgeous shade of light blue accentuated by his deep tan and I can see why my mother is smitten.

He gestures to the bench seat that's cracked and patched with duct tape, reminding me how important this interview really is. "Please join me, Abilene."

"I'll leave you two to discuss your business," my mother tells him. "Nice to meet you, Mr. Banks."

"My pleasure," he responds in a deep voice that has Mama all a-flutter. She blushes a pretty shade of pink that makes her appear young and sort of . . . wistful. My throat closes up when it occurs to me that my mother has been such a rock for Jesse and me and deserves to enjoy the softer, sweeter side of life.

As I slide into the cool vinyl seat, I notice that Mitchell Banks watches Mama walk away from the table, not in a leering kind of way, but with male appreciation. What makes me smile, though, is that my mother has just a hint of sway in her hips that I've never noticed before. "So, Mr. Banks, tell me about this ballroom dancing competition."

"You can call me Mitch," he says before taking a sip of his coffee. "Wow, this is good." He seems surprised, making me guess that fancy Starbucks is his usual choice.

"We use one hundred percent Colombian beans, real cream, butter, and fresh eggs here at Sadie's Diner," I inform him with a measure of pride. "Mama is a firm believer in using the real thing. She never cuts corners or sacrifices quality in order to turn a profit."

"Smart woman," he says with a smile.

I give him a serious nod but I'm feeling a bit foolish about my little speech. I'm not quite sure why I just told him all that other than the fact that I still don't really like that Misty Creek is going to be made fun of.

"You're proud of this town, aren't you?"

"Yes, I am," I admit to him even though I'm not sure where he's going with this.

"And you're not too keen on being laughed at."

With a slight hesitation, I nod again, realizing that I may have just given the wrong answer.

"But the chance of winning fifty thousand dollars is too good to pass up."

Feeling the color rise in my cheeks I give him an honest nod of my head.

"Do you ever watch Comedy Corner, Abilene?"

Crap. "I don't get the opportunity to watch much TV," I tell him, which is pretty much true. I decide to leave out the part about not liking or understanding some of the shows. "My brother is a big fan, though," I quickly add, trying to remember some of the buzzwords Jesse used yesterday. *Oh yeah . . .* "He enjoys the political satire and the . . . *um* . . . parodies and spoofs on pop culture." I give him a serious frown and lean forward to show my sincerity. I notice that his lips twitch and I wonder if I pronounced one of the words wrong . . . I do that sometimes. "Did I say something amusing?" I ask but then almost clamp my hand over my big-ass mouth. Oh, *why* did I have to go and say that?

"No, not at all," he assures me smoothly with a smile that makes his eyes crinkle. "I'm just enjoying your southern drawl. I love how you give words extra syllables."

"I do?"

He chuckles. "You doo-oo."

"Yankees love makin' fun of how we talk," I say with a sigh. "They think that having an accent means that you're stupid."

He takes another sip of his coffee and then says, "I'm not making fun, Abilene. I'm enjoying it. There's a big difference."

"Okay," I tell him with a shrug. "No offense taken."

"None intended. Listen, on Comedy Corner we poke fun at just about everything, sometimes just for laughs but more often than not to prove a point. *Dancing with the Rednecks* is supposed to be a spoof on reality television and how insane our culture has become. But you have to be willing to laugh at yourself, too."

"I understand." I want to tell him that I'm no stranger to being laughed at but I don't.

He rubs his index finger over the rim of the coffee mug

and looks at me thoughtfully. "But while we're poking fun at reality shows, this in effect *is* one . . . unscripted, so who knows what might happen? Sure, there will be humor but . . ." He shakes his head. "Then again you might be better than anticipated and show the audience a thing or two about Misty Creek, Kentucky. You just never know . . ."

Oh, I *know* all right that we're gonna suck, but I give him a serious nod like I'm buying into his scenario. I suddenly picture Travis Tucker or Betty Cook twirling across the dance floor and have to swallow the laughter that bubbles up in my throat. Luckily he's unzipping a fancy-looking leather case so he misses the amusement that's nearly choking me.

"Here is a packet of information for you. Please read it over carefully. I'll need everything signed and returned to me within the next thirty-six hours. The dance instructors will be arriving any day now and we hope to start rehearsals by the weekend. We've had a crew at Rabbit Run Lodge stocking the kitchen and setting things up."

"Isn't this moving kinda fast?" My heart starts doing a tap dance in my chest.

"Yes, but we need to film this show while the whole ballroom dancing craze is still hot. Yesterday's news isn't funny." He gives me a level look with those amazing blue eyes. "You do want to do this, right, Abilene?"

"Yes!" I quickly nod. "Oh, and pul-ease call me Abby. Mama is the only one who calls me Abilene . . . well, unless Jesse's mad at me and does it just to get my goat."

He smiles at my unexpected candor. "Your brother is a talented young man. His essay had me laughing my head off."

"Really? Jesse's usually so . . . reserved."

"Well then, he's got a hidden talent. With a little polish I could see him going places in this business."

Wow, I think to myself. Who knew? Of course Mama and I've been so consumed with keeping this diner afloat that life has been passing us by . . . including Jesse's childhood. What a sobering thought.

"Are you okay, Abby?" He sets his coffee cup down and gives me a concerned look.

"I must admit that this is all a bit overwhelming, but why do you ask?"

"For a moment there, you looked as if you had the weight of the world on your shoulders."

I shrug but I'm a bit unnerved that this stranger is reading me so well.

"If you're worried about your mother, well, she seems like she can handle things in your absence." He reaches over and pats my hand. "This will be an adventure, Abby. Fun. *Exciting.* Soak it all up and enjoy yourself."

"Okay," I answer with a smile. Mitchell Banks has somehow managed to calm my nerves and get me looking forward to this crazy thing I've gotten myself involved in. I notice that his gaze has shifted from my face to over my shoulder, and sure enough my mother appears with a coffeepot that she handles like it's an extension of her hand.

"Would you like a refill, Mr. Banks?"

"Yes, please. Your coffee is delicious . . . smooth and rich. My compliments."

"Why, thank you kindly," she responds with a proud smile. "I would have refilled your cup earlier, mind you, but I didn't want to interrupt." She fills his cup with a flourish. "May I bring you breakfast? On the house, of course."

"That would be most excellent," he says with a wide smile that shows off perfect teeth. I must admit that he's pretty danged hot for an older dude. "But on two conditions."

Mama arches one elegant eyebrow. How she manages to be a southern belle while waiting tables is beyond me. "And what might those be?"

"One, that you call me Mitch. And two, that you allow me to pay for my meal."

Mama inclines her head. "I will call you *Mitch* but breakfast is on *me*. Now, just what would you like?"

I'm watching this exchange like it's a tennis match and the two of them have forgotten all about me.

"Is there something special that you would suggest?" His voice is a smooth rumble and my mother gives him a look that I swear could melt butter!

"The all-American breakfast is a popular choice. We make everything from scratch, even the hash browns."

"Does it come with grits?"

Mama's mouth curves into a big smile. "Do you like grits?"

He smiles right back. "Never had them but I enjoy trying new cuisine."

Mama chuckles. "Here at the diner we think of it as good ole down-home cookin'. Now, how would you like your eggs?"

"Over easy."

"Bacon, sausage, or ham?"

He frowns. "Um, do you have turkey bacon?"

Mama taps her pencil on her cheek. "Now, just how could you wrangle bacon from a turkey?" She gives him a wide-eyed look but he somehow gets that she's joking.

"Okay . . . *bacon*, please."

"Biscuits or toast?"

"Whole wheat toast."

"The biscuits are to die for."

"You're tempting me . . ."

"All that low-carb nonsense is a bunch of hoo-ha," Mama tells him with a wave of her hand. "We have customers who eat a *real* honest-to-goodness breakfast here each and every day and who will live to be a hundred. It's all about hard work and clean living."

Oh, Mama . . . why did you say that?

Her eyes widen and she looks like she wants to clamp her hand over her mouth. "Oh *my*, I didn't mean to imply that *you* don't work hard or live clean . . . I meant it as a general observation," Mama says quickly, but of course the damage has been done.

"So I'm a damned Yankee, huh?" Mitch says but then smiles. "No offense taken, Sadie. You're probably spot-on in your general observation, anyway."

"Spot-on?" Mama frowns at Mitchell and I notice that the color is high in her cheeks.

"Correct," he tells her.

"Oh," she says, nodding slowly. "Again, I meant no offense . . . sometimes my mouth just rattles on and on . . ."

Mitchell shrugs his wide shoulders. "I think we all have preconceptions . . . perhaps misconceptions or prejudices if you will about people and places that we're not familiar with. This show will be an eye-opener in many ways, I'm sure."

"So, will you be in town for the entire production?" I ask, thinking surely he has bigger fish to fry. I notice that my mother is itching to get back to her tables but looks at him expectantly.

Mitchell cradles his coffee mug for a moment as if making a decision and then says, "Yes, I believe I will. I had intended to leave when the director and the production crew arrives, but I'm beginning to think that I won't want to miss a moment of this . . . adventure." He glances at Mama and I have to wonder if he is entirely referring to the show.

"I do have to get back to work," Mama says with a

smile even though the breakfast crowd has cleared out. "It was so nice to make your acquaintance . . . Mitchell."

I know that he said to call him Mitch but Mama always calls people by their full name. He must get this, because he doesn't correct her.

"Likewise, Sadie. Perhaps we can have dinner one evening." He stands up and politely shakes her hand.

Mama quickly withdraws her hand from his grasp and places her palm against her throat. "Oh . . . I . . . I don't *know*." She glances at me.

"Mama, I think that it would be very hospitable of you to show Mr. Banks around our town." I shoot her a look that says that I'm fine with her having dinner with him and that it would be entirely proper.

As if sensing that Mama is a bit flustered, Mitch says, "No pressure. I'll stop in and we can talk." He reaches in his leather case and gives her a business card. "Or you can call me."

"Why, thank you," she says and takes the card but I know that I have a better chance of seeing pigs fly than my mama calling up a man for a date. "Now, I really must get back to work." She turns on her rubber-soled heel and hurries away.

Mitch takes a sip of coffee and then says, "I made your mother uncomfortable, didn't I?"

"Mmm, a little."

"It wasn't my intention."

"Oh, I think she knows that." I take a deep breath and then give him a slow smile while shaking my head. "Things are gonna get all shook-up around these parts, aren't they, Mr. Banks?"

"I think it's safe to say yes. Are you ready to get all shook-up, Abby Harper?"

Hell yeah. A little shiver of excitement ripples down my spine and I grab the edge of the table. Jesse was right when he said that my life was in a rut. Well, I'm about to climb right up out of my danged hole that I've dug for myself. I give him a grin that's a bit shaky around the edges. "I think it's safe to say . . . *yes*."

"Good. Read through the packet of information carefully," he tells me. "There will be an orientation meeting tonight up at the lodge, but you can move in early today if you want to get settled."

"Today?" About a thousand questions pop into my head but I don't even know where to begin so I just blink at him like a ninny.

"If you wish," he says with a nod. "Just make sure that you're there for orientation. The instructors will arrive the following afternoon."

"Good . . . *good*." I smile even though my stomach feels as if it's spinning like a top. "Well, I'd better start packing," I say and scoot from the booth. Of course, he politely stands up with me and we shake hands.

"See you tonight, Abby."

Since my voice suddenly escapes me I simply nod. I pass Mama, who is bringing a tray laden with the all-American breakfast. She has a smile on her face and color in her cheeks and I'm thinking that I might not be the only one getting all shook-up.

3

Movin' Out

As I stop for the last red light at the outskirts of Misty Creek I glance in the rearview mirror. It feels so weird to be heading away from town instead of working at the diner. I feel sort of guilty like I'm playing hooky or something. Although I had been prepared to finish out my shift, Mama had insisted that I go up to my apartment and pack. I had argued a bit but when Mama insists on something you might as well just give in, so I did. Not knowing all I might need, I had packed almost every article of clothing that I own and it's now sliding around in suitcases and duffel bags in the bed of my truck. Luckily, I have a cap on my old pickup because it looks as if it might rain or, heaven forbid, snow. Although it's late in February and we've had some recent mild weather teasing us that spring is around the corner, I know that in these here parts that can change with how the wind blows.

My old truck climbs the steep and winding road like an old horse, pausing to cough and sputter now and then just to let me know how hard she's working. Finally, I reach the top of the ridge where the tall pine trees are cleared for Rabbit Run Lodge. While I've never been up here to hunt, the lodge doubles for summer camp in June and July and I spent many weeks up here as a kid so I know the layout and surrounding area very well. While other kids went to soccer or basketball or cheerleading camp, I was content to come here to make macaroni necklaces and crafts that always ended up becoming an ashtray and to sing silly songs around the campfire. Yes, I was a geek, not an athlete, and that has me completely worried I will never be able to master the complicated steps in ballroom dancing. I can't even remember country line-dancing routines.

Pushing that frightening thought from my mind, I park my truck near the entrance to the big A-frame structure. Weathered and rustic, the lodge blends into the woods like it simply sprang up from the ground. Two wings are attached to the main building and I remember that there's a huge deck off the back overlooking rolling hills and a deep valley below. To the left is a fishing lake where I used to swim and canoe when camping here as a kid. I lean against the steering wheel taking it all in and thinking that never in a million years would I have guessed that I would be coming to Rabbit Run Lodge to learn ballroom dancing for a reality TV show. "Life is pretty danged weird," I whisper.

Finally, I gather up the nerve to open my creaky door and step out of my truck. The cool breeze ruffles my hair and carries the scent of damp earth and pine. I inhale deeply, trying to clear my head and calm my nerves as I walk toward the entrance. A few other cars and trucks are here, so I guess that some of the other contestants have arrived as well.

But just when I've managed to calm myself down a tad with a little *you can do this* pep talk, I open the big double doors to the lodge and I have to stop dead in my tracks. It's as if I've entered a big beehive and there's a swarm of worker bees buzzing here, there, and everywhere. People are hanging huge lights, bringing in carts of food and skids of bottled water. The back of the A-frame building is the dining area and there's a crew polishing the hardwood floor with a big machine. Someone carrying a huge fresh flower arrangement bumps me from behind and after a hastily muttered apology hurries away. Orders are being shouted and even though it looks like utter chaos I'm guessing that the Rabbit Run Lodge will be totally transformed in short order.

"Wow," I say under my breath. I'm feeling like I'm in the way but at the same time going pretty much unnoticed by the workers. I'd dearly love to find my room, to unload my gear and read through the giant orientation booklet, but I have no idea who to approach. I'm looking around hoping to see Mitchell Banks when I spot none other than Julia Mayer. *She* doesn't have that deer in the headlights look that I'm sure I'm sporting. Oh no, she's got her sassy little cheerleader walk, big blond hair, and a bigger smile.

"Hey, Abby!" Julia gushes and hugs me like we're long-lost friends. "Isn't this excitin'?"

"Yes," I admit and give her a lukewarm smile. I've really got to get rid of this chip on my shoulder.

"Have you gotten your room yet? They're really, *really* nice." She leans in closer, totally invading my personal space. "I had a bowl of fruit, some fancy chocolates . . . Go-*di*-va, and some heavenly smellin' lotions." She waves her hands in front of my face. "Here . . . smell."

I don't want to smell but I take a polite, if very small, sniff and say primly, "Very nice." I want to know how she got the key to her room but it's hard to get a word in edgewise.

"I can't *wait* to learn to ballroom dance. Can you? It's so, *so* romantic. Can you imagine? In *Dancing with the*

Stars, they looked like they were floating on air." She sighs dramatically and I remember her doing multiple back flips and impressive round-offs across the gym floor. Jesse was right. Julia is going to be very good at this. I'm going to suck. Well, hell. She's blinking her big blue eyes at me and I realize that I haven't answered.

"Oh yes, I can imagine." I say this with a bit of a sarcastic bite but she doesn't get it. Oh, but *Lordy*, I *can* imagine and it makes me shudder. We have to step back out of the way when two guys push past us with a cartful of boxes.

"Wonder what's in that," Julia says and clasps her hands together. She gets on her tiptoes and angles her head to read what's printed on the side and then turns to me with a happy little gasp. "Oh, Abby, it's *dancing* shoes! Do you think they're for us?"

"That's a fair assumption," I tell her and somehow refrain from rolling my eyes. But I have to admit that her excitement is contagious and I'm thinking that maybe she isn't as bad as I remember in high school. I give her a genuine smile this time but take a step back when it looks as if she might hug me again. It's not that I'm opposed to hugging but I usually reserve my affection for family, friends, and a really hot guy if given the opportunity.

"Hey, girls," says a deep and sexy voice that will forever set my heart a-flutter. Of course I school my features into what I hope is nonchalance and turn to face Danny Becker.

"Hey there, Danny," Julia says and I fully expect Danny to fawn all over her but he gives her a brief nod and then smiles at *me*.

"How's your truck runnin', Abby?" he asks. "Make it up the mountain roads okay?"

"She was a little contrary, coughed and sputtered a bit, but made it okay."

"Good," he says rather close to my ear. I know that he's probably leaning in close because it's noisy but this feels a little flirtatious. "If she gives you any trouble just give me a holler and I'll give her a look." He gives me a wink and a grin and now there's no doubt that he's flirting. I flick Julia a glance under my lashes and since she's frowning I don't think that she likes this one bit.

Julia clears her throat, I suppose to get our attention, and says, "Are you excited about the competition, Danny? You always were *such* a good dancer." She gives me a look that I'm sure is to remind me that she knows this from personal experience.

Danny, though, just shrugs and doesn't give her the time of day and turns back to me. I want to feel superior about Danny's attention, thinking that this sort of turnabout is fair play, but my female radar tells me that there is something simmering beneath the surface.

"Well," Julia says with a breezy smile that seems a little forced, "I'm gonna head on up to my room and catch a nap. See y'all later."

"Okay," I tell Julia, and Danny gives her an absent nod. Suddenly it's just Danny Becker and me standing in the midst of the chaos.

"You want to get some fresh air?" Danny asks.

"Sure." I nod like I'm not at all nervous but of course I am. Being with Julia Mayer has me feeling like an awkward sixteen-year-old again. Danny grabs my hand (holy cow) and we weave our way through the crew until we're outside on the back deck.

"Wow, this is a great view," he comments as he looks out across the rolling hills dotted with pine trees.

"I've always loved it," I admit and take a deep breath of the fresh air. "It's even prettier when everything is all lush and green."

His dark eyebrows shoot up and he looks impressed. "You've been up here hunting?"

"Oh Lordy, no . . . summer camp. I was a nerd, Danny, not an athlete like you. Don't know why I let my brother talk me into doing this dance competition." I shake my head. "I have two left feet."

Danny glances down at my cowboy boots. "Doesn't look like it to me." His eyes meet mine. "And you sure don't look like a nerd."

"I was in high school but you probably don't remember that."

He leans back against the railing and then says, "Let me guess. I ignored you and you had a crush on me."

"Yeah, me and just about every other girl at Misty Creek High."

"Yeah, well, those glory days are long gone," he says dryly. "Instead of the hotshot hometown hero I'm just a mechanic. Sorry if I was an ass to you in high school. I was pretty danged full of myself, but I was just a big fish in a small pond."

Suddenly some of the pieces start to fall into place and it ticks me off. "Don't even tell me . . ." I narrow my eyes at him.

"What?"

I grip the railing next to him. "That you believe you're not good enough for Julia Mayer anymore."

"Now, what makes you think somethin' like that?" he scoffs with a wave of his hand but his gaze shifts from mine. Just then the breeze kicks up and ruffles his hair, making him look younger and almost vulnerable. Intuition tells me that I just hit the nail on the head.

"I can read between the lines, Danny. There was something going on between you two. I think you just might have been tryin' to make her jealous by flirtin' with me."

"Oh, come on . . ." he says with another wave of his

hand but there's a little color on his cheeks that tells me I'm on to him. "I was flirtin' with you 'cause you're a pretty woman, Abby." Then he frowns and says, "But you sure made it clear down at the shop that I didn't have a chance. Was it the grease on my hands?"

"You gotta be kiddin' me," I sputter hotly but he gives me a level look that says he's dead serious. "Okay, to tell you the truth, I was givin' you the cold shoulder because . . . oh, this is stupid . . . *because* you didn't even know my name back in school when I would have swooned if you had just said *hello*."

He gives me a grin. "Ah . . . so a little payback."

"Yeah, well, somethin' like that. But let me make it crystal clear that a hardworkin' man is damned appealing in my book."

His grin deepens, showing a cute dimple in his cheek. "And sexy?"

"That too," I assure him but feel heat creep into my cheeks. I hope he thinks it's just the cool breeze making my face pink.

"See, I'm hittin' on you and Julia is nowhere in sight, Abby."

"Yeah, but you're thinkin' about her. She's the one you want, not me. Admit it."

Danny shrugs his wide shoulders and gives me a look that has me almost swallowing my gum. "Maybe . . . maybe *not*."

"You two were joined at the hip in high school. Prom King and Queen. Y'all were the perfect couple. What happened, if I'm not bein' too nosy?"

He pauses for a moment and then sighs. "Everyone thought I was going to go on with a football career at some fancy college but I was just too small. Nobody would give me a serious look. I thought about walking on to a Division Two school but my family didn't have the money for college and I sure didn't have the grades for an academic scholarship. Julia suddenly decided that we should date other people and I chalked it up to the fact that I was no longer good enough for her. The damned woman has always been high maintenance and wanted a college frat boy on her arm. I felt like I couldn't compete."

"She's a hairdresser, Danny. We're all hardworkin' small-town folks. Nothin' wrong with that!"

"Damned straight," he says with a grin and gives me a knuckle bump.

"She seems to want you back now."

He sighs and then says, "Yeah, well, I guess I have a big chip on my shoulder about the whole thing."

"So you're making her squirm a little."

He looks out over the hills for a minute and then turns his gaze back to me. "Maybe that's what I'm doin'," he admits with another shrug. "But I don't want a woman who . . . what do you girls call it?"

I frown for a moment and then ask, "You mean settle?"

"Yeah." He looks serious for a minute but then gives me a lopsided grin and says, "I ain't as good as I once was."

I shake my head and chuckle while thinking that Danny Becker still sets my panties on fire. But I'm not about to go mooning over a guy who is smitten with someone else. Been there, done that, got the T-shirt. The air is damp and chill, making me shiver even though I'm wearing a jean jacket with a turtleneck sweater underneath.

"I'm sorry, Abby. I've kept you out here in the cold jawing your ear off. Why didn't you just tell me to shut up?"

A lock of his hair falls over his forehead, and his eyes are as blue as a cloudless summer sky and I'm thinking that Julia Mayer is a dumb-ass.

"What's that look for, Abby? What's on your mind?"

"You wanna know the truth?"

He nods.

"Julia is a dumb-ass."

He throws his head back and laughs. "I could just kiss you for that."

I must be looking at him like a bear lookin' at honey, because his blue eyes darken and he goes real silent. He steps a little closer and like a little hussy I close the rest of the gap and Lord knows where this nerve came from, and my mama would box my ears, but I pull him close and whisper, "Then do it, Danny Becker."

Danny's gaze lowers and then lingers on my mouth, making me swallow. When he lightly traces my bottom lip with his fingertip my eyelids feel heavy and flutter shut. A heartbeat goes by and *then* I feel the slight pressure of his mouth on mine. His lips are warm . . . just slightly moist and oh so soft. The very tip of his tongue touches mine, sending a slow tingle all the way to my toes. Tender and sweet, it's over all too soon, leaving me a bit breathless and wanting more.

Danny pulls back a fraction and grins at me. "Maybe we should just forget all about high school and start from here."

"Oh, high school isn't somethin' I want to relive, believe me," I tell him with a shy nod. He laughs, thinking that I'm joking, and I let him think that I am but in reality I'm dead serious. I also remember the wistful longing in his eyes while he was looking at Julia, so I'm not convinced that he's over her.

"What?" Danny asks, angling his head. "You've got that look on your face again like you think you know somethin'."

I'm thinking that he kissed me out of curiosity or maybe in an effort to get his mind off of Julia Mayer, but

I just give him what I hope is a saucy smile and say, "A girl's gotta have a few secrets."

"Yeah, well, I'll just have to make it my goal to find 'em out."

"That and winning the fifty grand, right? I think you have a good chance at it."

He cocks an eyebrow and says, "Man, winning the money and the girl . . . think I could be that lucky?"

"You are so full of it, Danny." I shove him on the shoulder.

"So I've been told. But hey, *remember* that this thing is a reality show and on the Comedy Corner Network of all things. It's safe to say that we can expect the unexpected. This might not be about who is the best dancer, Abby."

"What do you mean?"

"Do you watch much television?"

"No . . . I mostly rent movies," I admit.

He inhales deeply. "Reality shows are all about shocking the contestants and the audience to get ratings. Be prepared."

"Be prepared for what?"

"Anything."

I shiver again but this time not from the cold. Just what in the hell am I doing up here on this mountain kissing Danny Becker and putting my tush on a reality TV show?

"Let's get you inside before you catch your death of cold. You checked in yet?"

"No."

"Come on, I'll show you where to get your keys and then help you bring your stuff in. I'm guessing you brought every article of clothing you own, right?"

"How'd you guess?"

"I've got two older sisters. I know how the female mind works."

"So you got us all figured out, huh?" I ask as I follow him through the far door on the other side of the deck. As we pass by the big picture windows I peek in and see more activity inside.

He laughs as he pushes the door open for me. "I know *how* . . . just not *why*."

"I suppose if we understood the opposite sex it would take some of the fun out of the chase," I say breezily as if I know of such matters. I've dated here and there but I haven't had a steady relationship or ever felt as if I were in love.

"So true," he agrees.

I'm starting to think that maybe I'm learning the fine art of flirting. Who knew I had it in me? I give my hair a little flip for good measure and manage to elbow him in the gut. "Oh . . . sorry!" I gush, noting that he has rock-hard abs.

Danny rubs his stomach with a good-natured grin. "I'll live."

I'm thinking that I really like him. I hate that we're going to be competing against each other.

"What? You have a frown on your face again."

I shrug. "This is going to be hard competing against people that I know and care about. I hope that it doesn't get ugly."

"It's bound to, Abby. Just be prepared and watch your back."

I think he's teasing but when I see the serious look on his face my eyebrows shoot up. "You think anyone from the little ole town will try to get down and dirty?" I'm thinking of some of the contestants and can't imagine it, not even Julia Mayer.

"Human nature can get pretty danged weird, especially when there's fifty thousand dollars at stake. It's bound to get crazy and that's just what Comedy Corner is banking on. Remember that, Abby."

"Lord have mercy. Just what have we gotten ourselves into, Danny?"

"I don't really know but you can bet your bottom dollar that Misty Creek will never be the same."

4

Starting from Scratch

I'm sort of in a daze while Danny shows me where to register and pick up the key to my room. He helps me drag in all the stuff that I'm sure that I won't need but he's teasingly good-natured about it. When it starts to rain he insists that he will bring in the last load so I won't get wet and I'm thinking again that Julia Mayer is a complete idiot for letting him get away. Yeah, Danny might not be able to keep her in diamonds and pearls but he seems to be a hardworking, good-hearted man and in my way of thinking that's worth more than a million bucks. Oh *my*, and for a man who's so big and so strong he sure has a tender way with a kiss.

This gets me thinking about the kiss and I'm reliving it in my mind when he enters my room with two bulging duffel bags. His dark hair is damp, making it curl up a bit over the collar of his brown Carhartt jacket.

"Where do you want it?" he asks.

Oh, that's a loaded question. Something naughty comes to mind, making a hot blush creep up my neck. *Good God, just what is this man doing to me?* "Just toss it into the pile," I request and point to the mound of stuff in the far corner of the room. He handles the bags with masculine ease and a little sigh escapes me.

"You okay?"

"Just a little tired," I lie and fake a yawn. In truth, I'm more revved up than Dale Earnhardt Jr. at the starting line, making me wonder if I'll ever sleep again.

"I could use a nap, too."

I nod to him and I guess it's all this talk about sleeping that has me flicking a glance over to my huge bed. Something suddenly hovers in the air . . . and I can't quite put my finger on it but I wouldn't have been surprised if the lights suddenly dimmed and Luther Vandross music started playing in the background. I guess this is what you call sexual tension, but since I've never been in a hotel room with a man I just kissed before, I'm not exactly sure. Well, actually, I've never been in a hotel room with a man at *all*. This makes me feel a little awkward and unsure of myself . . . Wow, like *that's* never happened before.

I'm silent long enough that Danny clears his throat, breaking into my crazy train of thought, and says, "Well, I'd best be goin'. My bed is callin' my name."

"I hear ya," I tell him, trying to sound calm, cool, and oh so casual when of course I'm none of those things. Now, if I were a self-assured, sexually confident . . . Oh, hell, if I just had the nerve, I'd give him a saucy smile and tell him that *this* bed is calling his name. But of course I don't. Just telling him to kiss me was *way* out of my comfort zone and I really can't believe that I did it.

I make a big show of yawning and stretching and end up losing my balance. "Whoa!" I fall sideways onto the bed with an unladylike grunt, one big bounce and two little bounces. Rolling to my back, I squeeze my eyes shut in total humiliation. "Now, just how am I ever going to learn to do the tango? I'm just about the biggest klutz on

the face of the earth. Lord have mercy, I pity the dance instructor who gets stuck with me."

"I don't think getting stuck with you would be such a
hardship, Abby."

The low timbre of his voice washes over me like warm
summer rain and I slowly open my eyes. The heat in his
gaze makes me swallow hard. I realize that I'm lying here
like an open invitation, and I swear I'd move . . . but
when my brain tries to tell my body to roll from the
sprawled-out position my legs refuse to listen. *Move,
legs, you look like a hussy,* I silently scream, but my body
feels like a pat of butter melting into a hot frying pan.
Danny takes a step toward the bed and my heart starts
beating so hard that I think it might just jump right out of
my chest.

He wants me. Danny Becker wants me.

I'm about to lose my virginity right here, right now, at
the Rabbit Run Hunting Lodge. Well, okay, technically
I'm not a virgin . . . there was that time with Jimmy
Boone in the flatbed of his truck. We were fumbling and
bumbling after too much of his granny's homemade
wine and it was over before I knew it . . . Oh, and I threw
up afterward, making things worse. I *tried* to tell him it
was the strawberry wine and not *him* but he would have
none of it and our short-lived relationship was over.
There were a couple of other close calls and near misses
but until someone rocks my world I will think of myself
as a virgin.

I'm thinking Danny Becker could rock my world and
he sure is looking at me like he wants to. But with a sudden frown he runs his fingers through his damp hair and
blows out a sigh. "What's goin' on here, Abby?"

I swallow. "Um, I think we were havin' a moment."

Nodding, he jams his hands into his pockets, tilts his
head to the side, and says, "Yeah, but *why?*"

"Well . . ." I'm stumped by this odd question so I don't answer, but he seems to be asking himself more than me, anyway.

After clearing his throat Danny looks at me with serious blue eyes and says, "Look, I know that I've been comin' on to you . . ."

I hear a huge "but" and brace myself.

"But . . . well, I don't want to be a leftover crush from high school. In other words, I don't want to be what I once was or have to answer for what I could have been." Color goes to his cheekbones and he says, "I'm not making a damned bit of sense, am I?"

After mulling this over for a moment I say softly, "Yeah, you are, Danny." Scooting up to a sitting position, I take one of his big callused hands in mine. "I *get* it, Danny, and ya know what? Maybe we need to forget all about high school and start from scratch."

"Now, there's a plan."

When he gives me a slow, sexy grin I try to focus on the point that I'm attempting to make but it takes me a second . . . *oh yeah.* "I need to get rid of this chip on my shoulder about being ignored and not going to the prom and all that."

He frowns. "You never went to the prom?"

"Let's not dwell," I remind him.

"Right. Well then, I need to get over Julia Mayer once and for all."

I look up at him for a moment and, well, *damn*; I can't believe that I'm going to say this but I do. "Maybe . . . but then again maybe *not.* She's not in high school anymore either, Danny."

"And your point?"

Oh, this hurts but I feel that I must proceed. Schooling my features so that I'm not wincing I say, "Maybe she's grown up. Realized the important things in life."

While shaking his head he withdraws his hand from my grasp. "Yeah, right, when hell freezes over," he scoffs but something in his eyes tells a different story.

It sinks into my brain that he's been truly hurt by Julia and I do believe that he's afraid to open his heart to her again. I feel a stab of disappointment when I realize that he's still hung up on the damned woman. If I had it in me I'd pull him down on this here bed and make him forget that Julia Mayer ever existed. Of course I'm not exactly an expert in the art of lovemaking but I think I could wing it. I brave a glance up at him and think that maybe I'm on to something. Oh, but what if he called out *Julia* while in the throes of passion? Wow, that would really suck.

But then again what if fate has thrown us together and I'm wasting a perfectly good opportunity to be with the man of my dreams?

"Okay, I give," Danny says, breaking into my thoughts. "I have to know what's going on in that pretty little head of yours."

Get down here and let me make wild love to you until you forget that Julia Mayer even exists.

Do I dare?

Of course not.

Instead, I open my mouth for another fake yawn. But just when I start my fake stretch, Danny tugs me to my feet and threads his long fingers through my hair. Cradling my head, he slants his mouth across mine and turns my fake yawn into a long, hot kiss. Until this moment I thought the whole weak-in-the-knees thing was a bunch of hooey but my legs feel as if they're made of warm candle wax and I have to snake my arms around Danny's neck for support. I curl my fingers into the soft dark hair at the nape of his neck and kiss him back like there's no tomorrow.

I have the sudden need to feel his bare skin beneath the

palms of my hands and as if reading my mind he sheds
his jacket and then tugs at mine. Soft red flannel shirt
tucked into Wrangler jeans and designer clothes be
damned . . . there's nothing sexier than this. With a
thumping heart, I slide my hands up the soft fabric, loving the feel of the hard contours of his chest, the wild beat
of his heart. He sweeps my hair to the side and places
moist, nibbling kisses on my neck while I unbutton his
shirt with trembling fingers. A breathy sigh escapes me
when I feel his smooth, warm skin, the tickle of chest
hair, and the bump of his nipples. He's got the lean and
whipcord-hard body of a natural athlete and a hard
worker.

Danny inhales sharply and his stomach muscles
quiver. In the back of my mind I know I should end this
before it goes too far but I can't quite stop myself from
exploring every inch of his bare chest. When I run my fingertip over the top of his belt just grazing his skin he goes
very still and I immediately stop, figuring that I must
have done something wrong. Wow, if I'm bad at this part
just how bad will I be in bed? I'm guessing that it's best
he doesn't find out, so I try to take a step back but he puts
his hands on my waist, holding me firmly.

"Abby, baby, I'm only human," he tells me in a husky
tone and then inhales a deep breath.

"I know what you mean," I say with a nod. In truth I
have no clue what he's getting at but I'm thinking that
agreement sort of covers all the bases.

"If you keep touching me like that . . ." He stops and
shakes his head.

My gaze travels south and when I see the telltale bulge
in his jeans I understand what he's getting at. *Oh.* I suddenly realize that I'm at a crossroads and Danny is waiting for me to make up my mind and I have to say that I'm
leaning heavily toward the road less traveled . . .

Of course jumping into bed with him would probably be stupid and I suppose wrong and could complicate the competition. I wonder if there's something in that big packet that I should be reading about having sex with one of the other contestants. Good Lord, that would be totally humiliating to be disqualified for such a thing. Then again, this is Comedy Corner so anything probably goes . . .

"Abby, I'm sorry," Danny says, interrupting my decision-making process. Taking a step back he shakes his head and says, "What was I thinkin'?"

I don't know how to reply but since my face feels as hot as a match that's just been struck he must know that I'm embarrassed. I wouldn't be surprised if my hair suddenly burst into flames. While I was contemplating hopping into bed, Danny was looking for the escape hatch. I close my eyes for a moment and inhale a deep breath. Did I really just throw myself at him? I open my eyes and see his unbuttoned shirt.

Yes, I did.

My heart starts pounding and my legs tremble, making me plop down onto the edge of the bed. "I should be making meat loaf."

"What?" Danny looks at me like I'm one wrench short of a toolbox.

"I should be at the diner right now helping my mama make her meat loaf for the supper crowd."

"Abby, I'm sure she has the situation under control."

"Yeah, well, I don't. The competition hasn't even started and I've already made a fool of myself by throwing myself at you." I put my hands over my face.

"Abby . . ." Danny says softly.

When I don't respond he gently pries my hands from my face. I open my eyes to see that he's kneeling down in front of me and I try to swallow the tight ball of emotion clogging my throat but fail.

"Make no mistake, what just happened here was more than mutual. In fact I was the one who kissed *you*."

"Yeah, after I told you to." I would put my hands back over my face but he's still holding them.

Danny chuckles softly, leans forward, and gives me a tender, lingering kiss. "There," he tells me gruffly, "all my doing."

I hold on to the edges of his open shirt and ask, "Then what was the apology for and the 'what was I thinkin'?' comment all about?" My voice has a little hitch in it and I feel on the verge of tears. "We're moving way too fast, aren't we?"

"Yeah. There's no denying the attraction and you're a hellava woman but we've both got some issues, and then there's the whole ballroom dancing thing. As much as I hate to say it we need to cool our jets."

"Okay," I agree glumly but not because I know he's right. His mouth is so very close and he's looking at me with those deep blue bedroom eyes shaded by dark lashes that no man has the right to have, and I have to say that my resistance just isn't that strong. Without realizing it I'm leaning forward.

"Ah, Abby," he says and gives me a featherlight kiss that manages to pack quite a punch. My eyes are still closed when he says, "You're not making this easy."

"Nothin' worthwhile ever is."

He gives me a smile that makes my toes curl and says, "So true . . . and worth the wait."

At this point I'm ready to throw the whole waiting scenario out the window but he stands up and begins buttoning his shirt. After clearing my throat I say, "I guess I'll see you down at the orientation, then?"

Danny looks up from his task and nods. I watch him

walk toward the door, admiring his jean-clad butt, and sigh. He puts his hand on the doorknob but then pauses and turns around. "Ya know, Abby, I know that this is a competition and we could all use the money, but I want you to know that you can come to me if you need me. Okay? If anyone pushes you around or gives you a hard time, promise me that you'll come to me."

"Okay," I say softly.

With a satisfied nod he leaves, closing the door quietly behind him.

"Ohmigod." I fall back into the mattress and stare up at the ceiling. I'm touched beyond words that he wants to protect me. No guy has ever done that before and it makes me feel . . . *I don't know* . . . treasured or something. Since my daddy died Mama and I have had to fend for ourselves and I suddenly realize how hard it must have been for her to lose that security of having a man to look out for her. I think about how she blushed and flirted with Mitchell Banks and it occurs to me that she deserves to feel feminine. I mull this over for a few minutes and then think about how extraordinary this day has been . . .

"Wow," I murmur softly, "Danny Becker kissed me. Wanted to *be* with me." I could think this is all a figment of my imagination but I spot his jacket on the floor where he tossed it in our moment of heated passion. I swallow and close my eyes, reliving the kiss once and then again. I have the sudden need to call someone and tell them . . . but who? Calling Mama would be awkward and Jesse would just laugh.

I really want to call Misty Falls, my best friend since kindergarten. Yes, her mama named her after the town. I know her name sounds like it's a cheesy tourist attraction and should be painted on the side of a barn: See Misty Falls. She was Misty Morgan when we were kids but she's married with a baby on her hip and one on the way, so she tends to be a bit unstable and sometimes envious of my single status. Funny because I think that she's living the picket fence American dream. I suppose the grass is always greener . . .

With a huge yawn and a stretch I realize that I am a bit tired after all, but I glance over at the big packet that I'm supposed to read and I sigh. "Better get to it," I mumble. "Maybe I'll just rest my eyes for a moment or two. . . ."

5

Reality Check

"Oh, stop. . . ." I grumble when a thumping sound interrupts my dream that for some reason involves penguins sunbathing on a sandy beach. I turn to my side and cradle my head beneath my hands, wanting to see a penguin hang ten, but the darned thumping persists. It almost sounds like someone is knocking at my door.

"Oh no!" I jackknife to a sitting position and brush my tangled hair from my face. Someone *is* knocking! I scoot from the bed and head for the door, tripping over Danny's jacket, causing a stop, drop, and roll sort of tumble to the carpet. With a little groan I scramble to me feet and hobble to the door while rubbing my left knee.

"Danny!"

"I came for my coat and I thought I might walk you down to the orientation." With a frown at my disheveled appearance he adds, "You're going, aren't you?"

"Yes, I fell asleep," I breathlessly explain over my shoulder as I pick up his jacket. "I'll meet you down there, okay? I have to tidy up a bit."

"Okay," he says as he glances at his watch, "but you'd better hurry or you'll be late. It starts in just a few minutes."

"I will. Save me a seat."

"Sure thing."

"Thanks." I thrust his jacket at him, close the door, and then hurry to the bathroom. "Good Lord, would ya look at me?" My toiletries are somewhere in my huge pile of stuff but I don't have time to go digging for them. I manage to locate a comb in my purse and then begin tugging at the tangles in my bed-head hair while cursing at myself for letting this happen. "Just how in the world did I manage to sleep for two solid hours?" I cringe at my appearance but that will just have to suffice. Hopefully this is just an informal gathering anyway. As I hurry from my room I spare a glance at the unread orientation packet and hope that there isn't a test or anything, because I'll fail miserably.

While I hightail it down the hallway I hope that I'll meet up with someone else so I don't have to walk in alone, but since I'm a good ten minutes late that doesn't happen. After turning the last corner I know that I should just slip quietly into the room but I'm so dazzled by the touches of elegance in the otherwise rustic banquet hall that I stop dead in my tracks and put my hand over my mouth. Fat candles atop round linen-covered tables give the room a soft glow. Fresh-cut flowers are *everywhere*, filling the air with a sweet scent. I inhale deeply and have to smile.

"Miss Harper, how nice of you to join us," Mitchell says to me from the podium at the front of the room.

My smile fades when for a heart-stopping moment I think Mitchell's angry with me, but when he winks I breathe a sigh of relief. Everyone, though, looks my way and I hope that the dim lighting hides my blush. Danny discreetly motions with a sideways nod for me to sit next to him. With a grateful smile I head to Danny's table and slide into the seat next to him. This draws a bit of a frown from Julia, who is sitting directly across from Danny. I suppose if I think it's over between the two of them I had better think again.

"Hello," I say in general to everyone at the table.

Travis Tucker, the farmer, gives me a wide smile and a friendly nod. "Hey there, Abby." His beard is trimmed and his rather long hair is slicked back. He's wearing a white, neatly pressed dress shirt and it occurs to me that I've never seen him in anything other than worn overalls. I smile, thinking that he cleans up very nicely.

"Hey, Abby." Daisy Potter, the cashier from the Piggly Wiggly, gives me a friendly nod but then turns her undivided attention back to Travis. I'm used to seeing her in a uniform with her hair pulled back in a ponytail. But now she looks younger and pretty in a soft yellow dress with her brown tresses framing her face.

"Hello, Abby," Julia says a bit stiffly but I give her a smile anyway. Her hair is swept back from her face in a fancy twist and she's wearing a cream-colored silk blouse, making me feel frumpy in my jeans and turtleneck. For the first time I notice that servers are bringing around tossed salads. With a glance around the room I see that everyone else is dressed up, too. Swallowing a groan I realize that this information must have been in the packet that I didn't read. Deciding that I'm just going to have to wing it—and winging it is not something I'm good at—I take the fancy folded napkin and smooth it over my lap.

Patsy James, the florist, is sitting directly to my left. "Aren't the flowers amazing?" she gushes.

"They're lovely," I agree and accept a basket of bread from her. When I fold back the white linen the yeasty aroma makes my mouth water and I realize that I'm famished. I immediately tear off a soft, warm piece and pop it into my mouth.

"Hungry?" Danny asks close to my ear. His voice is low and teasing, making me all too aware of what almost transpired between us just a little while ago. I nod and almost choke on my roll when his leg presses up against mine and he says, "Me too."

An accident? I sneak a peek at him beneath my lashes but he's busy buttering a slice of dark rye bread. I notice that Julia narrows her eyes at me but quickly averts her gaze when she realizes that I'm looking her way.

I'm wondering whether Danny is cozying up to me to get to Julia while I'm glancing randomly around the room. I suddenly think to myself that as far as I can tell all of the contestants in the competition are single. With a frown I look around again, thinking that I must be mistaken, but I'm pretty sure that I'm right. I wonder if this is because being away from a family would be harder for married people, but then again maybe this is for added drama? Jesse never mentioned that you had to be single to be a contestant . . .

"Ranch?" Patsy asks, interrupting my thoughts.

"Yes, thanks." I accept the silver boat from her and drizzle some dressing over my salad before passing it to Danny. I pick up the smaller of the two forks and start to stab a cherry tomato when I hesitate. This isn't like any salad I've ever consumed before. I poke at it a bit and wonder just what some of these greens are. There's shaggy sprigs and purple leaves and not a carrot or radish in sight. The cherry tomato is the only familiar thing.

"Looks like a danged bunch of weeds," Travis remarks and Daisy giggles. He takes a big bite and wrinkles up his nose. "Tastes like weeds too."

"It's a spring mix," Julia says in a rather snooty tone but I notice that she isn't exactly gobbling hers up either.

"Yeah, a spring mix of *weeds*," Travis says and Daisy giggles harder.

I take a tentative bite and it's not too bad, just a little limp or whatever, but maybe it's just because I'm so hungry.

"I hope that the main course is a little more normal," Danny says, voicing what I had been thinking.

Servers hover, refilling our water, iced tea, and coffee. When wine is offered I decline, thinking that I need my wits about me and since my strawberry wine incident I've avoided it altogether. I'm hoping that we aren't given something that you have to crack open like crab or lobster since I know I would screw that up like Julia Roberts in *Pretty Woman*. I'm wondering if all of this elegance is put before us as a kind of welcoming gesture or to trip us plain folks up. I'm hoping for the former but since I see that cameras are quietly filming us I'm thinking the latter. When I'm served my main course I place my hand on the waiter's arm and ask in a low voice, "Could you tell me what this is?"

"Beef medallions, asparagus, and new potatoes."

"Thank you," I tell him, relieved that it's not veal. I can't stomach eating anything that's a baby. Had I been asked I would have told them to hold the yellow sauce artfully drizzled over the rounds of beef, but when I dip my fork in for a tentative taste I actually like the tart, buttery flavor. I notice that everyone else at our table is picking and tasting except for Travis, who is tucking into his food like it's his last meal.

"Well, this is just simply delicious," Patsy says with a satisfied smile.

"Yeah, I sure could get used to this," Daisy agrees.

I'm about to comment on the sauce when I suddenly remember that cameras are filming our every move. I wonder if there are hidden microphones in the flower arrangement or something.

"What's wrong, Abby? You look like you've seen a ghost," Danny said.

"I do believe that the cameras are rolling," I whisper to him.

"Yeah, you're right," he whispers back. "You think somethin's about to happen?"

"Didn't your mama teach y'all that it's not polite to tell secrets?" Julia asks with a little smile but there's a bit of frost in her tone.

"We were just noticing that the cameras are rolling," Danny says smoothly.

"Oh?" Julia looks around with wide eyes.

We all turn toward the front of the room when lights flash and music begins. A moment later Mitchell Banks steps up to the podium, the music fades, and he says, "Welcome, everyone! I'm Mitchell Banks, CEO of Comedy Corner and executive producer of *Dancing with the Rednecks*." Putting up both hands he continues. "First of all I want to tell you that we are using the term *redneck* with a sort of tongue-in-cheek fondness and not in a derogatory sense. In fact, I'm so impressed and charmed by the town and residents of Misty Creek that although I usually turn the show over to the director at this point, I've decided to stay on and watch the competition firsthand."

When he pauses we all applaud but I have to wonder if my mother is the one who charmed and impressed him. Mitchell is smooth, polished, and intelligent but if he does anything to hurt my mama I'll have to kick his butt all the way back to sunny California.

Mitchell takes a sip of water while the applause dies down. "Hopefully you've had a chance to read through the orientation packet so you know how the competition will work. You will have long hours of rehearsals throughout the week with an instructor from Starlight

Dance Studios, the top national chain of dance studios in the country. You will be allowed to leave Rabbit Run Lodge for emergency family or work-related situations but on a limited basis."

He pauses, raises one eyebrow, and then clears his throat. "In case you haven't already noticed, you are all *single*. We did this on purpose. First, it makes being away for weeks at a time easier, but second, this is a reality show. Part of the intrigue is the interaction between the contestants, and I will warn you that cameras will be rolling *everywhere* except of course in the privacy of your room. I'll remind you that you've all signed release forms to allow anything and everything to air to the general public. We also have rules. Read them carefully and follow them. I would hate for someone to lose the chance at fifty grand because of breaking the rules."

As I take a sip of iced tea, I make a mental note to read the darned packet as soon as I get back to my room. At the mention of the fifty thousand dollars Mitchell creates a buzz of excitement that seems to electrify the air. The music starts playing softly in the background and the bright fingers of light swirl around the podium. It's obvious that something's going to happen. I shift in my seat and my heart starts to pound.

"I know that I told you to expect the unexpected. In reality TV it comes with the territory. Well, a little while ago I was told that your dance instructors have already arrived and they are eagerly waiting to meet and greet you." He pauses again while excitement ripples through the contestants, me included. A shimmering curtain behind the podium begins to open slowly while the music gets louder. Finally all twelve instructors are revealed standing on a platform resembling a stage. The women are in sequined dance costumes and the men are in formal attire. With a bow they hook up with a partner and begin to dance.

I watch, spellbound, as they swirl and twirl, bend and sweep . . . gliding with grace and ease. I have to wonder who my instructor will be and if I will ever be able to master anything close to what they're demonstrating. When the music ends and they strike a pose, camera flashes are going off like strobe lights and I'm bummed that in my haste to get down here I totally forgot to bring mine. We applaud as loudly as twelve people can. In my exuberance I jump to my feet and thankfully others follow. This seems to please Mitchell since he's smiling from ear to ear.

"And now," Mitchell booms into the microphone, "let me introduce each of you to your Starlight Dance Studio instructors!" The light in the room goes from dim to bright as he begins calling out our names. I can see that the camera crew is catching all of this on film, and then something else is clearly evident:

The Starlight dance instructors have no idea what they have gotten themselves into.

The wide eyes and open mouths give them away. Most of them have the grace to recover and smile as they greet their students. Even the tall, leggy redhead in the purple sequins manages a big welcoming smile and deep bow to Mac Murphy, the big burly trucker. But then my eyes are drawn to one tall aloof man standing off to the side. His hands are folded across his chest and he has a—well, there's no other way to say it—a pissed-off look on his otherwise strikingly handsome face. Other than that he's tall, dark, and smokin' hot. Midnight-black hair is slicked back from a face that could grace the cover of *GQ*. High cheekbones, a full mouth, and a strong jaw shaded with dark stubble give him a dangerous sexy appearance that has me feeling warm all over and reaching for my water.

His billowy white shirt is open halfway down his chest, revealing tanned skin and a sculpted physique. Tight black pants and a bloodred sash at his waist give him the appearance of a swashbuckling pirate . . .

"Abby," Danny says, breaking into my sudden fantasy of being tossed over the pirate's shoulder, "they just called your name."

I gasp. "You mean the *pirate* is my teacher?"

"It appears so."

"I don't want him!" I turn to Patsy and say, "Let's trade."

"Oh baby, I'd take him in a heartbeat. Kinda looks like Antonio Banderas. But, hon, they don't allow tradin' dance instructors. Didn't you read your handbook?"

"Abby Harper," Mitchell says again, "come on down and meet your partner, Rio Martin, esteemed instructor and ballroom dance champion from Mexico City."

I swallow hard and stand up. Rio the dancing pirate looks my way and as luck would have it I stumble as I push my chair beneath the table. His pissed-off look gets more pronounced and it occurs to me that he probably doesn't possess a sense of humor. I force myself to walk toward the front of the room when I really want to turn and hightail it out of there.

"Hello, Mr. Martin," I venture, hating the little quiver in my voice, but I bravely stick out my hand in a formal greeting. "I'm Abby Harper. Nice to meet you." The touch of his warm hand and firm grasp sends a tingle down my spine. He's quite frankly the sexiest man I've ever come into contact with and I suddenly become tongue-tied. Now, just how in the world am I going to learn to dance with a man who makes my knees go weak? When I realize that I'm gawking with my mouth wide open, I snap my jaws shut and hope that I can gather my wits about me and say something remotely intelligent.

Judging by the expression in his deep brown eyes, I do *not* impress him much. Of course the fact that I'm in jeans and a sweater doesn't help matters.

"I—I didn't realize that this was going to be a formal dinner," I blurt out, but other than the deepening of his frown he remains silent. "I would have worn something more appropriate."

"Oh." This time he flicks a brief glance at my attire as if he hadn't cared enough to even notice what I'm wearing and then shrugs his wide shoulders.

Okay, all of the other instructors are chatting with their partners. I have to say that I'm getting a bit miffed that Rio Martin, my Antonio Banderas wannabe, refuses to speak to me. I might be a hometown hick and he might be some fancy-schmancy ballroom dancer, but darn it, I deserve better than this. My anger is quickly overcoming my bedazzled state concerning his extreme sexiness. As my mama would say, *pretty is as pretty does*, and he ain't being very pretty.

My heart thumps at what I'm about to say, but I've waited tables long enough to know how to deal with an arrogant jerk. "Look, Mr. Martin, I'm getting the impression that this isn't what you bargained for but—"

"I'm afraid you don't know the half of it," he interrupts with a wave of his hand.

His slight Spanish accent brings my bedazzled state back up a notch, but with determination I squelch it.

"Well, just what were you expectin' with a show called *Dancin' with the Rednecks*?"

His dark eyebrows raise and he shakes his head. "So *that's* what they're calling it?"

I step a bit closer so that no one can hear me except for him and admit, "Well, I'm hoping that it's a workin' title but as far as I can tell . . . *yes*."

"Dancing with the *rednecks*," he slowly repeats in a low tone. "I don't fucking believe it."

My sharp intake of breath draws his attention, and his brown eyes flash to mine. "Pul-*ease* refrain from using such vulgar language in my presence," I demand in a clipped tone that says I mean business. Of course as soon as I say this I regret my outburst. I suppose he's my boss in a manner of speaking and might somehow have the power to have me booted from the competition. But instead of backing down I jut my chin out and wait for his apology.

He blinks at me for a moment and I realize that I'm waiting in vain. His lips twitch and for a hopeful moment I think he's going to smile but then he scowls. With another dismissive wave of his hand he mutters, "Whatever."

Okay, let me explain that by and large I'm a very mild-mannered person, but right now I'm seeing red. There might actually be steam coming out of my ears, because it feels like my head is going to pop off my shoulders like a champagne cork. Some of this must be written on my face, because his eyes widen and he grabs my hand.

"Let's go somewhere private," he says and proceeds to tug me off the platform and out the back door to the deck.

"What do you think you're doing?" I sputter when the chill night air cools my hot cheeks and clears my head a bit.

"Salvar su asno dulce."

"What?"

"Saving your sweet ass."

"Excuse me?"

"You looked ready to explode and there were cameras everywhere. I didn't think you wanted *that* on the promo teasers for the show."

"Oh." I'm thinking maybe I should thank him, but then

I remember that his rudeness was my reason for going temporarily insane. An awkward moment passes and I try not to shiver in the night breeze.

"Look," he says and turns to face me, "I'm very sorry about my language."

"Okay . . ."

"But you were right when you said that this wasn't what I was expecting. My contract said that Starlight Dance Studios was going to be providing the instruction for handpicked students." He sweeps his hand in the direction of the lodge and continues. "And we were going to a private, secluded resort where we would give dance lessons for a nationally televised ballroom competition over the period of twelve weeks."

"Well, we *were* handpicked and this *is* private and secluded. *Resort* is a bit of a stretch, I suppose."

"Granted, but I was duped into thinking that this was a prestigious honor that would bring business in droves to Starlight Dance Studios. That's the only reason I agreed to do this."

"But, *Mr. Martin*, didn't the fact that Comedy Corner was doing the project give you a clue?"

"No, I didn't know that little detail. The contract said MB Productions with no mention of Comedy Corner." He shakes his head. "The money was huge and the opportunity seemed too good to pass up and I suppose I jumped on it before taking the necessary precautions. I should have had my lawyers dig deeper but it was all done in such a rush."

He looks so upset that my anger fades. "So you would have turned this down?"

"Of course! This will make Starlight Dance Studios a laughingstock and make a mockery out of ballroom dancing," he states hotly.

"Well, Mr. Martin, when you're given lemons . . . make lemonade."

"What?" He looks at me like I'm one taco short of a combo. Maybe I am.

I angle my head at him and explain. "Make somethin' sweet outta somethin' sour." I wave my hand in the direction of the big picture window behind us. "We might be rednecks from Misty Creek, Kentucky, Mr. Martin, but we are by and large hardworkin', good-hearted people. Given the chance we just might surprise *you*, Comedy Corner, and the rest of the world."

He gives me a you've-got-to-be-kidding look.

"Okay, granted it's a challenge."

"That's putting it mildly, wouldn't you say?" he asks dryly in his very cool accent.

The fact that Rio Martin has just shown a hint of a sense of humor makes hope blossom into a smile. "Well, yes. Admittedly we're lemons . . . but let's make us some lemonade. Whadaya say, Mr. Martin?"

He turns around and leans his elbows against the railing. He hesitates for a long moment as if assessing the situation, which gives me time to appreciate the fact that his partially unbuttoned shirt is gaping open, exposing his very fine chest. I'm trying hard not to imagine what his smooth brown skin would feel like beneath my hands and I'm suddenly feeling warm despite the cool breeze that's blowing my hair across my face.

When he unexpectedly reaches over and tucks a windblown lock behind my ear, I shiver, but not from the cold. "So, then, Abby Harper, *you* are my lemon?" He smiles, flashing white teeth in the moonlight.

I laugh to try to cover up my racing pulse. Let me tell you, Rio Martin's smile is something to be reckoned with. "Well, you'll have to squeeze pretty darned hard to get anything useful outta me."

He laughs. "Oh, I'm more than willing to give you a good squeeze."

I'm mortified to think that he might have taken my comment as a come-on. "I—I didn't mean that in a suggestive way."

"I didn't take it that way." He pushes away from the railing, takes a step closer, and says, "Forgive my earlier rude behavior. I was upset but that was no excuse."

"Forgiven."

"Good. Then tell me, Abby . . . are you ready to win this thing?"

I nod.

He smiles.

Oh my. I melt like soft-serve ice cream dripping down a sugar cone. "I'll give it my best shot," I assure him with such conviction that he chuckles.

"Good, then be ready bright and early." Rio walks toward the door and I follow until he pauses and turns to me. "I have to warn you that I'm a fierce competitor and I don't let up, so get a good night's sleep."

I give him a close look to see if he's teasing, but by the no-nonsense expression on his face I can tell that he's dead serious. "Got it," I reply, feeling like I should salute or maybe curtsey.

"Oh, and mark my words, *you'll* be the one using a few choice words before this is over."

When he grins, I have hope that he actually possesses an itsy-bitsy sense of humor.

"Never," I assure him with a lift of my chin. "My mama taught me better."

"We'll see about that." Inclining his head politely, he says, "Until morning, Abby. *Don't* be late."

"I'm never late," I assure him and then remember that I was late twice today already. "Well, almost never."

"Good, because ballroom dancing is all about discipline."

"Discipline is my middle name," I say firmly with a serious look of my own but thinking all the while that I'm really going to disappointment him with my skills . . . or lack thereof.

When I walk past Rio he stands to the side while holding the door open for me. Since I have to pass close by him I can feel the warmth of his body and then catch a delicious whiff of his aftershave . . . it's something spicy and manly but erotic and a sigh escapes me before I know it. When he shoots me a look I try to turn it into a yawn but unfortunately it becomes this weird noise that starts out high and then goes low. Thoroughly embarrassed, I add a cough at the end to throw him off.

"Do you have something caught in your throat?"

Think fast. "Um . . . yeah, maybe a . . . a *moth* or somethin'." I'm thinking that this is a good cover-up, but he appears horrified.

"You swallowed a moth?"

"Maybe just a tiny one." I pound my chest with my fist and politely cough.

"Let me get you something to drink."

"No . . . I'm fine, really."

He looks uncertain and still a bit horrified. I'm thinking that I should just come clean and tell him that his aftershave made me swoon and a moth isn't flapping around in my stomach, but he'd surely think I was crazy. What the hell was I thinkin'? Swallowed a moth . . .

"Okay then, see you bright and early."

"And bushy-tailed."

"Bushy-tailed?"

"Yeah, you know . . . bright-eyed and bushy-tailed?" I venture with a weak smile. Good Lord, this whole thing is going downhill as fast as a sled on a snow-covered hill.

He shakes his head and looks as if he wants me to explain, but I simply bid him good night and hurry up to my room. Once inside I lean against the door and groan. "So much for first impressions. Swallowed a moth? *Good God.*" With a weary glance at my pile of stuff and another tired glance at the unread packet, I shake my head. "I'll deal with it in the morning . . ." I say in my best Scarlett O'Hara voice, stumble into the bathroom to wash up, and fall into bed in my undies.

6

Just Rewards

"What happened to bright-eyed and bushy-tailed?" Rio asks with a hint of a smile.

"My doggone tail is draggin'." I try not to glare at him. While swallowing a groan, I blot beads of perspiration from my brow with a small towel.

"Okay, let's take five."

Oh, thank the Lord! Waiting tables is way easier than this! Plus, I'm surviving on a glass of orange juice and a hastily consumed bagel because it took me *forever* to decide what to wear this morning. Since Rio is looking classy in black pants and a formfitting white shirt I'm wishing that I had settled on something more stylish than gray sweatpants and a pink T-shirt.

"Okay, try again. A bit longer if you will. Keep your back straight and your chin up."

"What? It hasn't been five minutes, has it?" Again? Longer? Turning away I toss the towel into the corner of our rehearsal room and mutter, "Jerk."

"Excuse me?" Rio asks with the arch of one dark eyebrow, the same eyebrow that he has arched at me all morning long.

"Work. I said this sure is *work*." I add a sweet smile for good measure but when he turns around I stick out my tongue, deriving a small sense of satisfaction. I swear if I find him fast asleep somewhere I'm going to shave the doggone eyebrow right off. I giggle at the thought and he whirls around.

"Do you find something amusing, Miss Harper?"

I'm picturing him minus one eyebrow, so I sort of *do*, but I shake my head. "Not at all."

"Good, now let's try this again."

Again? How many times do I have to stand on one doggone foot and point my outstretched arms to the ceiling?

"You have to do this until you don't topple sideways," he explains as if reading my mind. "This is called *Pilates*. It will help you with balance, flexibility, and eventually strengthen your core muscles. Eventually you'll be able to control your muscles with your mind using this method." He points to his abdomen and *doggone core muscles* clearly defined by the tight shirt distract me from his instruction. This constant distraction has been happening all morning, making me appear stupid, but *hey*, the man should wear something other than butt-hugging pants and a shirt that shows each and every ripple of muscle.

"We'll work on endurance later."

Oh, goody.

"Now let me show you how to do this *again*. Inhale deeply while bringing your right leg up to your left thigh. Get your balance first, Abby. This is where you've been going wrong. Then slowly push your arms skyward, palms together like this. Press your knee back without moving your hips. Alignment is crucial. Hold this position for thirty seconds while pointing your fingertips to the ceiling. Stretch as far as your body will allow." He demonstrates this move with such grace and agility, none of which I have been able to master.

"Will I have to wax your car, Mr. Miagi?"

"What?" That one danged eyebrow goes up again and he looks at me still in the pointing-to-the-ceiling pose that has some crazy name that I've of course forgotten.

Oh yeah, the tree pose.

Rio's eyebrow slides back down to form a frown. "Wax my car?"

"You know, wax on . . . wax off?" I demonstrate with circular motions but when he shakes his head I realize that references to *The Karate Kid* are wasted on him. "Never mind."

"What's waxing a car got to do with anything?" he persists. His accent is getting more pronounced as the morning progresses. At one point he muttered a whole paragraph in Spanish and I don't think it was anything particularly flattering.

"I guess about as much as standing here like a tree!" Oh, crap . . . I said that out loud. I swallow nervously when a muscle jumps in his clenched jaw. He looks at me for a long heart-pounding moment and then says something under his breath. I strain my ears to hear but I do think it was once again in Spanish.

Now I know that this is where I should apologize for my outburst. And normally I'm a pretty mannerly, laid-back person but his saying things about me in Spanish *really* ticks me off. Being careful not to raise my voice I say primly, "Would you please speak in English? It's not right that I can't understand what you're sayin'."

"Well, half the time I can't understand what you're saying in *English*, so that makes us even," he says smoothly and raises that doggone eyebrow!

"Stop raisin' your eyebrow at me!"

"What?" This seems to take him off guard. "I don't do that."

"Oh, but you *do.*" I point to the offending eyebrow. "The left one."

He mulls this over for a second and I think he's going to apologize for the error of his ways but he says, "So it must be an involuntary habit. Get over it." He adds a shrug for good measure.

For a moment I'm admiring the play of muscle resulting from his shrug but then his rudeness sinks in and overpowers my good sense and I shove him with both hands right smack in the middle of his chest. *Both* eyebrows shoot up and he has to take a step backward to keep his balance.

Holy crap.

I swallow hard as two things hit me: One, that my hands are tingling from the contact with his hard, warm chest. And two, that I'm behaving very badly.

Rio goes still and gives me a long, silent look.

"I'm sorry . . . I—"

"Don't be," he interrupts in a low silky tone. He takes a step closer . . . so close that I can feel the heat radiating from his body. Suddenly I'm itching to touch him again but not to shove him away. He looks at me with those dark, fathomless eyes and I swear he must be the sexiest thing ever born. I remind myself that he's an arrogant jerk but my body has other ideas and I sway toward him. He steadies me by placing both of his hands around my waist and whispers, "Thank God."

Ah *yes*, I think as I release a long sigh. *Thank God!* My eyes flutter shut and I wait for him to lean in and kiss me but he doesn't. "Um, thank God for *what?*" I ask in a small, somewhat confused tone.

"You *do* have some fire and passion. I was beginning to wonder."

I let this sink in and then I get it. With narrowed eyes I ask, "So, let me get this straight. You were baiting me all mornin' to see when I'd crack?" I lean in so far that we're standing almost nose-to-nose. He's a couple of inches taller but I'm up on the balls of my feet.

"It took longer than I expected," he says calmly when he should be running for his ever-lovin' life.

"So posing like a warrior and a danged tree was to get my goat?"

"Not exactly . . . Pilates is going to be part of our training. But I admit that I was pushing you. I wanted to see some spunk . . . some personality so that I knew just what I had to work with. Ballroom dancing is all about passion, Abby. A monkey can memorize the steps. I wanted to see if sparks could fly," he says with a slow smile that does funny things to my stomach, "and they did." After taking a step back he says, "You've earned a break. Go grab a bottle of water."

"Wait a minute. I'm being rewarded for bad behavior?"

Rio throws back his head and laughs. "Yes, I suppose so."

I'm officially confused but I nod and then walk over to the cooler full of water and snag a bottle. I suppose I should be happy that I've somehow managed to please him but it bothers me a little that he planned the whole thing. And it bothers me a lot that I was feeling like grabbing him and kissing him silly when it was all just a ploy on his part to fire me up.

I make a mental note *not* to fall for my instructor. That would be really, really stupid.

Even so, while drinking my water I can't stop myself from glancing over at Rio. His dark head is bent while he jots down notes in a small pad. Gee, I can only guess what he might be writing . . . maybe something like *Hopelessly horrible but easily riled*. Something he writes makes him grin and I don't even want to think about it.

Am I just a joke to him? That thought hits me hard and I make another mental note, no, make that a *promise* to show Rio Martin, Mitchell Banks, and the rest of the damned world that I can do this. I stomp my foot thinking about it and slosh some water down the front of my shirt.

"Hell's bells!" This draws a look from Rio. *Great, that was classy.* His darned eyebrow starts to go up but he seems to think about it and stops himself. I can't help but grin and he smiles right back.

"Are you ready to learn some dance moves?"

"Yes!" I tell him with enthusiasm but then remember that my dancing skills suck. Maybe the tree pose wasn't so bad after all. "Unless you want to stick to the Pilates for a while longer . . . you know, to make me limber and strong."

"You're kidding, right?"

I force a laugh. "Of course."

"We drew the cha-cha as our first dance."

"Good." I nod like I know what the cha-cha is. "That *is* good, right?"

"I think so. Have you ever seen the cha-cha danced before?"

"Well . . . I . . . um . . ."

"I'm taking that as a no."

I shrug. "My knowledge of ballroom dancing is . . . limited."

"That's okay. I imagine that everyone else in this competition is in the same boat." He points to a stack of DVDs. "I'll give you some videos of dance competitions that I was in. It will give you an idea of what the dances are all about and to see how I move with a partner."

"I'll bet you're really good."

"I was."

"Was?"

"A knee injury put an end to my career." He shrugs again and gives me a nonchalant look that I'm not quite buying.

I take a step toward him. "Oh, Rio, I'm sorry. How—"

He waves one hand. "It's a boring story. Not to worry, though. Surgery and physical therapy have made me good as new."

"Then why—"

"The cha-cha is a lively, flirtatious dance," he says as if not hearing my question.

Something in his eyes makes me think that he's been hurt and not just physically, but I know when to shut my mouth. My mama taught me never to pry into someone's personal business.

"It's light and bubbly . . . all about the chase."

"The chase?"

"Between a man and a woman."

His eyes meet mine and I swallow. "Oh."

"You should have a catch-me-if-you-can attitude."

I nod but I don't quite get it.

"In other words . . . flirt. Tease. Draw me in and then push me away."

"Oh. Sure." I should probably warn him that I'm about as good at flirting as I am at dancing. Maybe worse.

"There are five steps to four beats of music. One, two . . . cha, cha, *cha*."

"Okay . . ."

Seeing my confusion, something I'm afraid he's going to see a lot of, he demonstrates, "Step, rock, cha, cha, cha. Two, three, four, and one. Rock the hips. Feel the rhythm. The cha-cha is all about the Cuban motion, strong hip action . . . and the chase."

"Right . . ." For a moment I'm a bit mesmerized by his hip action. Mercy, how does he do that?

"Stay on the balls of your feet. Steps are crisp. Quick.

Compact." He demonstrates, adding a hip motion that I just know I'll never master. Maybe he's double-jointed or something. "Our movements will be synchronized. We'll be working in parallel with each other. Ready to try?"

"Yes!" *Oh, hell no.*

"Okay, we begin by facing each other. Now join your right hand with my left. We must hold this position up at about your eye level. My right hand will rest on your shoulder blade. Your left arm should rest on my right arm in a comfortable, curved position. This is called the closed position and it will be our dance frame. It should always remain sturdy and well connected."

My head is spinning while I try to take this all in. It's not lost on me that I'm confused and this is just the standing-still part.

"Got it?"

"Sure." Not at all. *Crap.*

"Okay, now step forward slightly with your lead foot, which is always my left, and your right. Shift your weight forward like I did before. Shift your weight backward onto your other foot. Use your hips! Okay, now we do the chassé."

"The what?"

"The triple steps to the side."

"Huh?"

"The cha, cha, cha, Abby."

"Oh. Why didn't ya just say so?"

"Let's do it again. Slowly. Step, rock, cha, cha *cha*. Again."

"Okay."

"Two, three, four, and one. Balls of the feet, Abby. Step, rock, cha, cha, cha."

We do this about a million times . . . maybe two million . . . until I'm sweating like a pig and still totally messing up this basic move.

"Count with me, Abby. It will help."

"Okay, one, two, cha, cha . . . *Shit!*" I clasp my hand over my mouth. "Sorry 'bout my potty mouth. I'm gettin' frustrated."

"Try to relax. And by the way, you're about to break my hand."

"Sorry!"

"Okay, again . . ."

"One, two, cha, cha, cha," I whisper and finally manage to do it without faltering.

"Much better!" He gives me a smile and I think I *like* making him smile.

"Really?" Okay, I know I'm fishing a bit but it's been a rough morning.

"Yes, really. Now go take a short break."

"Thanks, Rio, for being so patient with me. I know that I'm a challenge."

He chuckles. "I imagine that there are others in this competition much more challenging than you. I consider myself lucky to have drawn you as a partner."

"Well, that was a backhanded compliment if I ever heard one, but I'll take what I can get."

He laughs as he unscrews his water bottle and I'm relieved to see a little bit of the earlier tension leave his demeanor. "Well, this isn't what I bargained for, but the contract is ironclad so I might as well make the most of it."

"You reread the contract for loopholes?" I'm a bit disappointed that he wants out so badly.

He gives me a guilty look but then grins. "In for a penny, in for a pound."

"Don't know about you, but I'm in for fifty grand."

"Now, there's the spirit, Abby Harper." He gives me a high five. "Now back to work."

He wasn't kidding and that's not an understatement. I

can squeeze a smile out of him once in a while, but for the most part he's all business. By lunchtime I'm plumb wore out and there is another session later that afternoon! Not that I don't need it, mind you, but I'm wondering how my calves are going to hold out.

At lunch everyone else seems a bit more chipper and not nearly as exhausted as me. I'm wondering if this is because Rio is working me harder or if I'm just that hopeless. The food is delicious and thankfully not some fancy-schmancy stuff but sub sandwiches on warm, crusty rolls and fresh fruit on the side. After my meager breakfast I'm ready to dig in.

"Hey there," Danny says and slides into the seat next to mine. "How's it goin'?"

I take a sip of tea to wash down my big bite of sandwich. "Rough. Who knew that dancin' was so hard?"

"Tell me about it." He agrees with a nod. "I'm doin' something called the jive. I feel like my feet are all over the place and in every direction. I was told to boogie while doin' this little wavy hand thing."

I snicker.

"Yeah, *boogie*. I told my instructor that I don't know how to boogie."

"What did she say?"

"She's one tough cookie. She said that I'd just have to learn to boogie."

"So, did you end up boogyin'?"

"Damned tootin'." He takes the top off his sandwich and checks out the contents before taking a generous bite.

"Howdy," Mac Murphy says as he eases his big frame into the chair next to Danny. His brown hair is curled up with sweat and he looks even more worn out than me. "This dancin' stuff is for the birds," he complains.

"Aw, it ain't so bad," Travis Tucker comments as he sits down. "I found it invigorating."

"You gotta be kiddin'," Mac grumbles. "*Invigorating?* What you been smokin'?"

"My dance instructor called it invigorating and I happen to agree."

"You sound like a girl, Travis," Mac tells him.

"Hey, I boogied," Danny admits with a grin and shows us his shaking hand wave.

Mac sputters on a swallow of sweet tea. "Get outta here. Okay, I admit that I was instructed to *twinkle.* Apparently while dancing the quickstep you must twinkle. Can you picture me twinklin'?"

I enjoy listening to them jaw back and forth while I eat my lunch. We collectively groan when warm chocolate chip cookies are delivered to our table.

"Damn, these are good," Travis says while licking a smudge of chocolate from his thumb.

I savor the gooey cookie. Mama makes wonderful pies for the diner but homemade cookies aren't something we get very often. I love to bake but I don't get the chance much. I think of how much Jesse enjoys my chocolate chip cookies and I'm suddenly feeling homesick.

"Hey, you okay?" Danny asks softly, close to my ear.

I nod and give him a reassuring smile. "I suppose. This is just all so . . ."

"Crazy?"

"Yeah, crazy is a pretty good way of puttin' it. This feels like I'm in a dream or something and I'm wondering when I'm gonna wake up."

"We're all out of our element, Abby. Just try to enjoy yourself."

"I know, I know." I polish off my cookie and then stand up. "I'm heading up to my room. Got homework to do," I tell everyone. "See y'all at supper."

Once I'm back in my room, I flop down onto my bed and watch several of Rio's dance videos. I'm amazed and impressed at how good he is. I can't believe that he gave up competing when his knee is obviously as good as new. I also notice how he moves so sensuously with his beautiful partner. Sexual tension seems to smolder as they glide across the dance floor and I have to wonder if the dark-haired beauty has something to do with his decision to retire from competition.

After a while my eyelids start to droop. A glance at the digital clock on the nightstand tells me that I have time for a short nap before the afternoon rehearsal begins. I set the alarm on my cell phone just to be on the safe side. Rio was quite clear with his feelings about tardiness.

Leaning back against the down pillows, I sigh and close my eyes. I stretch my arms and tired legs, hoping that a short rest will give me my second wind. "Set, rock, cha, cha, cha . . ." I mumble while going over the steps in my head. Step, rock, cha, cha, cha . . . Yawn. Step, rock, cha, cha, chaaaaaa . . .

7

Up for the Challenge

A loud banging disturbs my delicious dream where I'm cha-cha-cha-ing across the dance floor with Rio, doing a very find Cuban motion, like it's my business, I might add. I turn beneath his outstretched arm during an open break and perform a crossover walk-around turn with ease just like he did with the dark-haired beauty in the video. We end the dance with a flourish when Rio bends me backward, nearly touching my head to the floor. The crowd jumps to its feet, roaring approval, and then Rio lowers his head . . .

Bang, bang, *bang*!

"Go 'way," I grumble and sink my head into the soft pillow. I wait for Rio to kiss me but I'm awake now and . . . *oh, crap!* I jackknife to a sitting position and look over at the clock expecting to be way late for my rehearsal but thank God I've only been sleeping for twenty minutes. The banging on the door happens again and while brushing the hair from my eyes and, *ew*, the drool from the corner of my mouth, I hurry over to see what the commotion is all about.

After peeking through the peephole I see that it's a

young guy with a package for me. Cool. I swing the door open with a huge smile (he's kinda cute).

"Abilene Harper?"

"Yes?"

"These are for you." He thrusts a shiny red bag at me. "You *are* a size . . . *wow*, ten, right?" He glances down at my bare feet and I curl my toes into the carpet. I've always been a little self-conscious about my big feet.

"Yes," I admit stiffly and straighten up to my full height so that he has to look up.

"Mr. Martin said to inform you that you should wear the dancing shoes to the rehearsal."

"Gotcha." When he stands there and looks at me like he's waiting for something I say, "Oh, I'm supposed to tip you, right?"

"No, we're not allowed to accept tips from the contestants. Everything here is taken care of for you."

"Oh." I wait for him to elaborate.

"You're tall."

"Yeah, and my feet are big." I roll my eyes. "Anything else?"

"Are you a model? You look a little like Heidi Klum."

I blink at him for a minute waiting for him to burst into a fit of laughter and it ticks me off. I've had to deal with jerks like him since high school. But he doesn't laugh. *Oh. He's serious?* "Th-thank you."

After glancing right and left down the hallway, he leans in close and says softly, "And just between you and me . . . I've seen the other contestants and surely you've got a lock on this thing."

If he hadn't just refused a tip I would have thought he was playing me. "You think so?" I whisper back.

He nods and gives me a wink. "By the way, your feet are cute."

I glance down at my feet and then back at him, still not convinced that he isn't making fun of me.

"Good luck. I'm pulling for you."

"Thanks," I tell him with a smile and close the door. Heidi Klum? I look over at myself in the mirror and see . . . *me*, bed-head and sleep-rumpled. Still, I feel flattered. I'm smiling until I pull the shoes out of the box. "I'm supposed to dance in these?" I dangle them from my fingertips and look at the cream-colored, high-heeled shoes in horror. "I won't even be able to walk, much less dance!" There must be some mistake, but then I remember the shoes the dark-haired dancer wore in the video with Rio and I realize that these are indeed dancing shoes.

I examine them for a moment. They're lightweight and supple—I can see how they might be good for dancing. The heels are fairly high but sturdy and there is an ankle strap as well. Turning them over I run my fingers over the soft leather that's sort of fuzzy instead of slick. "Makes sense. Maybe I can pull this off." It's just that because of my height I've always avoided high-heeled shoes, so I'm worried about falling over or twisting an ankle. "Well, if Rio says I have to wear them I might as well break them in." I slip them on and buckle the ankle strap. Sitting on the bed I stretch my legs out and admire the prettiness of them before taking a deep breath and then standing up.

"Not so bad," I whisper and decide to parade around the room. Of course I wobble, not to mention that I feel like the Jolly Green Giant! The heels are a good three inches, putting me over six feet tall. I walk in circles, barely getting my balance, when the hotel phone rings, making me just about jump out of my skin. I teeter over to the nightstand. "Hello?"

"Abby, it's Rio. Did you get the shoes?" The low, sexy sound of his voice makes me feel all fluttery. "Abby?"

"Oh . . . yes, I got them."

"Do they fit?"

"Like a glove."

"Good. Wear them to practice but nowhere else, okay? They're strictly for dancing."

"Gotcha." Lord, like I'd wear these things anywhere else.

"Oh, and wear shorts or a skirt instead of those bulky pants you wore this morning. They'll be easier to move in."

"Okay. Anything else?"

"No, I'll see you in thirty minutes."

Thirty minutes! I glance over at my pile of stuff in horror. "Okay, if I were shorts just where would I be?" Of course the last duffel bag that I look into is where I find a couple of pairs. I didn't really think to pack summer clothes since it's February, so a pair of cutoff jeans is the best I can do.

So off I go in my Daisy Dukes, white T-shirt, and dancing shoes. What a redneck picture I'm painting, I think as I try to hurry down the hallway. It's not until I'm in the doorway of the rehearsal room that I remember that I shouldn't be wearing the danged shoes. I spot Rio at the other end of the room sorting through CDs and I'm thinking that I can slip the shoes off before getting caught, but of course he looks up and sees me. I give him a weak little wave of my fingers and try not to look guilty. As luck would have it, bad luck, that is, the first thing he does is look down at my feet.

"You're wearing the shoes. I told you that they're strictly for dancing."

Think fast. "Well, I danced all the way here . . . the cha-cha, of course. I even did the Cuban hip thing."

He looks at me to see if I'm kidding or serious and I try to keep a deadpan expression so he can't figure it out.

I'm good at deadpan . . . learned how in high school so that no one knew when my feelings were hurt. I wore a deadpan expression a lot.

"Interesting that you didn't even break a sweat dancing all the way from the other end of the lodge."

"I'm in pretty good shape."

His telltale eyebrow goes up and he doesn't even try to stop it. "Really? We'll see about that."

I look at him closely to see if he's teasing. Nope, I think not. "I'm up for the challenge," I bravely boast with a lift of my chin but then wobble a bit, ruining the effect.

"Very well," Rio says while he walks into the center of the room. He motions for me to join him. "So, show me this hip motion you're so proud of."

"I didn't exactly say I was proud of it . . ." I warn him.

Folding his hands across his chest, he says, "Show me."

I give my hips a tentative little wiggle.

"Surely, you jest."

I'm pretty sure that jest means joke. "All righty, then." I do another Cuban hip motion and this time I put some serious sway in it. He has the nerve to snicker. I narrow my eyes and—

"Stop!"

"Excuse me?"

"You look ridiculous."

"These were the only shorts I could find."

"Not that. I can deal with the shorts. It's your hip motion that . . ."

"Sucks?"

"I was going to say *needs work.*" His lips twitch and for a moment I think he might actually smile but then he catches himself and gives me his scowl that somehow manages to be sexy. Everything the man does is sexy.

I purse my lips. "Well then, *show me*, Mr. Fancy

Pants." I put my hands on my hips and tap one foot.
Oh . . . I suppose I should drop the attitude. What is it
about this guy that brings out the bitch in me?

"Ah, good." He takes me completely off guard with a
grin.

"What?"

"You're giving me some spunk, some emotion. That's
what we need for this dance. Cheeky is good, Abby."

"Cheeky?" I twist my head and look down at my tush.
Nope, my cheeks are covered . . . barely, but they *are*
covered. "Right," I say with a little head bop like I knew
what I was doing all along.

He smiles like he's on to me.

"Okay, I *give*. What is *cheeky*, exactly?"

"Mischievous, flirty. A bit of an attitude."

"Oh, sure, good. That's what I was goin' for. Cheeky."

"Excellent. You've done your homework. Keep it up.
Let's get some music going." Rio heads over to a boom
box and turns on some Latin music that has the distinct
cha-cha-cha rhythm. He comes back to stand very close
to me . . . so close that I catch a whiff of his cologne, and
as always my heart does a little pitter-patter. "Okay,
Abby. Move your feet apart and settle into your hips."

I don't really know what this means but I move my
hips a bit like I'm settling or whatever.

"Now bend your right knee and then straighten up."

I do this and he nods. "Okay, do the other hip but more
like this."

After he demonstrates I try to imitate his sultry movements but I teeter in the danged shoes.

"Again. Relax a bit. You're much too stiff."

"Okay." I bend and straighten but he shakes his head.

"Let me help. " With a sigh Rio places his hands on either side of my hips. "Step right," he tells me and guides
my movements with his hands. I'm trying to concentrate,

really, but he's so close! His fingers are curved around to my ass and his hips are moving in a very suggestive way with me getting me, well, all fired up and flustered.

"Abby, concentrate!"

"I'm tryin'!"

"Just do what I'm doing. It's simple."

"Easy for you to say," I grumble but he ignores me.

"Step, rock. Feel the music. Come, close your eyes and let your hips sway." His accent is getting thicker, so I know that I'm frustrating him. Well, he's frustrating me too . . . just in a very different way. "Are you feeling it?"

"Oh . . . yeah," I admit and I'm a bit embarrassed when my voice is breathless.

"Step, rock," he says close to my ear, making a tingle go all the way to my dancing shoes. "Other foot, step, rock. That's it. *Good*. Yes, much better."

"Really?" I open my eyes but then ruin the moment when I wobble and lose my balance. He catches me firmly around the waist and keeps me from twisting an ankle. "Sorry, it's the shoes."

He gives me a deadpan *yeah, right* look but says, "You'll get used to them. Now close your eyes again, Abby, and just let your body move with the music. Feel the rhythm."

I try to forget that a handsome, sexy male is standing so very close and force myself to concentrate on the music. It's difficult but after a few minutes my dancing becomes more in sync with the beat and I begin to feel more at ease. My body relaxes and my movements become more fluid. I'm not sure how long we do this, but it feels good and I *like* it.

"Okay, much, much better, Abby!"

I give him a shy smile. "Really?" Until now I hadn't realized how much I wanted to please him.

"Yes, now let's get into the closed position and put the hip motion with the basic steps that we learned earlier."

"Can I open my eyes, Obi-Wan Kenobi?"

He chuckles so I guess he gets the joke, or then again maybe he just thinks I'm a little off center. "Yes. Now let me count into the beat. Okay . . . step, rock, cha, cha, cha. Just follow my lead and let the music take over."

I stumble at first and groan. "Sorry, Rio. I'm such a klutz."

"After a few days of doing the same steps and the same sequence over and over you will have what we call muscle memory. It will be almost impossible to mess up."

"Oh, then you don't know me that well."

"No, not yet." He chuckles, low and oh so sexy, in my ear and of course I miss a beat.

"Time for a break," he abruptly announces and it might be my imagination but I think I hear a bit of huskiness in his voice as well. Is my nearness affecting him just a tiny bit?

I dance my way over to the water bottles as a joke but when I turn around to see if Rio's entertained, my heart kicks it up a notch. I do think that he was checking out my jean-clad ass.

"You have legs meant for dancing."

"I—I do?" I swallow hard.

He nods and gives my legs a once-over, but I'm disappointed when I suddenly feel like less of a woman in his eyes and more of a dancing machine. I realize that his interest is purely from a teacher's point of view and not male appreciation.

"What?" He frowns at me. "You're looking at me as if I've insulted you."

"Oh, no . . . not at all," I fib with a wave of my hand. I'm good at lying about my feelings. "I'm just surprised. Of course these long legs excited the high school basketball coach, but he was sorely disappointed in my performance and cut me."

"I have more faith in you than that."

"Well, as it is you're stuck with me."

He smiles and my heart turns over. "Not such a bad thing, Abby Harper. Give yourself some credit."

My throat closes up with unexpected emotion and I turn away and take a swig of water to hide it.

"Did I say something wrong?" He comes up close behind me and I turn around, hoping that I'll maintain my composure. Not trusting my voice, I simply shake my head. "Tell me, Abby."

I inhale a shaky breath and set my water bottle down. "What am I doin' here, Rio? I'm just a small-town waitress . . ." I'm mortified when a tear slides from the corner of my eye and down my cheek.

With a shake of his head as if to clear it he mutters, *"El bebé no llora."*

I don't know what he said but it sure sounded nice even though he might have just said shut the hell up. Why are foreign languages so much sexier than English? I'm touched when he wipes the tear away with his thumb. Then to my utter surprise Rio lowers his head and brushes his mouth across mine. He pulls back slightly and I think he means to end the brief contact, but with a low groan he suddenly captures my mouth in a head-swimming kiss.

8

The Rut Is Officially Over

The touch of Rio's tongue to mine sends liquid fire through my veins and I wrap my arms around his neck to steady my trembling legs. He pushes me back against the cool wall and kisses me with a wild, hot hunger that has me melting. I thread my fingers through his hair and press my body to his, crushing my breasts against his chest. In my heels we are almost the same height, making his hard body mold to mine in all the right places. I move sensually against him, making desire flare and begin to build. Rio moans and kisses me even more deeply.

I've never been kissed like this . . . with so much heat and passion. When he tugs on my bottom lip with his teeth a warm ripple spreads out to my fingertips and down to my toes. Then his moist lips, hot mouth, discover the sensitive side of my neck and with a soft sigh I angle my head to give him better access.

Needing to feel his bare skin, I tug his silky shirt from his pants and then slide my hands up his back, loving the supple ripple of muscle beneath my palms. "My God, Rio . . ." My voice doesn't even sound like my own and I'm wondering how I suddenly became this sultry, sex kitten. It occurs to me that I've really blown my being in a rut all to hell in very short order. I chuckle at the thought and even *that* sounds low, sexy, and inviting . . . Wow, who knew that this could be so easy?

But then Rio suddenly goes very still and I'm thinking that maybe my laughter must have been a mood killer. "Rio . . ." I begin but he shakes his head and then takes a giant step back.

"¿Mi Dios, qué hago yo?" he mutters as he threads his long fingers through his hair.

I don't know what that meant but it didn't sound good. I'm really gonna have to invest in a Spanish dictionary. He looks confused and I'm thinking vulnerable. "Rio?" With my hand outstretched I start to close the distance between us but he stops me in my tracks when that damned eyebrow shoots up.

"Well," he begins in a smooth and emotionless tone that is void of all the earlier heat. "That was a plus."

"What?" Color me confused.

"There's a bit of a spark."

A bit? More like an inferno. I know I'm blinking at him in total confusion but I can't help it.

"We'll need that passion in our routine. Now that I know you can pull it off we'll use it to our advantage."

My heart plummets to my toes like a fast-moving elevator making my stomach lurch. "So, that was a little . . . *test?*"

He avoids looking at me but says, "Yes, and you passed with flying colors. Good for you. Now let's put some of that heat into the cha-cha. What do you say?"

I open my mouth to say just what I'm thinking of him and his little test but I'm so pissed that all that comes out my mouth is a feeble sputter. I want to put some of that *heat* into a slap right across his handsome face. Okay, I've never even come close to slapping a guy before . . .

not even in the diner when Cooter Buckthorn pinched my butt, but boy oh boy, I'm thinking that a loud smack would be mighty satisfying right about now.

This isn't the first time that I've been made a fool of by a guy, but for some reason this one really has me seeing red. While I'm thinking maybe a swift punch in the nose might be an excellent follow-up to the slap Rio points a small remote at the boom box, turning on the music. "Do you remember the basic steps from this morning?" he asks smoothly as he takes me into the closed position. Maybe he wouldn't be so calm if he knew he was about to get his butt kicked. One, two, slap, slap, *punch.*

"Of course," I tell him in a clipped tone while racking my brain to recall the first sequence. Slide basic, cross over, walk around, underarm turn . . . or was it the open break? And do I go right or left in the solo turn?

"Now remember that the dance is a sexual pantomime. I'm seducing you and you're pushing me away."

"No *problem*," I tell him through gritted teeth but if he notices my sarcasm he chooses to ignore it. In fact, I'm *so* ticked off that I dance to the music while following his lead without even thinking about the steps because I'm so busy fuming. I guess there's something to the muscle memory theory. My anger makes my steps short and crisp, but despite my anger I still have to try my damnedest not to be affected by his nearness, the heat of his body, and the possessive feel of his hand on my back. When he cha-cha-cha-chases me I retreat with a haughty lift of my chin and fire in my eyes. I wouldn't be surprised if smoke was curling out of my ears.

Take that, Rio Martin. Ha.

"Abby, stop." He ceases dancing and mutes the music with the remote that was in his front pocket.

Oh, so *that's* what that was. I was wondering. "What?"

"This isn't the tango."

"I know that." This means nothing to me but I nod. "Your point?"

"You need to be bubbly . . . flirt with me. *Tease.*"

I look down at my fancy shoes that are beginning to hurt and shrug my shoulders. Just when I was feeling proud of my dancing he has to go and ruin my moment. Hanging my head I say rather glumly, "I'm not very good at flirting."

"You've got to be kidding."

I snap my head up at his tone. "Why do you say that?"

"Look at you," he says with a wave of his hand. "Surely you have to fight guys off with a stick. Those legs alone are enough to—"

When he suddenly ceases my heart begins to pound. "To what?"

"Oh, come on, Abby." He sounds a little irritated. "What game are we playing? You must know your appeal."

I laugh without humor. "My appeal? Rio, my whole life I've been a gangly, clumsy geek. I've never even had a steady boyfriend. And I don't know how to play games unless you count poker, which I'm pretty good at, but I don't think that's what you mean."

Rio frowns at me for a second. "Are you serious?"

"As a heart attack."

"Come on. You look like you should have been . . . what do they call it? . . . prom queen or whatever."

"Didn't even get asked to go." I chew on the inside of my lip and then blink away the moisture burning behind my eyes. "Doesn't matter anymore but it still hurts to be played like a fool."

"Abby, I wasn't playing you for a fool. About before—"

I halt him by putting both palms up like a cop directing traffic. If I had a whistle I would have blown it too.

"Forget about it, Rio. It ticked me off but I get what you were doing."

"Mi Dios." He runs his fingers through his hair and looks at me for a long moment before giving me a slow smile. "Okay, who cares about being prom queen? You're going to be the Redneck Ballroom Dancing Queen."

"Ya think?" I joke but I was secretly hoping that he was going to say something different . . . like he found me irresistible and couldn't stop himself from kissing me, but I force a smile, anyway.

"Yes, *I think.* After all, you have me as your teacher." With a teasing wink he jams his thumb toward his chest.

"Oh, how lucky can I get?" I tease back while I'm thinking *not nearly lucky enough* but then mentally chastise myself. *Don't go there, Abby!* I try really hard not to stare at the nice slice of exposed chest that felt so supple and smooth beneath my hands. He really should button that danged shirt up.

"Ah, now you're seeing things my way." He points the small remote toward the boom box and the music starts up again. "Now back to work."

I groan. "But my dogs are barkin'."

"What?"

"My feet hurt."

He shrugs. "You want to win this thing, right?"

"But—"

"No buts. Now show me some Cuban motion! Balls of the feet! Swing those hips, Abby. *Flirt.* Make me want you and then shove me away."

Oh, I want him all right. It's the shoving away part that's gonna be tough. I have to laugh even though my feet are killing me and the muscles in my calves are as tight as hard-packed snowballs. I'm still a little miffed about the kissing test that he gave me but every once in a while I catch him giving me an unguarded glance that tells me that our little interlude might not have been as one-sided as he pretended. Not that I'm about to go there again . . . once bitten twice shy and all that. But his belief in me is something I've latched on to like a pit bull. This whole competition might be a joke or a spoof or whatever Comedy Corner wants to call it, but to me this is serious stuff and I aim to win or at the very least give it my best shot.

"One more time, Abby."

Groan. "Okay . . ." One more time turns into ten. I'm grinding my teeth and biting my tongue but I refuse to cry uncle.

"Good job," Rio finally tells me and I notice that he's actually broken a sweat. *Imagine that.* After glancing at his watch he says, "Wow, we danced right through the afternoon break. Time for dinner."

"Thanks for working extra with me, Rio." I'm smiling even though my feet are on fire and I think that even my skin is tired.

"No problem," he replies with a smile and I'm thinking that we're sharing a warm and fuzzy moment until he says, "Um, Abby, take your shoes off unless of course you plan on dancing all the way back to your room."

"I was considering it," I lie.

"Yeah, right," he says with a chuckle but then his smile fades and he gives me a look that I can't quite decipher. "You're something else, you know that?"

"Is that good or bad?" I act like I'm joking but I secretly want to know.

"Bad . . . all bad," he answers with a frown. Of course my eyes must be as big as twenty-five-cent gum balls, because he laughs. "Abby, I'm just kidding."

"I knew that," I lie and purse my lips for good measure.

"Right." He draws out the word and gives me a knowing grin. "I do have a sense of humor, you know."

"Right . . ." I mimic and he laughs again. I sit down on a nearby bench with a wince as I begin to unbuckle one shoe. "Ah, that feels so good."

"Your dogs still barking?"

"No, they're too *doggone* tired. All they can manage is whimperin'," I answer with a weak grin.

Rio gives me a look that's actually laced with sympathy. "Here," he says softly. Brushing away my hands, he kneels down in front of me on one leg and props my foot up onto his thigh. I try not to dwell on how his silky shirt is molded to his damp skin but, heaven help me, I *am* dwelling and I have to grip the edges of the wooden bench so as not to reach out and touch him. He bends his dark head and eases my shoe off my foot. Good Lord, I hope that my feet don't stink! I'm thinking that he's going to lower my foot and undo the other shoe but instead he grips my heel in his palm and then *ohmigod*, he begins to massage the ball of my foot with his thumb.

"Is this making it better?" Without looking up he massages deeper using both of his thumbs to work his magic. When he looks up in question I nod because speaking is beyond me at this point. My tired body is about to slither right off the bench like melted butter on a hot griddle. I grip the bench so hard that I wonder if I'm leaving fingernail marks.

"Relax, Abby."

"I'm relaxed," I lie.

Rio glances at my white-knuckled grip and shakes his head. "Lean back against the wall and close your eyes."

"'Kay," I say weakly.

"Now breathe deeply and try to release the tension."

"'Kay," I lamely repeat and suck in a big breath of Rio-scented air. Can a girl have an orgasm from getting her feet rubbed? I'm thinking yes. The cool wall feels good against my shoulder blades and his warm hands are easing the pain while making my feet feel tingly and pliant. "Mmmm," I groan long and low in my throat. It's kinda embarrassing but I can't help it.

When he finishes with my now limp, droopy foot I'm disappointed and thinking of protesting until he starts working on my other foot and I'm suddenly wishing I had two more feet instead of hands, but then again that would be weird . . . Bottom line is that I don't want him to stop. Ever.

"Feeling better?"

"Mmmm . . . if you ever give up teaching rednecks to dance you could make millions doin' this."

He chuckles. "Millions, huh?"

"I'd fork it over in a heartbeat at the end of a double."

"What's a double?"

"Back-to-back shifts. Basically workin' from mornin' till night."

"You have to do that very often?"

I hear a frown in his voice but I'm too weak to open my eyes to find out. "Um-hmm, more often than not."

"That's got to be difficult." His hands still for a minute and I wiggle my foot in impatience.

"I'm used to it." With my eyes still closed I shrug, making my shoulders slide against the smooth wall. "I'm not alone. Most of the folks here in Misty Creek are in the same boat . . . working overtime or moonlightin'. A lot of the farmers have second jobs when farming is enough work for an army. We might be rednecks but let me tell ya, Rio Martin, we're the backbone of this country."

Rio remains silent and I think I might have gone overboard with my little speech so I sneak a peek at him through my eyelashes. He has a thoughtful frown on his face and seems to have totally forgotten about my tired feet. "Um . . . whoof, whoof."

His frown disappears and he grins. "Okay, okay. So your dogs are still barking."

"Yes, uh, but not stinkin', I hope?"

Rio waves a hand over my foot. "Now that you mention it."

"Oh!" I try to pull my foot from his firm grasp and he laughs.

"Just kidding, Abby."

"You're becoming quite the jokester. Ha, ha, *ha*."

"I guess you bring it out in me."

"In other words I'm an easy target."

"You said it, not me."

"Mmmm . . ." Whatever comeback I was going to shoot at him is lost when he starts the magic massage once again. "You must know what's it called . . . ? Oh yeah, *reflexology*."

"Some," he admits and sounds surprised that I asked. "The feet and hands are much more sensitive than most people realize. There are detailed charts about places on the foot that mirror organs in the body and are supposed to deal with all sorts of ailments. There are claims of everything from losing weight to removing toxins from the body."

"Do you believe in all of that?"

"I simply think that it relieves stress and feels good," he admits and continues to massage my foot.

"Y'all got that right."

He chuckles.

"What?"

"You talk funny. Long and lazy with extra syllables."

I sit up from the wall. "And you don't?" He does something to the arch of my foot that makes me shiver and I slide weakly back against the wall.

"I speak a foreign language. That's different. Don't be offended. I think it's cute."

"No offense taken," I tell him but for some reason I suddenly think of him dancing with the dark-haired beauty and cute isn't how I want Rio to view me. I don't want to be cute and sweet. I want to be hot and sexy. Then I remind myself that I shouldn't be thinking in those terms anyway. Closing my eyes I let my mind and body relax and simply enjoy his hands on my feet . . . Oh, it feels so good . . . I could do this for a living. "Mmmm . . ." I inhale a deep breath and try to control the silly smile on my face while the tension drains from my body like water through a sieve.

"Abby?"

"Mmmm?"

"Are you asleep?"

"Course not!" I tell him but do believe that I dozed off for a moment there. "I was . . . practicing my dance moves in my head."

"Ah, so that explains the snoring."

Of course I gasp. "Oh no, *really*?" I sit up straight and check the side of my mouth for drool. It's dry, thank the Lord. I hope it was a girly snore and not like a freight train. "Was I loud?"

"I was merely teasing," he answers with a chuckle. "You're easy."

"You!" I give him a playful shove in the shoulder but because he's holding my foot on one leg he loses his balance and topples sideways. "Whoa!" I squeak. Since he's still holding on to my foot I'm pulled from the bench with him, giving him an unintentional elbow to the gut and a knee to the groin in a pro-wrestling-worthy move.

With a hiss and a grunt he says, *"La mierda santa que usted me agarró en la ingle."*

Oh, that can't be good. "Ohmigod, Rio, you okay?"

"No todavía. ¿Deme por favor un minuto, bueno?"

"I'm not sure what you just said but I'm taking that

strained sound in your voice as a no. Did . . . did I catch your family jewels?"

"*Sí, tengo miedo que usted hizo.*"

"That means yes . . . right?"

"Yes, Abby. *Yes* . . ." With his eyes closed he does a pitiful little moan that has me biting my bottom lip between my teeth. "Please, mother of God, get off me."

"Oh . . . right." After rolling off him I prop myself up on one elbow and ask in a very timid voice, "Is there something I can do?"

"No. Please, dear God, no."

"An ice pack maybe?"

He groans. "Abby, *apenas me da un minuto y permitió que mí agarrar el aliento que jode.*"

"You have to speak English," I patiently remind him.

"I said give me a minute to catch my fucking breath."

"Oh."

Wincing, he squeezes his eyes shut. "Sorry."

"That's my line."

"About the"—he pauses to gasp—"language. It just . . . slipped out."

"Think nothing of it. And if it's any consolation my elbow smarts. Your gut is rock solid."

He manages a half grin. "That helps a little. So, how is your knee? Must hurt too."

I think about this for a second and then start laughing so hard that my elbow slips on the hardwood floor and I land on my back. When the laughter ends there is an awkward moment of silence and I have this compelling need to reach over and hold his hand. Of course I don't but I feel a sudden emotional tug that I don't quite understand. There is just something about Rio Martin that makes me want to fall into his arms. I know that he's my dance instructor. I know that he's out of my league. And I just bet that he more than likely has a hot Latina girlfriend waiting for him somewhere. But that doesn't stop me from wanting him.

"You should head on back or you'll miss your dinner," Rio says.

I'm relieved that his strained voice is sounding more like his raspy sexy self. "I can wait for you."

"There's no need," he tells me in a casual and dismissive tone that's disappointing.

"Oh, okay." I mentally chastise myself for thinking of him in any other way other than my instructor. I'm only setting myself up for heartache. When am I gonna learn?

"See you bright and early, Abby."

I scoot up to my feet and smile down at him, hoping that I don't look too wistful. God, he's gorgeous.

"What?" He props himself up to his elbows with a slight wince.

"What do you mean?" I try to look innocent but it's hard when I'm feeling anything but.

"You were giving me a funny look."

"Goes hand in hand with my funny talkin'."

With a low chuckle he shakes his head. "Scoot, Abby. You need your dinner."

With one last look over my shoulder to make sure he's okay I leave him and hurry to the dining hall. It looks like I'm the last one to enter the room but I notice a vacant chair next to Danny. When he spots me, he smiles and waves me over. Wow, what I would have given for him to do that back in the high school cafeteria. But then I tell myself that those days are over and that I need to live for today. With that thought in mind I head to his table and sit down to a very nice tossed salad.

"Hey there," Danny says with a weary smile. "Tough day, huh?"

"Tough doesn't even begin to describe it," Daisy Potter chimes in with an exaggerated groan. Then again maybe it's *not* exaggerated. She looks too pooped to pop. "Who knew that dancin' was so hard?"

"I hear ya," I agree with a sympathetic nod. I'm met with tired greetings from everyone else as well. Travis Tucker looks plumb, well, tuckered out and even Julia doesn't look so cheerleader perky.

Looking around I notice that several cameras are placed around the room but no one seems to care. Muted background music and the tinkling of silverware against glass as the servers bring out some sort of chicken dish are just about the only sounds in the big room. For long-winded southerners this quiet conversation, yawns, and scattered groans are unusual but understandable. It's good to know that I'm not the only one dead on my feet, but then again it tells me that we are all taking this competition seriously. But with fifty thousand dollars on the line, who wouldn't? I only hope that this remains friendly and that no one gets hurt during what I'm sure is going to become the adventure of a lifetime.

One thing is for sure: my rut is officially over.

9

Keep Your Eyes on the Prize

The next week can only be described as a whirlwind and of course before this *nothing* I've ever been involved in could ever be described as such. When we aren't rehearsing, which fills up the bulk of the day, we're getting fitted for costumes, or being interviewed for the clips that will be shown as teasers for the upcoming show or for fillers in between the dancing just like they do on *American Idol*. It's all so . . . surreal. I still can't get over the fact that there are cameras *everywhere* filming *all* of the time. It seems like a waste to me but I suppose it's how reality shows are done. Jesse called to tell me that the families and friends of the contestants are also being interviewed and that a film crew has been hard at work all over Misty Creek. They were in the diner yesterday doing little snippets about me! I can only hope that people are kind and don't divulge my rather clumsy nature.

With a long sigh I prop my sore feet up on a couple of pillows and lean my back against the headboard wishing I had the nerve to call Rio and beg for one of his magic foot massages. But I don't since nerve is something I'm sorely lacking, so instead I point the remote at the

temperamental television and surf through the channels.
Like everything else in this here lodge the TVs need some
serious updating. At least they have satellite so I have
about a million channels to choose from but nothing
seems to catch my attention until I reach channel 69
which is Comedy Corner, and . . .

"Ohmigod. Th—there I am! There I *am!*" I point the
remote at the TV and giggle when the caption THE WAIT-
RESS waves across the bottom of the screen. For the few
seconds that I'm dancing I look hometown and dorky
while bumbling around with the suave and sexy Rio . . .
Hey, when did they film that anyway? Those cameramen
are a sneaky lot. I can cha-cha better than that, can't I?
Then I trip and Rio has to catch me. Oh no, I guess not.
"They should have cut that part," I mutter with a little
sniff.

"Oh no!" I have to laugh when huge Mac Murphy "the
Trucker" does this twinkle-toe thing that I think is supposed to be the quick step. He's surprisingly light on his
feet but the contrast between his twinkle-toe dancing and
his size is too funny. Betty Cook "the Lunch Lady" has a
bug-eyed Olive Oyl expression as she does the tango with
her very tall, serious-looking instructor. The commercial
blends into a scene with Mary Lou Laker "the Maid."
Mary Lou is led into a spin with a move that for a shin-
ing moment looks pretty impressive but unfortunately she
keeps spinning right out the door while squealing. Her
horrified partner stands there with his hands to his
cheeks. When we hear a crashing noise he then hurries
out the door after her.

"Oh, so *that's* why she had that bandage on her forehead," I mumble as I watch. The clips end with a "more
to come" promise from the deep-voiced announcer followed by the Web site address and the upcoming date for
the reality TV spoof *Dancing with the Rednecks.* The

commercial concludes with one more shot of Mary Lou spinning out of control. I have to laugh but then feel guilty and put my hand over my mouth to hide my grin. "Oh my Lord," I mumble behind my hand.

My cell phone rings, bringing me out of my oh-my-God-this-is-really-gonna-be-on-TV shocked state. I smile when I see that it's Jesse.

"Abby! I just saw you on Comedy Corner."

"I know, *I know*! I caught it too."

"That was so damned sweet!"

I'm so excited that I don't even tell him to watch his language. "Did Mama see it?"

"You know it's past her bedtime but I rewound it and taped it for her."

"Good." The cable television remote is still a mystery to me but Jesse had TiVo mastered the very first day we got it. I lean back against the headboard and close my eyes. "Oh, but, Jesse, we all looked so . . ."

"Redneck?" He has the nerve to chuckle.

"Yes! And heaven help me but I admit that I laughed. Jesse, when Mary Lou twirled out the door . . . *Lord have mercy* . . . but until now it didn't hit home that this is really gonna be on TV, ya know?"

"It'll be fun, Abby. It's just entertainment."

"At our expense."

"Aw, get over it, Abby."

"I know," I grumble. "How's Mama? The diner? I've talked to her briefly a few times but we've mostly played phone tag."

"She's fine."

I swallow the sudden emotion clogging my throat. "I miss her."

"Hey, how about me?"

"Never, squirt," I say but my darned voice cracks like a CB radio.

"Even grumpy old Pete was asking about ya."

"No . . ."

"Way!"

I giggle while swiping at a tear but then say, "Hey, you're doin' your homework and everything, right? Not fallin' behind?"

He sighs loudly. "Don't worry. It's handled. You just concentrate on dancin'. Look, we'll see you in a couple days when you come in for the show. Mama and I have front row seats."

"How did you manage that?"

"Mitchell Banks. You know he's kinda sweet on Mama? Can you believe it? *Mama?*"

I smile at the thought. She deserves some attention and pampering.

"They even went out to dinner. Mama got all gussied up in a dress I've never seen before and made her hair bigger than I thought possible."

"Well, good for her. I guess she's broken out of her rut too."

Jesse chuckles and I'm glad that he seems okay with Mama dating. "It would appear so. I'm keepin' an eye on him, though," Jesse assures me in a manly way that reminds me that my baby brother is growing up.

"That's good to hear. I love you, squirt. And I have to admit that I miss you terribly."

"I love you too, sis. Sleep tight."

"You too and go to bed right this minute. It's late."

He chuckles. "Okay. Oh, and, Abby, I'm really proud of you."

Jesse says this in his usual laid-back way but his comment makes my heart swell. "Really?" I ask and then feel foolish like I'm fishing for compliments.

"Of course," he says like he can't believe I'm asking. "I always am. Mama is too. You know that, right?"

"Sure I know," I scoff but I really don't. "Course you haven't seen me dance yet. You might change your tune after that."

"I know you'll do us proud."

"All I can promise is my best."

"I know you always do."

"Why, thank you." My heart swells a bit more. "Night, Jesse." I flip the phone shut, ending the call before I burst into tears and upset him. Jesse can't stand to see Mama or me cry. With a shaky sigh I lean back and stare at the small phone for a moment. "They're proud of me," I whisper. "Well, whadaya know?" I realize that I'm the daughter and the big sister, so their love is unconditional, but pride? See, I've never really excelled at something special the way most kids do. I sucked at sports and my grades were average at best. I don't play a musical instrument and my singing voice could make a grown man weep. I actually mouth the hymns instead of singing in church. In other words I have no talent whatsoever.

I work hard and I'm quick with a smile or a joke but other than that I go pretty much unnoticed in Misty Creek. Sure, I'm aware that I've recently blossomed into some curves that turn male heads but I still feel like the geeky old me, so to hear Jesse say that he and Mama are proud of me makes me get all choked up. "Oh . . . bless their hearts." I burst into noisy tears, *so* noisy that at first I don't hear the knocking at my door.

"J-just a m-minute," I try to yell, sounding sort of garbled. While sniffing and swiping at my eyes I head over to the door and peek through the peephole. Rio? I glance down at my Pink Panther oversized sleep shirt that has a little yellow mustard stain from eating cheese-filled pretzel bites in bed and wish I was wearing something slinky and sexy with my hair flowing in silky disarray instead of pulled back into a sloppy ponytail but then remind myself for the hundredth time not to think of him in that way! After inhaling another shaky breath I tug the door open and attempt a smile.

I fail.

"My God, what's wrong?"

"Whatever do you mean?" I try again to muster up a bright smile but it trembles at the corners, ruining the effect.

"Have you been crying?"

"Why, no."

He gives me a disbelieving frown.

"Only a little." I step back for him to enter the room and then play with the hem of my sleep shirt.

"Right." He gives me an I-don't-believe-it-for-a-minute look.

"It's no big deal."

"Sure it is," he insists and takes a step closer to me.

Really? Hope blossoms. Does he really care? Unable to help myself I give him the once-over. Instead of his usual dance attire he's in faded, low-slung jeans and a white V-neck T-shirt. His long dark hair is damp like he's just recently showered and man oh man, he smells good . . . like mango and spice.

"Tell me about what's bothering you."

Feeling silly I shake my head.

"Abby, your emotional state will have an effect on how you perform. Now, please, tell me what's bothering you. Are you nervous about the rehearsal at the dance hall tomorrow?"

My hope fades like a shooting star falling from the sky. When will I understand that this is all about winning with Rio? I'm his student, end of story.

"Abby?" He takes a step closer and puts a gentle finger beneath my chin, forcing me to look at him.

"It's just a little touch of homesickness, that's all. I promise it won't mess up my dancing."

"Is that *all*?" He searches my face for clues and if I didn't know better I would swear that he cares.

I so want to lean my face into the palm of his hand but instead I step back from his touch and nod. "Yeah, that's all."

He clears his throat and jams his hands into his pockets. "So, are you missing anyone in particular?"

His question surprises me. "You mean like . . . a guy?" Hope rears its ugly head again.

Looking a bit uncomfortable he clears his throat. "Yes, and whoever he is you need to forget about him and focus."

"There's no guy, Rio."

"Oh." He looks so relieved that I have to smile. Looking a little flustered he says, "Good. You don't need that kind of distraction."

I peer at him closely, wishing I knew if he meant this strictly on a professional basis, but of course I don't have the nerve to ask. "Right. Um, why are you here at this late hour?"

Instead of answering he seems distracted by my attire. He glances at my Pink Panther shirt and his mouth twitches in amusement.

"It was a Christmas gift," I explain.

"There's no need to be embarrassed. I think it's, ah, how do you say? . . . cute."

Cute. Right. I'm beginning to hate that word. To my horror I feel my eyes well up. God, he's going to think I'm a crazy person. Maybe I am.

"What's wrong, Abby?"

"I told you. I have a touch of homesickness."

"Bull. Be honest with me."

I hesitate, thinking that honesty is *not* the best policy,

but then blurt out, "Okay . . . maybe I don't want to be *cute*. Maybe I want to be—" Luckily I stop myself but he looks at me expectantly.

"Maybe you want to be *what*?"

"Nothin'," I insist but I can tell by his expression that he's not going to give this one up, so I continue in a very small voice, "Sexy."

"Sexy?" Rio angles his head at me for a second and then does something I didn't think possible. He bursts into a fit of laughter. At first I think it's kind of cool that Rio can cut loose and laugh like that since I didn't think he had it in him, but then it hits me that he's laughing *at* me! So of course I shove him. Well, okay, I *don't* shove him but I want to and I sort of imagine it in my head. Instead, I stand there with my hands fisted at my sides and try to at least muster up a glare but it's darned hard to do while blinking back tears.

"Why are you looking at me like you want to smack me?"

"Well, let me think. Oh yeah, because I *do*."

"Why?"

"Because you're . . . laughing at me, Rio."

"Is that what you think?"

"Uh . . . *yeah*. Your huge guffaws were a big clue."

Sobering, he shakes his head and bravely takes a step into smacking range. "Abby, I'm not laughing *at* you. I happen to find the fact that you don't consider yourself sexy quite amusing."

"Really?"

"Why must you always doubt yourself?"

Not knowing how to answer I just shrug.

"I've as much as told you so. You *are* a desirable, *sexy* woman, Abby, and we will use that to our advantage on the dance floor."

My heart sinks a bit and I look down at the shaggy

brown carpet. "Oh, so . . . you mean that I'm sexy in like a general observation kind of way?" I know I'm fishing again but I just can't seem to stop my wayward tongue.

"Yes," he begins but then hesitates before growling, "No, *hell no.*"

Of course my head snaps to attention and I wait for him to explain.

"Abby . . . *listen.*"

Oh, that firm tone didn't sound good but I say hopefully, "I'm all ears."

"Hardly." He gives me a look that once again sets my panties on fire . . . Oh, but then I remember that I'm not wearing any panties beneath my sleep shirt. Or a bra. Holy cow, does he know? I swallow hard and my gaze locks with his. I'm acutely aware of the bed directly behind me. His gaze flicks in that direction and I'm thinking . . . *so is he.*

"Rio . . ." My voice sounds like a husky invitation and perhaps it's because he closes the gap between us so that we're almost touching. I can feel the heat of his body, smell that tang of his aftershave, and I so want him to touch me.

Kiss me.

A muscle jumps in his clenched jaw as if he's fighting his own feelings in that same direction. Closing his eyes he inhales a deep breath. "Ah . . . Abby."

Unable to help myself I reach out and put the palms of my hands on his chest. Beneath the thin cotton I feel his heartbeat, his warm body, and I suddenly imagine his bare skin sliding next to mine. "Rio . . ."

His eyes open but he shakes his head harder. "Abby, we shouldn't do this."

"I know. But then why are you here, Rio?"

"I came armed with the flimsy excuse that I needed to see the color of your costume so I could match my sash."

"Excuse for what?" My heart begins pounding like a jackhammer.

"For this." Rio wraps his arms around me and captures my mouth in a tender kiss that has my toes curling into the shaggy carpet. Instead of hot and wild this kiss is long and languid as if he's savoring something that he knows must end. But when I feel his lips begin to pull away I thread my fingers through his cool, damp hair and hold his mouth captive.

With a groan of surrender Rio deepens the kiss and when his tongue touches mine a jolt of heat has me melting into his embrace. He tastes like mint and I think to myself that maybe he really did have kissing me on his mind. I find this so endearing that right here and now I fall a little in love with Rio Martin.

After kissing me so tenderly that my heart aches Rio pulls away and leans his forehead against mine. *"Yo no puedo creer que haga esto."*

"I don't know what you said but it sure sounded pretty."

"Ah, Abby, I said that I can't believe I'm doing this."

"Oh. Well, I guess it wasn't so pretty after all," I try to joke to hide my sharp stab of disappointment.

He chuckles and then steps back to look at me. *"Yo le encuentro irristable."*

"I'm afraid to ask."

"You're irresistible," he says and then puts a finger to my lips. "Don't you dare say, *really*?" His imitation of my southern drawl makes me chuckle even though I know where he's going with this.

"I'm hearing a great big *but*, Rio."

"Oh, Abby," he says sadly and traces my bottom lip with his fingertip, giving me a hot shiver. I wish I had the nerve to suck his finger right into my mouth but I don't.

"Getting romantically involved with your dance partner can be a disaster."

When his brown eyes darken with what looks like hurt I have to ask, "Was this from personal experience?"

"I'm afraid so," he replies and I wonder if his sadness has anything to do with the dark-haired woman in the dance tapes with him, but my southern upbringing has me too polite to ask.

"I shouldn't have come here. Shouldn't have kissed you." He blows out a sigh. "But as I was trying to choreograph our next dance all I could *think about* was kissing you. I thought if I came here and did just that I could get it out of my system."

When his eyes linger on my mouth I swallow hard and ask, "So . . . did you?"

"No. It only makes me want you even more."

Okay, this is like being on a doggone roller coaster ride. First I'm up and then I'm down. "So now what do we do?"

"It's quite simple. We resist."

"Sure. I understand." I nod like I think this is the right thing to do but I really want to grab him and kiss him again. And again.

"Good. You have my apologies, Abby. From now on I promise to be professional."

I nod but I'm thinking that this professional nonsense is way overrated.

"Tomorrow we have dress rehearsal and then our first live dance competition. I don't want to break our concentration again. We're on the same page, right?"

I hesitate because he's giving me a look like he's half hoping that I'll grab him and fall onto the big bed right there behind us. I'm liking that plan a whole lot better.

"Abby? We're on the same page, *right?*" he repeats.

"Oh . . . sure. *Yes.* Of course."

"Good," he murmurs with a crisp nod, but is that disappointment I read in his dark eyes? "I'll see you tomorrow at the dance hall. I'm heading over there early to check it out. Good night, Abby."

I open my mouth to tell him good night but then clamp my lips together because what is about to come out of my mouth is an invitation to stay. But before I can muster up the nerve he turns on his heel and leaves.

"Well . . . *wow.*" I sit down on the bed and relive the encounter in my head a couple of times just to make sure that I didn't get it all wrong. I'm flattered and, well, flabbergasted that Rio is attracted to me when I was convinced that he was all about the dancing. I'm wondering if I could have convinced him to stay but then I remind myself that I'm not here to find a guy. I'm here to win this competition.

"Get your priorities straight," I tell myself firmly. "Just do as he says and resist. How hard can it be?"

10

Driven to Distraction

I suppose that it's human nature to want something even more when you know you can't have it. I want Rio Martin. I went to bed wanting him. I woke up wanting him. Now here I am in this amazing stretch limo with half of the other contestants on my way to the rehearsal at the Bluegrass Dance Hall and I'm still mooning over him when I'm supposed to resign myself to the fact that I can't have him.

"Lord have mercy," I mutter as I stare unseeing out the tinted window.

"I know," Mary Lou Laker says, thinking that I'm talking to her. She smacks her knee. "Isn't it amazin'? Looks like most of Misty Creek is lined up on the streets just a-wavin' at us. Lookie at the signs! It's almost like bein' in a parade. I've always wanted to be in a parade. How 'bout you, Abby? You ever been in a parade?"

"Can't say as I have," I reply absently. I don't point out that this isn't a parade.

"Oh, lookie, there's your mama and Jesse." Mary Lou nudges me with her elbow and I snap out of my mooning state of mind and wave to Mama and Jesse, who are standing right outside the diner sporting big smiles and snapping pictures with one of those throwaway cameras. Even crusty old Pete is standing there with a cigarette hanging out of the corner of his mouth. Of course they can't see us since the windows are tinted black but we're all waving like they can. Mary Lou's right. Main Street is lined with people cheering, waving, and holding up hand-made signs.

"Lordy, I feel like a rock star or one of them *American Idol* people," Mary Lou says and then giggles.

I have to admit that it's enough to make a person feel special.

"Hey, look at this," Travis Tucker says and pushes a button to open the sliding sunroof. "Ain't that sweet?"

Betty Cook, the lunch lady who served me gummy macaroni and cheese and various versions of casserole surprise, suddenly stands up, pokes her head out the roof, and begins to wave to the crowd. She's rewarded with cheers and whistles. With a little squeal, Daisy Potter joins Betty and they proceed to throw kisses and wave like they're Paris Hilton and Nicole Richie when they were still friends.

The Bluegrass Dance Hall is on the opposite end of town, a big barnlike structure that's mostly used for square dancing, clogging, and country line dancing on Saturday nights. Ballroom dancing here, I'm sure, is a first.

When we arrive cameramen are waiting to film our each and every move, but we're all getting so used to this that we barely pay them any mind. We're all chatting and laughing in an excited but nervous kind of way. Danny, who was riding in the other limo, heads in my direction but is sidetracked by Julia. Oddly enough, I'm relieved.

And then I'm annoyed. I've been waiting all my life for Danny to be interested in me and then Rio comes along, a guy who will be in and out of my life in just a few weeks, and he's all I can think about. Danny is a hometown boy, a hard worker and successful in his own right. He is the kind of guy I need to be setting my sights on. Not a Spanish-speaking, world-class ballroom dancer who makes me melt but is way out of my league.

I need to do more than *resist* Rio Martin. I need to not think of him in that way at all. I'm only setting myself up for a fall if I do. So from here on in I'm really going to start thinking of Rio as my dance instructor and nothing more. *There*, I feel better already.

"Hello, Abby," says a deep, smoky voice laced with a doggone Spanish accent that can only belong to one person.

My traitorous heart begins beating triple time but I carefully school my features into a nonchalant smile and turn around to face Rio. "Good mornin'." I incline my head politely. He gives me an equally bland smile and a crisp all-business nod. Good. We're still on the same page. Perhaps this won't be so hard after all. I just won't think about how hot he looks in tight black pants and an ice blue formfitting shirt or how sexy his long hair is pulled back in a short ponytail. Where I come from guys don't do this, but on Rio it works . . . *not* that I'm noticing or anything. I'm certainly not going to think about how his inky black hair feels sifting though my fingers. Nope, not me. Shaking my head as I follow him inside I ask, "Did you get here early?"

He nods. "Yes. I wanted to get a feel for the layout of the dance floor. We'll all get turns rehearsing and I'm happy to say that we're first. Are you ready?"

"I was born ready."

Rio chuckles at my comment and flashes me a grin that makes it so darned hard to remain aloof. Note to self: no more jokes. His broody bad-boy scowl is hard enough to resist but his laughter lights up his face and warms my fast-beating heart. But there's a hint of sadness about Rio that has me wanting to make him smile in spite of my resolve to resist my growing attraction to him. There's so much more that I want to know about him but then I remind myself to concentrate on the competition that's important to my family.

As I pass by him into the dance hall he says, "Are you okay? You look so . . . *serious.*"

"Got my game face on."

He frowns like he doesn't understand and then I realize that he probably doesn't.

"I'm concentratin' on the task at hand, Rio. That's the plan, right?"

"Ye're danged tootin'," he says, making my head whip around. When I raise my eyebrows he explains, "Heard that big truck driver use that phrase a couple of times. Seemed like an appropriate time to use it. You know, when in Rome . . ."

I roll my eyes but have trouble not smiling. "Um, you'll have to work on that accent to be convincin'."

"Ye're danged tootin'," he repeats, attempting to sound southern but ending up sounding like a Spanish John Wayne.

I have to laugh, which is a mistake because when Rio joins me my resistance starts to dissolve as quickly as a sand castle slapped by a big wave. I'm thinking that I don't have a lot of willpower when it comes to chocolate chip cookies or Rio Martin. In fact, he looks good enough to just gobble right up and I'm sure I'm gazing at him like I want to do just that, but resist I must. That's the plan. Clearing my throat I say, "Okay, well, let's get this show on the road."

"Pardon?"

"Let's get this party started."

He shakes his head. "Party?"

"Let's *dance*, Rio."

He grins. "Now you're speaking my language."

I return his smile, glad that I'm able to keep things lighthearted and upbeat. We go through a series of stretches and warm-ups when Rio turns on the music. Finally after he decides we're limber enough we settle into the closed position with my hand resting lightly on his arm, and I suddenly understand the meaning of sexual tension. The brush of his fingertips down my back raises goose bumps on my skin, making me wish I had worn something more substantial than this thin cotton T-shirt. I try to concentrate on the sequence of the dance steps and to ignore the hum of desire that being in his arms creates, but the beat of the music, the Cuban motion of our hips sends a sensual message that my body will not deny. My heart beats faster and faster while my breathing becomes quick and shallow. I follow Rio's lead, feeling the rhythm and dancing the routine without even thinking about the steps.

"That's good, Abby. You're improving by leaps and bounds."

"Thanks." I hope he thinks my breathlessness is from the exertion.

"We want to dance closer to the judges if possible. I'll have to adjust where we begin the dance." He points to a long table set up where there are usually high tables with bar stools. The huge dance hall is rustic, with a western flair, and I'm guessing they will leave it this way to contrast the elegant dancing with the hoedown atmosphere. Lighting is being set as we speak and I notice for the first time that a camera has been filming us.

"Ignore the media," Rio says, noticing my gaze. "You can't allow yourself to be distracted by the cameras or the crowd."

"I'll try not to."

"But at the same time we must play up to them."

"Okay." I nod but I'm a little confused. How can I play up to them and ignore them at the same time? "Shouldn't I just concentrate on the dance?"

Rio shakes his head. "I wish that were the case. But this is a reality show, Abby. The most popular couple will win. Unfortunately, we can be the best dancers and still come up short, so we have to play both angles. Am I making sense?"

"Yes," I answer slowly but I can't suppress a little nervous quiver in my voice. "People watch Comedy Corner to laugh so they might vote for the funniest couple, right?"

"Exactly. We don't have any control over that."

"That won't be our angle, will it?"

"Funniest?" Rio chuckles. "Do I look like a funny guy?"

"Uh . . . no."

"Exactly. I couldn't pull that off if my life depended on it. But we can entertain. I've won enough competitions to know how to work the audience and the judges."

"Yes, but I haven't. Rio, I don't have a *clue* as to how to do this."

"Remember the chase of the cha-cha. Show some of that cheeky personality. Woo the judges and wow the crowd."

"You really think I can do that?"

He takes a step closer. "I *know* you can."

But then he gives me an intense look that has me asking, "Oh boy, there's something more, isn't there?"

Rio nods but remains silent as if what he has to say is going to make me uncomfortable.

I sigh. "It's okay. Lay it on me."

"Lay it on you?" He frowns and seems to mull this over.

"Spit it *out*, Rio."

"Spit *what* out?" He runs his tongue over his teeth as if he's afraid he's got some food stuck there.

"Mercy me. Just tell me straight up, will you? I'm a big girl. I can take it."

He throws his hands up in the air. *"¡Para la consideración de Dios, habla inglés!"*

"Speak *English*, Rio."

"That's what I just told *you* to do."

"I'm speakin' English!"

"But I'm hearing you in Spanish and the literal translation of your redneck lingo isn't making sense."

I narrow my eyes and thin my lips. "Did you just call me a redneck?"

"Is there a problem with that? I mean, you *are* a redneck, right?" He gives me another confused look.

"Yes, I *am*," I tell him and add a little head bop but I'm suddenly wondering why the hell I'm getting all fired up. I think it has something to do with suppressing the need to kiss him senseless. Still, I take a step closer and try to look all big and bad like when I try to intimidate Jesse even though it never works. I don't think it's working now, either. Suddenly remembering my train of thought that was sidetracked by Rio's too sexy self, I add, "And I'm proud of it." I feel the need to jam my thumb toward my chest for emphasis.

"And I'm proud to be Mexican. Just where are you going with this, Abby?" His voice is a low, exasperated growl and Lord help me, I want to kiss the man.

"I—I don't rightly . . . *know*." My own voice is barely above a whisper and I can't help but stare at his mouth that is so very close to mine. "I guess I'm a bit confused and feeling . . . um, frustrated."

After glancing over at the cameras Rio takes my hand. "Come with me."

Like he'd have to ask twice. Weaving past the tables and bar stools, I let him lead me out the side door away from the prying eyes of the media and camera crew. Once outside I take a deep breath of cool morning air and give Rio my attention. "Okay, spill."

"Spill?" He rolls his eyes. "I'm guessing that translates to tell you what I mean."

"Yes." I sigh. "I'm going to have to refrain from pop culture references and redneck slang."

"That would help."

I shrug. "Sorry, it's who I am."

"No need to be sorry, Abby. I like who you are."

"Real—" I begin but then stop myself.

He tucks a finger beneath my chin and says gruffly, "Yeah, *really*."

Swallowing hard I back up a step and come up against the brick wall behind me. "So . . . so, what is this thing you need to tell me?"

"We have something that, as far as I can tell, no other couple in this competition has."

"And just what is that?"

He takes a step closer and rests his palms on the wall behind me. Mere inches separate us. He blocks out the bright sunlight and replaces the cool breeze with the warmth of his body and yet I shiver. "We have chemistry, Abby. Something smoldering between us." He leans in even closer but not yet touching and whispers in my ear, "Do you feel it?"

I nod. "You know I do. Just . . . just what are you doin', Rio? I thought resistance was the plan."

"It is, but only *off* the dance floor. On the floor we must sizzle. This is the thing that will separate us from the pack. I think the only way we have a chance to win this is to play up our chemistry. What do you say, Abby?"

"I reckon I'm down with that."

He gives me a half grin. "*Down with that* means that you're in agreement, right?"

I start to say yes. I should say yes. But instead I put a hand on his chest and shock myself by saying, "I suppose. But why? We're both adults and there *is* something between us that we can't deny. There's no rule that says we can't be together, Rio. I checked. Why fight it?"

He goes very still, making me regret my outburst. His heart is pounding beneath my hand and for a moment I think he's going to throw caution to the wind and lean in and kiss me. "It would be a mistake, Abby. We've already discussed this."

"A mistake, Rio? Or a risk? There's a big difference."

"It would be both." A shadow of sadness passes over his features. "A mistake I'm not willing to make and a risk I'm not willing to take for both of our sakes."

I open my mouth to protest but he places a gentle finger on my lips. "I do care about you, Abby. But I know what this money would mean to your family. I was so wrong to let my desire and my feelings overcome what I know is best. Now let's get back in there and rehearse before our time is up."

Although I nod in agreement I see regret in his eyes and deep down inside I know that I'm not ready to give up.

11

Dancing with the Rednecks

You might think that there is a limit to how nervous a person can get, but with each passing minute while Rio and I wait our turn to dance in the first live competition at the Bluegrass Dance Hall my nerves stretch tighter than a rubber band on a slingshot. My stomach feels like it's sailing over the first hill of a roller coaster . . . rising up and hovering near my throat before plunging like a bat outta hell.

"I have to pee." We're waiting our turn in what they call the greenroom but in reality is a big storage area that's been cleared of beer cases and *hello*, the walls are white. "I'll be back in a minute . . . or maybe never."

"Abby, how can that be?" Rio takes his gaze from the television monitor where we can watch the performers dance and gives me another worried once-over. "You've gone twice in the past thirty minutes. There couldn't be anything left in your bladder."

"The second time I didn't pee. I barfed."

"Barfed? What is barfed?"

"Threw up. Blaaah." I demonstrate with a hand motion from my mouth toward the floor and then rest my hand on my sequined stomach. "In fact I think I might have to do it again."

"You don't have to pee or . . . *barf.*"

"Oh yes, I do. I have to do both. Maybe at the same time."

"You *don't*," he quietly assures me and takes my shaky, cold hand in his firm, warm grasp. I hang on for dear life, hoping that we won't need a visit to the hospital for crushed fingers. "You don't have long to wait. After this dance there's one more and then us." He nods toward the monitor. "Take your mind off your nerves and watch."

I inhale a deep breath in an effort to calm myself, but the stench of stale beer and cigarettes hovering in the storage room, excuse me, the greenroom, makes me cringe. "'Kay," I say weakly. "Sorry for bein' so crude."

"How so?"

"Sayin' pee and barf and everything. I'm just not thinkin' straight. I've been raised better than that." I smooth my hand over my hair to make sure that it's still in place, but there's so much hair spray holding it back into the tight bun at the nape of my neck that there is really no need. A couple of snappy little no-nonsense wardrobe women are flitting around touching up makeup and checking our costumes. I tug at the top of mine, thinking that it reveals a little too much cleavage, but it's double-taped in place to avoid any wardrobe malfunctions. Other than that it's amazing. The teal sequins glitter beneath the lights and silver fringe swishes when I spin and turn. It's tight like a swimsuit but stretchy and surprisingly comfortable except for where the tape is stuck to my boobies and my butt.

Rio gently squeezes my hand. "Don't worry. You look gorgeous. Those long legs of yours will impress the judges. You have the look of a champion, Abby."

"So do you," I reply and he sure does. His tight black pants have a teal satin stripe down the leg that matches my costume. And Lord have *mercy*, you could bounce quarters off his very nice ass. His snowy-white shirt has full-sleeved arms but fits close to his torso and is unbuttoned halfway, revealing a generous portion of his tanned chest. A teal sash adds a bit of flash and with his hair slicked back into a short ponytail he has that Antonio Banderas pirate look that's going to drive the ladies wild.

Turning my attention back to the television, I have to be a bit impressed with big trucker Mac Murphy's twinkle-toed quickstep that's both powerful and light on his feet. He looks a bit like a gangster in a dark blue pin-striped suit, and the crowd is eating it up with a spoon. I guess his instructor whipped him into shape, because he hardly misses a beat.

"He could be the dark horse in this competition," Rio comments while rubbing his chin.

"You mean like the underdog?"

Rio nods.

"I thought I was the underdog."

Rio chuckles. "I think it applies to just about everyone in this competition."

"We can't *all* be underdogs."

"I didn't think so until now. I'm seeing a lot of fight in all of you." He gives me a grin. "I have to admit that I'm impressed."

"So you're eatin' your hat, huh?"

"I'm not sure what that means but I'm guessing, *yes*."

I give him a warm smile and think to myself just how much I'm coming to like Rio. He's a lot more down-to-earth than what I had originally thought. Maybe he grew up a regular Joe in Mexico City so he gets where we're coming from. I make a mental note to ask about his childhood.

"Wow, that was a cool move," I comment after Mac and his partner do some springy, fancy footwork, ending their dance with a flashy flourish that brings the crowd to their feet. Sure, it was far from perfect but who would have thought that Mac could move like that? In fact, except for Mary Lou Laker, whose dance ended in another disastrous out-of-control spin all the way off the dance floor and into the crowd, and burly Jimmy Joe Porter the plumber, who slipped during a turn and ended up on the floor twirling on his back like an upside-down turtle, the dances have been surprisingly well executed. I feel a measure of pride over this and it settles my stomach a tiny bit.

As we wait for the judges to hold up their points I go over the previous dances in my head, wondering where Rio and I will stack up. Ex-cheerleader Julia Mayer was very good as Jesse had predicted, but Rio had whispered to me that she was too mechanical and lacking in emotional appeal. Travis the farmer was clunky and comical but charming. Gangly Betty Cook, looking more like Olive Oyl than ever, brought the house down with her serious attempt at the tango. With pursed lips and one eyebrow cocked she gave it all she had and actually looked kinda pretty without that hair net on her head and a ladle in her hand. If I had been watching instead of participating I would have enjoyed the entire show.

"Oh my goodness!" I clamp my hand over my mouth when Ben Sebastian, the cocky Ryan Seacrest wannabee, announces Danny Becker, the Misty Creek mechanic, and his champion dance partner, Anna Fandango, who will perform the jive. Danny is dressed in black jeans, a black T-shirt, and a thin black belt. His hair is slicked back 1950s style, making him look like John Travolta in *Grease.* His blond partner looks like Sandy in her poodle skirt and letter sweater, and sure enough they begin danc-

ing to the energetic song "Greased Lightnin'." They
begin with the hand-pointing, knee-popping part and the
audience loves it.

I giggle as Danny hams it up for the crowd and the
camera. The dance is fast-paced with lots of kicks and
spins, but being a natural athlete, Danny can handle it.
"Wow, he's good."

Rio shrugs and flicks me a glance. "He's okay. A little
rough around the edges."

"Well, yeah. After all, he's a mechanic. He's an athlete, though. Always was a good dancer."

"Let me guess . . . high school football?" Rio says this
a little smugly and I have to wonder who suddenly put a
bug up his butt.

"Yes," I admit a little defensively but I have to wonder
about Rio's attitude. Could he be jealous? My heart
thumps at the thought.

"Was he your boyfriend?"

Is his question a little too casual or am I desperately
trying to read something in this? "Ha, only in my dreams.
I was a geek, remember? I didn't date much." Okay, at *all*
really, but I don't feel the need to share that part.

"I still have a hard time believing that, Abby," he says
but keeps his eyes on the dance.

"Remind me to show you my yearbook." I'm about to
elaborate a bit more on my high school geekness when
Ben Sebastian announces our names.

Holy crap.

Rio gives my hand a squeeze. "Well, Abby Harper,
you're not a geek *now*. You ready to kick some serious
butt?"

I have to chuckle at his attempt at American slang. It
just doesn't sound badass with his delicious accent. "You
know it." I extend my fists for the double knuckle bump
that I've taught him and give him a quick, confident nod

of my hair-sprayed head while I'm actually wondering if my legs will function.

Thankfully, they do in a wet noodle kind of way, and a moment later we're standing in the wings while Danny and Anna are getting their scores from the three judges. Carson Sage, the silver-haired, resident snarky judge, gives them a snooty seven, saying that they had showmanship but lacked proper technique. Ha, I'd like to see him change the brake pads on a car as effortlessly as Danny. Bet his technique would *suck*. I'd give him a two! Of course I realize that he is giving an over-the-top spoof on mean judges but it still rankles.

Myra Jones is a really hip black chick with big hair and a warm smile. A bit more forgiving, she gushingly gives Danny and Anna a solid eight, earning loud approval from the hometown crowd.

Peter Kelly, the third judge, is flamboyantly gay and outrageously funny and holds up another eight, putting Danny one point behind Mac and his partner, who scored three eights.

Great. We get to follow the best performance of the evening.

"We can do better," Rio whispers in my ear.

I muster up a nod and a smile but I have my doubts.

When Ben Sebastian announces our names my heart starts doing a pretty good version of the quickstep against my rib cage. When I refuse to walk out onto the dance floor, Rio gently tugs on my hand and without knowing how I got there I'm suddenly standing beneath the hot lights before the crowd. I'm seriously thinking of bolting when I spot Jesse and Mama standing on their feet clapping wildly. Their faces are glowing and Mama, who never does anything remotely unladylike, puts her thumb and pinkie in her mouth and lets out a shrill whistle. Jesse shoots her a wide-eyed *who knew you could do that?* look

but she gives him a shrug and a huge smile, making Jesse
tip his head back and laugh. They are positively glowing.

It hits me again that they're proud of me. *Of me.* Closing my eyes I swallow hard, thinking, *I can do this.*

I have to do this.

Taking a deep breath, I lift my chin and *will* my knees
to stop their damned knocking but they just won't. I can't
do this no matter how much I want to. My hand trembles
in Rio's grasp and he gives me a reassuring squeeze that
should but doesn't help.

I'm trembling like a stop sign in a hurricane and cold
sweat is rolling down my back and I do believe that I'm
about to hurl in front of God and everybody. I'm gonna
be the laughingstock *and* the film clip on Comedy Corner
that will run longer than Mary Lou Laker's crazy out-of-
control spin into the crowd. They'll show it on *Good
Morning America* and I'll be the talk around the watercooler. But worst of all I'll be the very first one voted off
and totally disappoint Mama and Jesse.

And lose a shot at the money!

Oh God, this sucks! How in blue blazes did I get my
sorry self talked into doing this? Fear and anger roll
around in my stomach and start to bubble up in my throat
in the form of hysteria.

But then I hear this gruff voice in my head saying,
"Abby girl, you can do this. I know you can, sugarplum."

My daddy. He always called me sugarplumb.

All of a sudden I can feel his presence like he's looking down and smilin', proud of me too, and here I am
about to choke.

So I dig down deep. Really deep. There's gotta be
courage in there somewhere, doggone it! After inhaling a
cleansing breath I lift my chin a notch higher and give
Rio a crisp nod that I'm ready.

"That's my girl," the voice of my daddy whispers and

a sudden feeling of calm washes over me, warming my freezing hands and steadying my trembling legs.

When the sultry beat of the music begins, I dance without thinking, feeling the rhythm, the emotion. Step, rock, cha, cha, *cha*. On the balls of my feet with my movements crisp and sure, I let Rio lead me, chase me. Rocking my hips, I give new meaning to the Cuban motion, teasing, flirting, and then pushing him away. When we do the open break and underarm turn I give it all I've got. In the background I can hear the roar of approval from the crowd and I play it up with a sassy, cheeky attitude.

Rio is sexy, dashing . . . pursuing me with a tenacity that leaves me breathless. When he dances closer our bodies brush and his touch is firm, lingering, with the hint of a promise. He leads me into an underarm turn and I do a teasing walk-around to face him. Release and open, cha, cha, *cha* . . . He lures me back with heat in his dark eyes and pulls me in close for a near kiss and then moves to a side basic, rock, step, side to side, opens the position up right next to the judges while I do a teasing walk-around to face him. We ham for the camera and play up to the crowd and I can feel it working. Suddenly I feel confident . . . yeah, me, *confident*. Sexy. I purse my lips, arch an eyebrow, and let Rio come in close before dancing away.

As the song ends, Rio spins me in, finally catching me flush against his body with another near kiss, and then bends me backward over his arm in a dramatic finish that brings the audience to its feet. Wow, no one has ever clapped for me before unless you include when I'd drop a trayful of food in the diner and I don't think that counts.

Rio tilts me back up, spins me next to his body, and I fling my arm skyward just like we rehearsed. We bow, milking the moment until breathless and panting we wait for our scores.

Ben Sebastian hurries over to us sporting his toothy trademark smile. "That was *hot*." He thrusts the microphone at me and says, "You were smokin', Abby Harper. Any thoughts for the crowd?"

I blink at the microphone for a second while my heart hammers in my chest but I suddenly know what I need to say. "I owe it all to Rio Martin," I tell Ben while trying to control my breathing. "My awesome instructor." I smile up at Rio, who returns my smile and hugs me close.

"Abby is a hard worker. The credit belongs to her."

I beam up at him and I know we sound cheesy but it's the truth.

Ben turns from us to the camera and says in his deep announcer voice, "Well, we know how the crowd feels. Let's see what the judges have to say about Abby Harper and Rio Martin's sizzling cha-cha." Turning to the judges he says, "Carson, let's start with you."

Of course my knees start knocking and I'm glad for Rio's strong arm about my waist. Pursing his lips Carson rubs his chin for a long moment, making me want to climb over the judges' table and knock him a good one. But I stand there clinging to Rio with a smile that's starting to wobble around the edges. This is by far the most nerve-racking thing I've ever experienced in my entire life.

Finally, Carson takes a deep breath and in his clipped British accent that I'm beginning to think is fake he says, "There have been moments in this competition that have been painful to watch. Sort of like passing a wreck on the highway . . . you have to gawk even though you want to turn away in horror."

A gasp rises up from the audience and I think I might

have heard my mama booing. Rio tightens his arm about my waist.

Carson waves a dismissive hand at the audience. "You know what I'm talking about. Don't deny it. Chill, people."

The crowd collectively boos, not just my mama this time.

Holding up his hand to quiet the crowd, Ben rolls his eyes. "Carson, this is a live show. Get to your point."

Again I know in the back of my head that this is drama for ratings but it's enough to make me sweat on top of already sweating!

"Very well. While Abby the waitress is somewhat lacking in finesse, she more than makes up for it in moxie."

I'm not sure what moxie means but it seems to please Rio because he gives me a squeeze and smiles down at me.

"Since Ben is giving me the hurry-it-up look I'll simply say that I enjoyed the performance. It was sexy and smart. Rio and Abby, my hat goes off to you." He holds up an eight.

"Myra?" Ben asks. "What are your comments for Rio and Abby?"

"Oh," she gushes while shaking her head, making her huge hair sort of flop around, "that was delicious. Rio, honey, you made me sweat. What have you done to this little ole waitress from Misty Creek? Abby, baby, you rock, girl. I give you a solid nine!"

Rio inclines his head and I follow suit with a polite nod. I was instructed to be gracious with criticism and classy with praise. Under no circumstances are we to whoop it up and of course my nature is to do just that but I hold it in by swallowing and trying to keep my grin under control.

"Peter?" Ben asks. "You look ready to explode over there. What do you have to say?"

Peter is smiling and squirming with excitement. "Listen. When I was asked to do this show I was, like, no way. Misty Creek? Redneck ballroom dancing? Sure, it could be *amusing* . . . but come on, people. How much can a person endure? Okay, I have to confess that it *is* entertaining. I mean, when that Jimmy Joe the plumber spun around on his back like a dead cockroach, I about lost it." Peter puts his hand to his mouth and shakes his head.

"Peter," Ben warns.

I'm not sure where Peter is going with this and I do some squirming of my own. I feel Rio stiffen, so he's wondering, too.

"Okay, okay. I'll get to my point. Rio, you sexy beast, you have worked a miracle and turned this little waitress into a dancing machine. Abby girl, you put the motion in Cuban. I give you a nine!" He flicks up his sign with a flourish and the crowd roars.

Ohmigod, we're in first place! I sway a little with giddy relief and really wish I could give Rio a huge hug but I'm afraid that it might be unprofessional when I'm not really professional anyway. Ben is explaining to the television audience how to text-message votes or to go online to vote for a favorite redneck.

"Now we'll show you a short clip from each dance to refresh your memory. Remember that your votes count! For the first three weeks we will eliminate the bottom two couples, leaving the final six, and then *one* each week after that until we have our champion, who will be awarded *fifty thousand dollars*! So call, text, or vote online for your favorite couple because tomorrow night two of these couples will be voted off the show. Until tomorrow, I'm Ben Sebastian . . . see ya!"

I still want to hug Rio but when the show ends the

crowd rushes forward and it's mass chaos. There are way too many hugs and flashbulbs flashing for my liking but I smile and hug all those who approach me. But what I'm not prepared for is when a youngster thrusts a pen and paper at me and she asks for my autograph! Can you imagine? Me?

I start to write my name after I remember it but she stops me and says, "Make it out to Carrie."

"Oh, okay." I try to act famous and all but my fingers tremble a bit. Luckily Carrie stands there beaming and doesn't seem to notice.

"Oh, thank you. *Thank you!* I'm votin' for you and"— she points at Rio—"the pirate guy."

Of course I'm tongue-tied but Rio comes to the rescue. "Thank you very much, Carrie."

She scurries off and I watch with my jaw hanging open.

Rio leans in and asks in my ear, "How does it feel to be famous?"

"I'm not famous," I scoff with a wave of my hand but it sure feels like it. Cameras are going off like strobe lights. Rio smiles his crooked smile at me, the one I like the best, and I'm remembering that I still didn't get a hug from him. I'm about to ask him for one when I suddenly spot Mama and Jesse weaving through the crowd in an attempt to reach us.

"Rio, there's Mama and Jesse." I grab his hand and move in that direction.

"Oh, Abby!" Mama hugs me hard and then pulls back to kiss me on both cheeks. "I was so proud of you!" She promptly bursts into tears and of course I try to hold back but I join her.

"And you, young man, were absolutely wonderful!" she says to Rio while dabbing at her eyes with a hanky.

Mama is in her highest heels but still has to crane her head back to look up at Rio.

"Why, thank you."

"Oh, you are so welcome. My, *my*, handsome and polite too!" She dabs at the corner of her eyes carefully, keeping her mascara from running, and then steps forward and gives Rio a fierce hug. He looks a bit startled at the intensity of her affection but when it comes to emotions Mama rarely holds back.

Jesse gives me a double knuckle-bump and then a big bear hug. "You were amazing, Abby. I knew you would be."

"You did not."

Jesse laughs. "Well, let's say I was hoping that you would be amazing and you were." He thrusts his hand out to Rio. "Nice to meet you, Rio. I'm Jesse Harper."

"Likewise." Rio clasps Jesse's hand and they both smile but Jesse gives him a bit of a look that says that he had better be good to me. Rio seems to get the unspoken message and instead of smiling like he could, he gives Jesse a serious look and a nod, telling him that he understands.

This seems to satisfy Jesse and he breaks into a more kidlike grin. "How in the world were you able to teach my sister to dance like that?"

Mama gives Jesse an elbow but Rio laughs. "Your sister is a hard worker. Never gives up."

"Oh, like you would let me."

Rio chuckles. "See, we understand each other."

Out of the corner of my eye, I catch Mama watching us, and she arches one delicate eyebrow. I see her wondering if there's something more between Rio and me than dancing but of course she's much too polite to ask. But she's wondering. Before she can draw me aside and ask privately it's announced over a loudspeaker that our limos are waiting to whisk us back up the mountain to the lodge.

I give Mama a quick hug and then turn to Jesse and do the same. "The inns are full, Abby," he whispers in my ear. "Business at the diner has been booming. I haven't seen Mama this happy in a long time. Keep up the good work, sis."

I pull back, on the verge of tears again, and Jesse is doing some major league blinking as well. A typical guy, though, he gives my shoulder a shove, clears his throat, and then says, "Good luck! I'm going home to vote."

"Oh yes, we havta vote!" Mama says but then frowns. "Oh." She puts her hands to her cheeks. "I don't know how! Just what is tex-mexing? I thought that was spicy food. You know, tacos and whatnot."

Jesse chuckles. "Text-messaging. I'll show you, Mama."

Tears well up in my eyes as I turn to go. I miss them so much. Being famous might be fun and all but I suddenly realize that I wouldn't give up my life for the world.

Rio escorts me out to the limo. All of the dance partners are chatting and hugging once we are outside and it reminds me that I never did get my hug. I'm about to ask but Rio suddenly seems all business like he knows that I'm about to throw myself into his arms. I guess it's written all over my face.

"I'll see you bright and early, Abby. Get a good night's sleep, okay? And a good breakfast too. Be ready to work hard."

I nod and somehow muster up a smile, trying not to show my disappointment at his businesslike demeanor. I know he's keeping his distance and sticking to our resistance pact . . . but would a little ole hug hurt? I'm thinking that I'm going to just throw caution to the wind and hug him anyway but he turns on his heel and walks away. I have the urge to run after him, grab his arm, and swing him around for a hug and a kiss, but of course I don't. With a sigh, I slip inside the limo. By rights I should be on cloud nine and although I'm thrilled that our dance went so well, there just seems to be something missing.

My damned hug!

The ride back up to the lodge is full of whooping and hollering and I try to join in even though my heart isn't really in it. My doggone heart is too busy mooning over Rio Martin.

I mentally tell myself to *stop*. I'm in the thick of this competition and I owe it to my family to focus on dancing. "Keep your eyes on the prize," I say to myself but Daisy Potter the Piggly Wiggly cashier hears me and turns her gaze my way.

"Now, there's the spirit, Abby." She thrusts a flute of champagne that I didn't realize had been popped open into my hand. Raising her glass she says to everyone, "Here's to keeping your eyes on the prize!"

"Hear, hear!" we collectively shout and of course I join in, not wanting to bring attention to my Rio state of mind.

"Here's to fifty grand!" Travis Tucker adds. He tips back his flute to take a drink, just as the limo lurches, and sloshes it down his chin. Everybody laughs. Everyone is in a good mood.

I should be in a good mood. After all, I'm in the running for the money.

Yeah, fifty grand. Think with your head and not with your heart, I tell myself firmly. Of course my heart just doesn't *get it*.

12

Easier Said Than Done

"Look, Rio, I did a lot of thinking last night and while I know there are valid reasons why we should resist this attraction between us, well, I got to thinkin' that we could have both. Right? I mean, who is to say that being together would harm our chances at winning? Maybe it would help!" I exclaim with a bright smile. "Let's just go with the flow. Whadaya say?"

I wrinkle my nose at myself in the mirror. No, he won't know what *go with the flow* means, and leave out the dorky smile. This is serious stuff. Clearing my throat I begin rehearsing the end of my speech again. "Let's let the chips fall where they may." Grrr. He probably won't know what that means either. "Let's throw caution to the wind," I venture with a dramatic wave of my hand. "Oh, that sucked!" And sounded way too risky. I'm so bad at this. *So very bad.*

Licking my lips, I flip my ponytail over my shoulder and open my mouth to start again but I'm beginning to have my doubts that this is a wise thing to do. Then again, I went to sleep with Rio on my mind and woke up the same danged way, so how could giving in to my feelings for him make things worse? I think this resistance thing is just way too hard. I mean, why fight it? It occurs to me that I should ask him just who hurt him in the past to make him so cautious but I simply don't have the nerve. Some chick must have done a number on him.

With a sigh I decide to give it one more shot. "Rio, I know that we decided to resist this growing attraction between us and I fully understand the reasons why, but the fact is that I can't stop thinking about you. I've never felt this way before. You'll only be here for a few weeks and I don't want you to leave Misty Creek without giving our relationship a chance. I do believe that I would regret that for the rest of my life."

There. I nod my head at myself. The end might have been a little heavy on the drama but it's the truth. If I don't tell Rio Martin how I feel I *will* regret it. With the sudden passing of my daddy I truly know how fragile life can be and there should be no regrets. The saying "nothing ventured, nothing gained" comes to mind and I think it's about time that I start venturing.

"Oh no!" The red digital numbers on the bedside alarm clock tell me that breakfast is almost over. Knowing that Rio will be working me harder than ever, I grab my bag with my dancing shoes and extra towels to mop my sweat that is sure to come and hurry out the door. Sure enough, they're closing down breakfast but I manage to snag a chocolate doughnut and a bottle of apple juice. I wanted orange juice but it's all gone.

While chewing on bites of doughnut and sipping the sweet juice I all but sprint down the hallway not really tasting my breakfast because I'm rehearsing my little speech in my head instead of thinking about eating. Not an easy task. When I reach the rehearsal room door, though, I get skittish, causing the doughnut to do swan dives into the puddle of apple juice sloshing in my tummy. I put a hand to my stomach in an effort to stop the flipping and flopping and then take a deep breath. "Nothing ventured, nothing gained," I remind myself and armed with that thought I push open the heavy door.

"Rio, I know we decided . . ." I begin but my perfect little speech dies on my lips when I see Rio talking in rather loud and rapid Spanish to the dark-haired woman from the dance videos. Their conversation is so intense and heated that they don't even notice me.

She's beautiful . . . dark and exotic, petite and curvy— everything I'm not. Her cleavage is all but spilling out of her low-cut top, a deep ruby red that matches her pouting lips.

My heart of course plummets like a sky diver whose parachute fails to open, and it feels as if it lands with a dull thud somewhere near my toes. With a long sigh I mentally rip my speech to itty-bitty pieces and imagine it falling to the ground like confetti. For a moment I simply stand there wondering if I could slowly back up without being noticed. I used to be pretty good at that as a teenager but I'm a little rusty.

I'm contemplating doing just that but when the dark-haired woman places a small hand on Rio's bare chest where his shirt gapes open and looks up at him with doe-like pleading eyes I've officially had enough. I clear my throat to get their attention but it sounds a little gurgled so I clear it again, more forcefully this time, and they simultaneously swivel their dark heads in my direction.

"Abby . . ." Rio begins, his eyes stormy, but the pouting little siren interrupts him.

"Ahhh," she says, placing her hands on her rounded hips, "so *this* is the little redneck waitress that you were talking about." Her voice is heavily accented with lots of long *e*s and dripping with . . . *venom* or something equally not nice.

"Angelina . . ." Rio warns in a frustrated low voice but she ignores him and gives me an amused grin like she knows some joke that I'm not in on. I don't like that feeling and I have to wonder just what Rio said about me.

I'm feeling like a dorky country bumpkin in my jean shorts and T-shirt, but luckily my southern manners kick in and I stick out my hand. "Hello, I'm Abby Harper." I do my best to sound friendly but it's not easy.

"Oh," Rio says, "forgive me. Abby, this is Angelina Perez. She will be taking the place of Anna, Danny's partner, who had to leave due to a family emergency."

I swallow, wondering if this is good news or not. On one hand, Angelina is here on business, not to see Rio. *Good.* On the other hand, not only is she here to stay, but she's also Danny's partner. Poor Danny. *Bad.*

Angelina gives me a quick dead-fish handshake, confirming my suspicion that she can't be trusted. My daddy always said that a firm handshake is an indication of good character. Not that I like to prejudge people or anything but she's giving me some bad vibes.

"Rio," Angelina says, dismissing me and turning her full attention to him with her pout back in place, "we need to talk."

"Our rehearsal time is tickin' away, Rio." I tap my watch, drawing a glare from Angelina, who certainly isn't angelic even though the morning sunlight is beaming in the big picture window, casting a weird halolike glow over her head. This almost makes me giggle, so I cough instead to mask the impulse. I tend to giggle at odd times like when I get nervous, and, unfortunately, more often than not it's not appropriate.

"You can just wait a few minutes," Angelina informs me and I would have given her a little static but I suddenly notice something. She's kinda old. Not like *really* old, but in the glare of the sunlight I can see fine lines, making me guess that she's maybe early thirties. I remember reading in Rio's bio that he's twenty-seven. Yes, she's definitely got him by a few years. Interesting.

"Angelina, Abby's right. We need to rehearse."

I give her a *there, now hit the door* look.

"Just a minute of your time, Rio," she pleads, once again placing her hand on his chest.

I have this almost uncontrollable urge to get in her face and say, "Don't you go messin' with my man." But then I remember that Rio isn't my man. Hey, but he *is* my dance partner and I give Rio a look that says so.

"Angelina, *esto tendrá que esperar.*"

At that she narrows her dark eyes at him. Then she trails her hand down his chest in a suggestive way that makes me want to growl the don't-go-messin'-with-my-man thing again. But just when I think I might do that except say *partner* instead of *man*, she flips her hair over her shoulder, pivots on her high heels, and wiggles her hips out the door.

For an awkward moment there's silence.

"So, she was your dance partner." My voice is a little clipped but I can't help it.

Rio nods. "Yes."

"And she dumped you when you hurt your knee."

"That's old news, Abby. Let's get to work."

I nod and sit down on the bench to strap on my shoes. Rio remains quiet as he gives his attention to his notes. At first I think that I should just let it go and concentrate on the dancing but I just can't. "So, are you still in love with her?" I say this in a conversational tone even though my heart is beating wildly. I know it's rude of me to ask such a personal question but if I'm not going to let it go, then why beat around the bush?

Rio's head snaps up. At first I think he's going to tell me to mind my own business and I suppose he would be right, but he surprises me by slowly walking over and sitting down on the bench next to me.

"I'm sorry for being so nosy," I tell him.

Rio looks at my nose with a frown but then he must catch my meaning because he says, "I don't mind telling you. Angelina was a dance instructor at my family's studio in Mexico City. She and I became dance partners when I was eighteen. She was twenty-five at the time . . . beautiful, sensual, a woman when I was used to giggling girls . . . and I immediately fell for her. We became world-class dancers, winning some major ballroom dance competitions. I was wild about her and we eventually became lovers."

When he goes silent I slide a glance at his face. His dark eyes are stormy once again and a muscle is ticking in his jaw.

"She hurt you, didn't she?"

Rio turns his head to look at me. "I was young and stupid."

"Bull. You weren't *stupid*. You were young and in love." I say this so hotly that he grins. "So what happened?"

"You're right. She dumped me when I blew out my knee."

"That *bitch*!" I sputter and then clamp a hand over my mouth.

Rio chuckles but then gives me a look that makes my heart kick into high gear. "Not something you would ever do, is it?" He says this like a statement rather than a question and gives me a look I can't quite figure out.

Not on your life, I think but I don't say it because I don't want it to seem like I'm trying to score points. "So, she broke your heart?" *That stupid bitch,* I think again but refrain from voicing my opinion out loud. I would have been bringing him breakfast in bed and giving him back rubs and stuff.

Rio shrugs and then leans back against the wall. "I thought so at the time. I brooded and drank lots of tequila."

I wrinkle my nose. "Ew, that stuff is rank."

He raises his eyebrows. "Ah, then you haven't had the good stuff."

"Guess I haven't," I answer and something suddenly hangs in the air between us like we aren't really talking about booze.

Rio's gaze drops to my mouth and for a heart-stopping moment I think he might kiss me. He even leans slightly in my direction but then straightens and says, "As it turns out it was for the best. My father fell into ill health and I had to take over running the studio."

"So, you got over her?"

"Yes." Rio nods. "It turns out that my father had been ill and in my damned self-indulgence I didn't realize how serious it was. We were in danger of losing the studio *and* my father, so I took over and threw myself into saving them both."

I think of my own father's death and I put a hand on Rio's thigh. "And did you?"

"My father is a fighter," he says with pride. "After open heart surgery he regained his health, thank goodness." But then he shakes his head. "Had I been around to help instead of wallowing in my misery perhaps it wouldn't have come to that."

"I understand where you're comin' from. I never thought my big strong daddy would up and die, so I guess I took him for granted. And my mama? She worked her tail off makin' ends meet for me and Jesse. Until recently when Mitchell Banks was flirtin' with her I didn't realize how much she gave up when Daddy died. Don't beat yourself up about it, Rio. We were kids. We didn't understand."

He gives me a warm smile. "Thanks. You have, as you say . . . a good head on your shoulders. But I bet you were always there to lend your mother a hand working those double shifts and helping raise your little brother, right, Abby?"

Looking at the floor, I shrug.

"Just what did you give up, Abby Harper? What are your dreams?"

"M-*my* dreams?"

He tucks a finger beneath my chin, tilting my head up to look at him. "Yes. You want college for your brother. The diner renovated for your mother. Tell me, what do *you* want?"

I want you, I think but I don't say it.

There is this *one* thing but I've never told anyone, so I say instead, "A new pickup with all the trimmings would be danged sweet."

He gives me a level look. "Okay, so you want a truck. But what are your *dreams*, Abby?"

I look into his brown eyes that seem so sincere and caring and confess, "Well . . . I've always loved helping Mama bake her pies."

He raises his eyebrows like he thinks that's interesting . . . or maybe weird. "Go on."

I nibble on my lip for a second and then admit, "Um, there's this school, Sullivan University, in Louisville, Kentucky, where you can study culinary arts and baking." I feel my face grow hot but I continue. "See, I always wanted to learn how to bake fancy cakes, cookies, and pastries. I have a weakness for chocolate chip cookies."

"So, do you bake a lot?"

"I've fiddled around some in the kitchen, only after everyone else was gone, mind you, but there's never much time. See, we have a dead period after lunch and I thought that if we had fancy cakes and such and got one of those cappuccino machines we could draw in some of the late shoppers for dessert and coffee." He's not laughing yet, so I continue. "Maybe add some music? Tourists could drop in and relax, you know?" When he nods I get excited. "Coffeehouses are *so* popular and both would be good take-out items, too." But then I shake my head. "Silly . . . I know."

"No, it's not silly at all. Abby, did you ever approach your mother about this?"

I swallow hard. "No. She has enough on her mind. Plus, if I go off to school, who would help her? She needs me, Rio. And . . . and where would the money come from? Jesse is the smart one. He deserves to go to school, not me."

He gives me a slow smile. "I think fifty grand might help. Let's get to work, my little future baker. We have the jive to learn."

"The one Danny did?"

"Yes."

"Do I get to wear a poodle skirt?"

"That's not my department but I'm guessing yes."

"How fun! Oh, but that dance is fast."

"Yes, it is," he says, pushing up to his feet. "In fact, it is the fastest of the Latin dances with lots of kicks and twirling of the woman," he says, circling his index finger in the air.

I groan but he ignores my distress. What if I twirl into the crowd like Mary Lou Laker?

"It will look like our feet are all over the place in every direction but the dance is actually very controlled. The feet should be under the body and the knees should always be close together."

"Okay . . ." I'm trying to picture doing this and I have to warn him, "But my big feet aren't easily controlled."

"That's about to change. We'll be doing the flick, ball

change a lot." At my confused look, something he's getting used to, he demonstrates, standing on one foot and kicking down at the same time. Holy cow. "Keep in mind that your toes are always pointed to the ground when kicking."

"Sure," I say with a nod knowing full well that I'll forget until I do this a million times and the thank-the-Lord muscle memory thing starts taking over. God had his thinking cap on when he put that little memory chip in our brains.

Rio tugs me to my feet but before we begin I have to ask, "Rio, the studio. Did you save it for your daddy?"

He hesitates as if this question sort of stumps him and then answers, "You could say that."

"Good for you. I know how you feel. I would hate to have my mama lose the diner."

"We have that in common, then."

I'm thinking that Rio and I have more in common than I once thought. At first he had seemed so sophisticated and out of my league, but now I feel yet another connection and it gives me hope. It's good to know that we aren't such worlds apart after all. Although I'm not totally convinced that he's still not hung up on that Angelina chickie, I feel like there's a chance for us. Now all I have to do is get past this silly resistance thing he insisted on. But first thing's first: I have to learn the jive.

13

A Force to Be Reckoned With

Just when I think I've reached the pinnacle of how nervous I can possibly get I'm put into a situation that's worse than the previous one. Like now, here I am standing beneath the lights and cameras mangling Rio's hand once again while we wait to see the first two couples to get the heave-ho. Given our high scores I think we're safe but then again this is not only a reality show, but also a reality show *spoof*, so I'm thinking that anything can and will happen just like Mitchell Banks and Rio warned. As it is they're doing all of the rotten things from reality shows combined . . . putting us in so-called bottom three and all that nonsense. Twice now Rio and I have been made to think we're goners. While I realize that Comedy Corner is going over the top with this for the laughs it's still just as hard on us as any other reality show. We all could use the money and we all want to win. Not to mention that although not every contestant is what you'd call my friend, they're all good people. I'd even feel a little bad if Julia got the boot.

The dance hall is packed and I can see Jesse and Mama looking as nervous as I feel. No, I take that back. No one could look as nervous as I feel without being a quivering puddle on the floor. My knees are so weak that I'm standing here with them locked and I know that that's a sure-fire way to find yourself passing out. It happened just like that to Mary Lou Laker during the rehearsal, bless her heart. But it's either locking my knees or flapping like a flag on a windy day, so my knees are locked.

If that isn't bad enough, on a giant screen behind us are interviews with Misty Creek residents who were obviously extremely eager to get on TV. Now, you'd think that Comedy Corner would have asked our friends and family . . . but oh no, they decided on interviewing random people from our places of work, teachers, and so forth. You get the idea . . . people you don't really remember and who barely remember you. Now, just who-daya think they interview about me? You guessed it. Crusty old Pete Jenkins. Yep, there he is up there on the big screen in his grease-stained apron having a smoke out in back of the diner. When a microphone is thrust in his face he's more than happy to flap his jaws.

"Yesiree," he says and pauses to take a long drag on his cigarette. After blowing out a long curling stream of blue smoke he says, "I know Abby Harper. Never thought I'd see the day she'd be ballroom dancin', though. Why, that girl has trouble walkin' and a-chewin' gum. Spills somethin' on someone most every day. Once she knocked over a full glass of lemonade on a baby." He slaps his knee and goes into a wheezing fit of laughter. "The baby was a-wailin' and her mama was a-hollerin'. Never seen such a sight."

I narrow my eyes at the screen wishing I had an egg or better yet a tomato to hurl at bigger-than-life Pete. But then he scratches his grizzly chin and says, "Yep, no one was more surprised than me that she done so good. Did us right proud."

I swallow. I made Pete proud? Well, shut my mouth. But before I have time to get all choked up Ben Sebastian is suddenly thrusting a microphone in my face.

"Well, Abby Harper, waitress at Sadie's Diner. Pete was impressed. The judges were impressed. Do you think the American public was just as impressed with your steamy cha-cha?"

Steamy? Lord have mercy, I think I might pass out. Ben is looking all fuzzy and the microphone resembles a slithering snake. Yes, locking my knees was a big mistake. I sort of sway . . . and feel icky. Oh, crap, I'm gonna hurl as I pass out. No . . . dear God, *no*.

But then I feel Rio's strong arm firmly support me about my waist. His voice, sounding sort of far away, says, "I can tell you that I was certainly impressed. Abby's smart, gifted, and a hard worker, a combination that's going to be difficult to beat."

My vision is still wavy but I see Ben's very white teeth flash as he smiles, snapping me out of it. "Well, Abby Harper, America agrees. You are *safe*. Go have a seat with Danny, Julia, Mac, Travis, Daisy, Jimmy Joe, Hank, and Brandon."

With Rio's arm still offering support, I go over to the safe contestants and flop down onto the seat when my legs all but give out.

Rio whispers in my ear, "You okay?"

I manage a nod, wishing Rio would grab my hand, but he doesn't so I turn my attention to the final bottom three. My heart goes out to them. I didn't realize how awful this would be.

Ben gets this serious look on his face and says in his deep MC voice, "Betty Cook the lunch lady, Patsy James the florist, and Mary Lou the maid, one of you is safe and the other two will go back to your regular jobs." He pauses while the three women cling to each other. "Betty

Cook?" Ben pauses again and Betty's Olive Oyl eyes get as big as moon pies. "You are . . ." He pauses so long that even I start to sweat. The audience gets restless, and even cool-as-a-cucumber Rio shifts in his seat. Someone in the audience yells, "Come on, get on with it," but Ben, being the professional that he is, ignores the outburst. Instead he waits even longer.

"You are . . . safe!"

Betty just stares at him and starts blinking rapidly, looking more like a cartoon character than ever. I'm wondering if she made the mistake of locking her knees too.

"Betty, you are *safe*," Ben says a little louder but it's his wide smile that seems to break through to her. "Take a seat."

"Oh!" Betty gives Ben a big hug that lasts a bit longer than it should, but then Ben is pretty *hot*. She clasps her hands to her chest Olive Oyl style and hurries on her long, loopy legs over to the last vacant seat.

"Mary Lou and Patsy, I'm sad to say your stay on *Dancing with the Rednecks* is over. Is there anything you'd like to say to the American public who didn't vote for you?"

There are a few suggestions shouted from the crowd that on any other station than Comedy Corner would have been bleeped. I'm thinking that it's coming from some four-wheel-drive tailgaters I spotted earlier in the parking lot.

"Yes," Patsy says and hiccups, clearly holding back tears. She swallows three or four times and then says, "Well, yeah, thank y'all so much. I know I wasn't good but I had a blast." She turns to us and says, "Good luck to y'all!" She hiccups again and then places a hand over her mouth.

Mary Lou giggles and I fully understand her nervous laughter. My heart goes out to her, too. I figured the out-of-control spin would do her in although I thought she might gain some sympathy votes. After all, she still has the bandage on her forehead. "I . . ." Mary Lou says with her hands clasped close to her chest, "I . . . I had the time of my life. I wouldn't trade a moment of it for a thing, not even my crazy spin." She touches her forehead. "I think I might have a scar but that's . . . that's *okay* because it will remind me of this experience."

The crowd eats this up and she gets whistles and wild applause. "How else was I gonna make it on *Good Morning America*? And have Jay Leno tell a joke about me on *The Tonight Show*?"

The crowd stands up and cheers.

We stand up and cheer.

My eyes fill with tears. I'm proud of us all. Even Ben looks a little choked up.

Rednecks are a force to be reckoned with.

Rio squeezes my hand and I instinctively lean over and kiss his cheek. "Thanks for believing in me," I whisper in his ear.

"You make it easy," he whispers back. His warm breath tickles my earlobe, making me shiver. I so want to throw my arms around him and give him a big hug but I give him a smile instead. He looks as if he might say something else but we notice that we're supposed to be part of a big group hug for Patsy and Betty, who are both swiping at tears. I find myself doing the same thing.

In the background on the big screen are highlights of Mary Lou's and Patsy's short-lived stint on *Dancing with the Rednecks*, ending with Mary Lou's out-of-control spin, first the one during rehearsal, and then the one during her dance. At one point they show both spins on a split screen. The crowd is both laughing and cheering and I imagine people watching from their living rooms are doing the same thing. Mary Lou takes a good-natured bow and I think to myself that no matter how much we're poked fun at, I will always be proud of who I am and where I come from. America might have voted, but in my book we're all winners. With that thought I throw myself into the group hug, thinking that no matter what, I will remember this moment forever.

I shamelessly take this opportunity to turn and throw my arms around Rio, finally getting my much-needed hug. Whether by instinct or better yet because he wants to, he hugs me back. I soak up the moment, loving the feeling of being in his arms, lingering as long as I can before becoming too obvious, and then turn away before he can see the hunger and need that must surely be written all over my face.

As I weave through the crowd to get over to Mama and Jesse, I'm stunned when I'm stopped for pictures and autographs . . . me, *autographs*!

"My little superstar!" Mama gushes and gives me a big hug. "Abilene, I'm so proud of you!" She squeezes me so hard that I think my head might pop right off.

"Hey, Abby," Jesse says with a grin.

"Squirt." I hug him as hard as Mama hugged me. I miss them so much but I don't say so because Mama will cry and I'll cry and Jesse will roll his eyes.

"They feedin' you okay?" Mama asks and looks me over to see if I'm losing weight. "If not I'm gonna send some real food up on that mountain to you if I have to bring it up myself."

"The food is good, Mama. Not as good as the diner, but good. You doin' okay without me at the diner?"

Mama nods. "Everybody keeps askin' after you, hoping you'll come in for a shift, but I tell them you aren't allowed. Business is booming, though! We had to have Norma come in and I might have to hire another waitress for the lunch shift. But don't you worry. Just concentrate on your dancin'."

"I will," I assure her just as they call for us to head for the limo. I give Mama and Jesse another quick hug.

"Good luck, Abby," Jesse says and gives me a little shove.

"Call me when you get the chance," Mama says and starts blinking rapidly, trying to hold back the floodgates.

"I will." I nod and start blinking too and then turn to hurry out the door before I lose it. I'm usually a steady-as-she-goes kinda girl, not an emotional wreck! I close my eyes and take a deep breath of crisp air, trying to clear my head, and vow to get a hold of myself. Of course walking with one's eyes closed leads to running into things . . . *something warm and solid.*

"Whoa there," Rio says in that smoky voice of his that makes me think that whatever he's selling I'm buying. He steadies me around the waist and his hands feel warm through the thin silk blouse I'm wearing. I finally read through the packet so I knew to dress up for tonight's occasion.

Of course my eyes are wide open now and looking into his. The night breeze kicks up, filling my head with the scent of his cologne and leather jacket. I shiver but only partly from the chill air.

"Where's your coat?" Rio asks.

His voice is a low sexy rumble and his hands are still holding me close, making my brain refuse to formulate an answer. The best I can come up with is "M-my coat?"

"Yes, didn't you wear one? It's cold out here."

Cold . . . coat . . . suddenly my brain decides to function. "Oh, my *coat.* I left it in the limo." I look over his shoulder into the lighted parking lot. "Hey, where *is* the limo?"

Rio shrugs. "They were waiting for you so I told them I would drive you back to the lodge."

"Oh." I notice that we are completely alone in the back parking lot.

"I hope that's okay?"

I nod, fully aware that his hands are still holding me close. "You have a car?"

He grins and motions with his thumb over his shoulder.

"Okay, stupid question."

When Rio laughs his hands tighten on my waist and I stumble forward . . . It was an accident, I swear, but suddenly I'm flush against him. He stumbles as well, takes a step back, and lands against the door of a shiny black car. So now I'm leaning on him and he's leaning on the car and I think he's going to push me away but with a low growl in the back of his throat he dips his head and captures my mouth with his.

The kiss is long and hot and oh so deep. I hang on to the lapels of his butter-soft leather jacket, and his hands go from my waist to my back, pressing me even closer. His tongue strokes mine, sending a hot shiver of excitement coursing through my entire body. I tug on his lapels and he slides his hands down to cup my ass, pushing me closer so that I can feel how much he wants me.

While still kissing me Rio fumbles for the door handle and we tumble onto the backseat . . . all legs and arms and heavy breathing. My silk shirt slides against the cool leather and I bend my knees to accommodate his body on top of mine. When his mouth moves to my neck I thread my fingers through his long hair. His warm kisses move lower to the swell of my breasts and with a sexy moan he shifts his weight to the back of the seat and then begins to undo the pearl buttons until my blouse falls open, revealing my bra.

"Ah . . . Abby, what are we doing?"

"Makin' out in the back of your fancy car."

He chuckles. "I know that. My God, I haven't done this since I was a kid."

"Well, you're one up on me 'cause I've never done this, *ever.*"

"You're kidding."

"Well, there was this time in the back of a truck but it ended really badly."

"I won't ask."

"Smart thinkin'," I say and then gasp when he rubs his thumb over my nipple.

"This is insane, doing this. We should stop."

My heart sinks. "Oh . . . I—I know. We keep going down this same road, Rio. I think it's inevitable."

"I think you're right. Abby, I've tried not to think about how silky your skin feels." He slides his hand up my thigh, stopping just shy of where I want him to be. "Or how you taste." He runs the very tip of his tongue over the soft swell of my breast. "And I can't stop imagining how it would feel to be buried deep inside you."

I look into his eyes and whisper, "Then do it, Rio. Make sweet love to me."

"But—"

I stop him with a fingertip to his lips. "We can't deny this thing between us, Rio. I know I'll regret it if we don't see this through."

"Ahhh, Abby."

"Were you hoping this would happen?"

He nods slowly. "In the back of my head, yes."

I fleetingly wonder if this has anything to do with Angelina. Is he using me to get her out of his head? But suddenly it doesn't matter. The future doesn't matter or even the competition. I cup his cheeks between my palms and say, "All that matters is right here and now."

14

Taking the Lead

"I've never known a woman like you, Abby Harper."

"How so?"

He runs his fingertip over my bottom lip. "There is sweetness and honesty about you that tugs at my heart. The last thing I want to do is hurt you."

"I'm not made of spun glass, you know."

"Ah . . . that I can see."

"Then just what are you waitin' for? A written invite?" I try to sound sassy and confident but it comes out breathless. I search his eyes for his answer.

He chuckles. "No, that's not necessary."

"Then I think I need a little less talk . . . and a lot more action." There, *that* sounded sassy, well, except for that little quiver in my voice.

He shakes his head, laughing. "Be careful what you wish for, my little lemon."

I chuckle but it's really to hide my reaction to him referring to me as *his*. I realize now how much I want to be his and his only but I also know how unlikely that is to happen. Making love to him will be risking my heart but it's a risk I'm willing to take. For once in my life I refuse to worry. But then a sudden thought occurs to me. "No one can see us, can they?" I whisper like someone can hear. I'm willing to risk my heart but not my reputation.

"The windows are tinted and the parking lot is empty. Here we don't have to worry about cameras or microphones," he adds with a grin but then turns serious. "Abby, are you having second thoughts? Because if you are—"

I shut him up by pulling his head down for a long delicious kiss. It's about time that I take the lead for once. Needing to feel his warm smooth skin, I begin to unbutton his shirt but of course my fingers are shaking. He gently brushes them away and leans back to remove his leather jacket and then shed his shirt.

"Ouch!" When Rio bumps his head on the ceiling I giggle. "I can't believe I wanted to do this for two weeks and I end up in the backseat of a car with you."

"You want to go back to the lodge?" *Please say no.*

He raises his eyebrows. "And wait a moment longer? I don't think so." To prove his point he leans in for another scorching kiss. I put my hands on his bare shoulders and slide my palms down his back, loving the ripple of muscle while he moves. I want to cup his ass but I don't have the nerve. Then I think, *oh, to hell with it*, and just do it anyway, adding a squeeze for good measure. He chuckles low in my ear and then deftly unhooks my bra.

"Beautiful," he says after leaning back to gaze at my breasts, instantly squelching my instinct to cover myself.

"You make me feel beautiful, Rio," I shyly tell him.

"Because you *are*," he says and I think he gets it that no one has ever called me that before.

My heart races when he leans down and captures a nipple in his hot mouth. He licks me with his warm, wet tongue and then nibbles sharply, sending a jolt of desire through me that has me arching up for more. Sucking and teasing he moves from one breast to the other, driving me wild. When he scrapes the soft yet prickly stubble on his chin over my sensitive nipples I suck in a breath, wondering if I might have an orgasm right here and now.

He begins a hot trail of kisses between my breasts and then down my abdomen, making my belly quiver. His long hair tickles my skin and I thread my fingers through the baby softness. He finds the zipper on my skirt and I lift my hips for him to tug it off . . .

"Rio . . ." I protest when his tongue circles my navel and then, God, suddenly his hot mouth is between my legs and he kisses me *there*, making my panties moist. I want to tell him to stop, this is too much, but I'm shameless with wanting him and I arch my hips upward against his mouth.

With a groan Rio hooks his thumbs on the sides of my panties and slides them down my thighs and over my ankles. Cool air hits my hot body and I shiver.

"Your legs are *amazing*," he says in my ear and slowly slides one hand up my calf, making me so glad that I shaved my legs. When he reaches the tender inside of my thigh I tingle all over. He teases, circling his index finger closer to where I so want to be touched but stopping just short.

"Rio?" I open my eyes when the teasing stops. He's unbuckling his belt and I notice in the dim light that his hands are none too steady and this knowledge goes straight to my heart. He removes his belt with a whoosh and tosses it to the floor. When he leans against the seat I undo the button on his fly and then unzip his pants. While he braces himself up on one elbow I tug his pants and boxers over his hips, sucking in a breath when his penis springs forward hard, proud, and erect.

Unable to stop myself I grasp the long length that pulses and comes alive in my hand. I marvel at the silky soft skin of the smooth round head, thinking that even his penis is perfect . . .

"Abby," he says in a strained husky voice, "you're driving me over the edge."

"Oh . . ." I stop my exploration while he fumbles in his pocket and is suddenly sheathing himself in a condom, something I hadn't even considered. This makes me think of how inexperienced I am and that maybe I'll somehow mess this up.

Noticing my sudden silence he tucks a knuckle beneath my chin. "Hey, you okay?"

I nod but his dark eyes continue to search my face. "I just want to please you."

While shaking his head he looks down at me with such tenderness. "You do please me, Abby. Just let yourself go . . . your inhibitions," he says, nibbling on my neck. "Your worries," he continues hotly in my ear and then tugs on my earlobe with his teeth. This must be my personal erogenous zone that I was unaware of, because when he suddenly sucks my earlobe into his mouth it drives me wild and all I can think of is having him inside me. My inhibitions go flying out the window and I open my legs and wrap my arms around him.

Rio enters me in one deep, delicious stroke, taking my breath away. He's so hot, so hard and powerful, but he moves slow and easy, letting me adjust to his size. Intense tingling pleasure, warm and liquid, begins to build. I can tell by his bunched muscles, his ragged breathing that he's holding back for my sake and I fall a little more in love with Rio Martin. I ease into a slow and steady rhythm with him while running my hands over his sleek, smooth back.

With each long and lazy stroke my excitement builds until I wrap my legs around his waist so he can go deeper, faster. He whispers Spanish in my ear and I don't need to know what he says . . . all I need to do is feel. Sweet, hot pleasure winds tighter and tighter . . . exquisite, almost painful in the intensity. I arch my back so that we are skin to skin, heart to thumping heart, while I climb higher, searching for blessed relief . . .

"Rio, *God,*" I say and he slides his hands under my ass, going faster, deeper, *harder* until an orgasm bursts upon me like a wave cresting and then crashing to the shore. Rio thrusts deep, stiffens, and comes right along with me.

"*Mi Dios,*" he mutters weakly and I'm pretty sure that means *my God.* Still buried deep within me he captures my mouth and kisses me thoroughly while I'm reeling with little aftershocks.

My world has finally been rocked.

Finally, he leans against the back of the seat, giving me room to lie next to him, and I really wish we were in bed so we could snuggle and then fall asleep together maybe to wake up in a couple of hours to do it all over again. As it is I have to be content with him holding me close in the cramped confines of the car. I kiss his chest where his heart is still beating wildly.

When he chuckles and kisses me on top of the head I tilt my face up and he looks at me for a long moment as if wondering just what to say. Then he leans in and kisses me tenderly, which is nice and all, but I get the feeling it's to avoid what needs to be said. "You were amazing, Abby."

Of course I blush hotly, enough that he can probably see it in the dim lighting.

"You *know* that, right?"

I shrug, not to be modest but because I really *don't* know that, and then brace myself for what he's about to say because I'm hearing a really big *but* in all of this. Why does there always have to be a *but*?

"But tomorrow we need to go back to instructor and student."

"Y-you mean and forget this ever happened?"

He shakes his head. "I couldn't forget this ever happened if I wanted to . . . and I don't." He runs his fingertip down my cheek and I wait for the next big *but* to come. "But we need to concentrate on the dancing. This was bound to happen," he says and then hesitates.

"But . . ." I prompt, and he finishes, "We have to get back to business."

I lick my lips and then ask softly, "So, was this an effort to get me out of your system? Like the kiss?"

"No," he says firmly, "but if it *had* been, it would have been a dismal failure."

I'm confused. "So . . . we're back to the resistance plan?" *I hate that plan.*

"I'm afraid so but now it's even worse."

I raise my eyebrows. "How so?"

"Because now I know that being with you was even better than I had imagined . . . and I have quite an active imagination," he tries to joke but we both know that this situation royally sucks.

"So, it's like we're damned if we do and damned if we don't?"

"Yeah, like that."

"Well, hellfire. I don't see any way to make lemonade outta this one without getting squirted smack dab in the eye."

He mulls this over for a second and then chuckles a bit

sadly. "You know, I'm finally starting to understand your language."

"Well, I still don't understand a word of Spanish except for the fact that it really turns me on. You could be telling me off and I would still melt."

Rio laughs and says, *"Posterguemos el plan de la resistencia para un pequeño más largo. Vendrá mañana por la mañana pronto bastante."*

"Were you telling me off?" I joke. Isn't it funny how you can joke when your heart is sort of breaking? Must be a defense mechanism or something.

"I'm not sure what telling you off means but I don't think so."

"Then what were you sayin'?" I ask when I pretty much have it figured out.

Rio hesitates like he doesn't want to say what he really *has* to say so I bide my time, drawing little patterns with my fingertip on his bare chest. He has a really nice chest. Finally I decide to help him out. "I get it, Rio. We're good together but can't *be* together because of complications beyond our control. Like the fact that there is a ballroom dancing competition that means so much to me and shouldn't be compromised by having a relationship with my instructor. Oh, and beyond that there is the fact that we're from totally different backgrounds . . . different countries, for goodness' sake. *Oh yeah*, and you'll be leaving here forever in just a few short weeks. What else is there to say?" I ask sadly, totally leaving out Angelina because I hope she isn't part of the complications even though I think that she might be.

"I basically said that tomorrow it's back to business, but it's not tomorrow yet . . ."

"Oh."

"So, are you, how do you say, catching my drift?"

I answer him with a long hot kiss. In the back of my

brain I know that taking my relationship to this level with Rio might not have been the smartest thing I've ever done. I've already developed feelings for him and this is going to make it so much harder when he's gone.

But I won't think about that now while I'm in his arms and he's whispering Spanish love words in my ear . . . at least I think they're love words.

Tomorrow will come soon enough.

15

Blame It on Rio

"I know, I *know*, I just can't believe it," Julia says to me as she tops off my glass of wine. *"Angelina,"* she says, drawing out the dreaded name and adding a head bop followed by a finger wave, "is hardly Danny's type."

"Oh, I wholeheartedly agree," I assure Julia and then take a sip of wine. I know that I've sworn off wine but it's been such a tough week that I couldn't resist a glass . . . or two. "I just don't know what he's thinkin'."

This draws a snort from Julia. "Well, I'll tell ya. He's thinking with the little head instead of the big one."

"What?" I don't get it.

"His *dick*, Abby. Angelina is leading Danny around by his dick."

"Oh, the little head . . ." I say and then giggle behind my hand when I sort of picture it in my mind, but Julia doesn't think it's all that funny and frowns at me.

"Sorry," I tell her, feeling bad that I laughed when she is in such distress. "I had just never heard that expression before."

She waves a hand in my direction. "You're such a nice girl. Sorry I was such a shit to you in high school."

I shrug it off because I realize that it truly doesn't matter anymore and it makes me smile. Wow, the chip on my shoulder is officially gone. How about that?

"You really weren't a shit . . . just basically ignored me." It's hard to believe, though, that I'm sitting here in Julia's room sharing a bottle of white wine and some little cheese squares and thin round crackers that she brought out neatly arranged on a plastic tray. In fact, everything in her room is neat and tidy, unlike my own, but after a long day of dancing I really haven't felt the need to tidy up.

And the days have been long, not to mention difficult. After steaming up the windows in Rio's fancy rental car, he has felt the need to stick to the resistance plan of action, which translates to *no* action. I fully understand why and all but it doesn't make it easy. On top of that, the jive is damned difficult. There are tons of flicks, kicks, and twirls with lightning-fast feet movement. My big feet just weren't meant to move fast as lightnin'. I have fallen on my ass no less than each and every day. Today I tripped Rio and we both ended up in a tangled heap that I had hoped would lead to some hot and heavy kissing but he merely tugged me to my tired feet and demanded we do the whole dance over even though it was lunchtime.

"So, do you think Danny and Angelina are *doin'* it?" Julia asks and her lips tremble like she's on the verge of tears.

"No," I assure her firmly, but in truth I'm *not* so sure. Danny and Angelina were all over each other at dinner. Well, she was all over him but he didn't seem to mind. "I think he might have been trying to make you jealous."

Her lips stop trembling and she perks up. "You think?"

"Well . . ." I begin as I pick up another slice of cheddar and a cracker. Dinner was this weird stuffed fish drizzled with sauce that smelled funny. I only pushed it around my plate, so this is a welcome snack. I'm dying for some of Mama's meat loaf.

"Abby!"

"Oh, sorry." I stop daydreaming about Mama's cooking and say, "I really do believe that Danny might be tryin' to make you jealous." I leave out the part that he was going to try that very same plan only using me. I know that I'm sticking my nose in where it doesn't belong but the wine has loosened my lips. Besides, I didn't like him flirting with that dark-haired hussy either. Not that I have any designs on Danny anymore. My sights are set on Rio. "He's not over you, Julia." This much I know is true.

"I know that, I guess. He's just bein' hardheaded and stubborn." She leans back against the headboard and takes a sip of wine.

"He thinks—"

"That I don't think he's good enough for me," she interrupts with a shake of her head.

"You already know that?" I ask from the other bed where my tired feet are propped up on two feather pillows.

"Oh, Abby, Danny thought I wanted a frat boy on my arm when he got cut from Eastern Kentucky football. But I really wanted to go to college to cheerlead. Could you imagine cheering in front a huge crowd like that? On national television?" She sighs as if she's imagining it right now.

"No, I can't. Of course I couldn't imagine ballroom dancing in front of a crowd on national television either."

"Well, I wanted it so danged bad. I even had a partial scholarship to Eastern Kentucky but . . ." Her cheeks turn pink and then she admits, "My grades and my ACT scores weren't good enough. I always struggled in school, Abby. The whole blond bimbo cheerleader thing wasn't an act. I really thought I was a dumb blonde."

"You're not dumb!"

"No, I'm dyslexic."

"What? Dyslexic?" I think about this for a moment. "Like, you get letters backward or somethin'?"

"My case is mild compared to others, but yeah. I always had a hard time reading and I would get directions wrong even in cheerleading. My mom thought I was a screwup and my daddy called me lazy." Her blue eyes cloud over. "In grade school I would have to miss recess or stay after school to finish things and I used to shake when I had to read out loud. I never got the point of reading out loud anyway."

She pauses and then says hotly, "I wasn't lazy or a screw-off. In reality I had to work so much harder than the other kids to accomplish the things I did. To compensate I felt the need to be the most popular girl in school and the best cheerleader ever. Pretend that it wasn't cool to get good grades when I *so* wanted to be on the damned honor roll just once."

"When did you find out what was wrong?"

"In cosmetology school. My teacher had it and knew immediately what my problem was. I could learn when I watched but had difficulty with the reading comprehension." Julia shakes her head and chuckles. "Mercy, I thought I was gonna be a beauty school dropout."

We both break into the song from *Grease* and then burst into laughter.

"Abby, did we just bond?"

"I think so."

"Good, 'cause I could use a friend."

I take a sip of wine and ask, "So, are you over the dyslexic thing?"

Julia shakes her head and sighs. "You don't outgrow it

and there isn't a cure or even a pill. You just have to live with it. Hey, there are plenty of famous people with dyslexia. Thomas Edison, Picasso, Leonardo da Vinci, and even Jay Leno to name a few."

"Wow, Jay Leno?"

"Yeah, I think sometimes we overcompensate," she says with a laugh.

"So, what are you going to do about Danny?"

"I dunno. What are *you* going to do about smokin' hot Rio? You two light it up on the dance floor. You been lightin' it up between the sheets?"

I almost choke on my wine.

Julia grins. "Yeah, it's that obvious. Damn, y'all are gonna be hard to beat."

"Not unless I can master the doggone jive. That dance is hard. I keep falling on my ass," I tell her, steering her away from her question.

"It's gotta be better than the boring fox-trot!" Pursing her lips she says, "Danny is doing the very sexy rumba with that *bitch*."

"Tell me how you really feel, Julia. Don't hold back, now."

Julia giggles. "I can't help it. I always cuss when I drink," she admits and then suddenly sits up from slouching against the pillows. "Hey, maybe I should make Danny jealous. Two can play that card."

"With who?"

Tapping her cheek, Julia ponders this for a moment and then brightens. "Ben Sebastian."

"He's pretty danged hot," I have to admit. Not broody-bad-boy hot like Rio but *hot* in a hip surfer-dude way. "Wouldn't you feel bad using him like that?"

"Are you kiddin'? He's been flirtin' with anyone with boobies. He even flirted with Mary Lou Laker *after* the whole spinning-out-of-control thing."

"Maybe he was just being nice. I think he's really friendly."

Julia rolls her eyes. "Abby, he was flirtin' with ya."

"Oh."

"Hey, you're not gonna tell Danny about my plan, are you? 'Cause the two of you were gettin' pretty cozy there for a while. I havta say that it was pissin' me off big time."

"Danny's a great guy, Julia. I admit that I had a huge crush on him in high school and I thought I might have had a chance with him here at first, but I know he's still carryin' a torch for you."

"You really think he is, Abby?" Her eyes fill up with tears. "I know I messed up all those years ago, but I was a kid and I didn't know what I wanted. Why can't he believe that?"

"Well, you'll just have to bring him around to your way of thinkin'."

"Yeah," she says and sets her glass down with a thump.

"And," I begin but then think better of what I was going to say.

"What?"

I shake my head. "Nothin'."

"Spill, Abby. Don't hold out on me."

"You promise to keep this under your hat?"

"Cross my heart and hope to die." She actually crosses her heart. "Stick a needle in my eye."

"Ew, I always hated the hope-to-die and needle-in-the-eye part. Take that part back and I'll tell you."

"Okay, I take it back."

"Except for the promise part, right?"

"Except for that," she says so seriously that I believe her.

"Okay," I begin, really hoping I'm not making a big mistake by divulging this information.

"The suspense is killin' me, Abby."

I swallow and then say in a rush, "Rio and Angelina used to be dance partners."

"That's it?" She looks disappointed in my scoop.

"They were a little more than that."

Her eyes widen. "Oh . . . they were *lovers* . . ."

I can't bring myself to say it, so I merely nod. "Angelina's mean, Julia. She dumped Rio when he hurt his knee and couldn't dance!" I lean toward her bed and whisper, "Remember to keep it under your hat." Oh, curse the wine for loosening my lips.

Julia shakes her head. "Who would ever dump Rio Martin?"

"That's what I was thinkin'," I say but then give her a you're-not-having-any-designs-on-him look of warning.

"Don't worry, I won't go messin' with your man."

"I wasn't thinkin' that."

"Were too."

I giggle. Girl talk is fun.

Nibbling on her bottom lip Julia suddenly raises her eyebrows. "Do you think that Angelina is using Danny to make Rio jealous?"

"Could be," I answer but I'm not liking the thought of Angelina using Danny or Rio getting jealous.

Julia must see this written all over my face, because she says, "Not that I think Rio is gonna get jealous or anything. I mean, you've got so much more going for you than *Angelina* anyway."

"I do?" I'm hoping for examples but none are forthcoming.

"Sure," is all Julia can manage but she's frowning like she's trying to come up with more. "And do you think that Comedy Corner *knew* about Rio and Angelina's past and deliberately brought her onto the show to stir things up?"

"Likely, don't you think?"

"Yeah . . ." she says very slowly. "So what are we gonna do about it?" She cocks one eyebrow like Rio.

"Danged if I know."

Her eyebrow slides back into place. "Well, we're gonna havta think of something to thwart their evil plan."

I don't think I've ever thwarted anything before but I nod like I'm willing to try.

"Thanks for keeping me company, Abby. I hope you get your man, too."

I shake my head as I set my empty glass down next to hers on the nightstand and scoot to the edge of the bed. "We're worlds apart," I tell her, unable to keep the sadness from my voice.

"So what? Are you sayin' you're not good enough for him?"

"No . . . but—"

"No buts!"

"Julia, it's not that easy."

"Love never is."

Love? My heart thumps at the word. Do I love Rio Martin? "How do you know if you're really, truly in love?"

Julia shrugs. "You just do."

"Well, I'd best be goin'. Morning will come way too soon." I stretch and start for the door but before I leave I turn and say, "Thanks for the snack and the wine. And, Julia, it was good to get to know you."

"Still think I'm a bitch?"

"I never thought that."

"Liar."

I have to laugh. "Maybe a little." I hold up my thumb and finger about an inch apart.

"Well, good luck with smokin' hot Rio. But I won't say *good luck* with the dance 'cause I want to beat your long-legged butt. You're like Stacy Keibler in *Dancing with the Stars* and I'm like Tatum O'Neal, who was the underdog."

"I'm the underdog," I insist. Why can't I be the underdog?

"Well, one thing is for sure. We gotta beat the pants off Danny and *Angelina*!" She sort of spits the name out with the emphasis on *lina* and then wrinkles her nose.

I give Julia a thumbs-up and open the door. As I head for my room I'm thinking that life sure takes some weird twists and turns. Oh, but then thinking of twists and turns has me remembering the jive, which I suck at, and that the doggone dress rehearsal for the second live show is tomorrow! If it weren't for the two glasses of wine making me feel mellow I just might have a panic attack.

After scrubbing my face and brushing my teeth I slip beneath the covers hoping that I'll fall right asleep because I know that tomorrow is going to be stressful. Not that I'm complaining or anything. While I'm not sure how this will all end up, my life is changing in ways I never thought possible. I'm starting to dream . . . to want things that I should have been going after all along, and I pretty much have Rio Martin to thank . . . or to blame.

16

Fancy Footwork

"What if I fall?" I ask while Rio and I wait in the wings at the dance hall.

"You're not going to fall, Abby," he says with more conviction than needed, which leads me to believe that he thinks I might fall.

"I've fallen every day this week. It's all of those dog-gone kicks and spins."

"But you won't tonight. Muscle memory will take over."

"Yeah, my muscles will remember to fall!" I tug on his fifties-style bowling shirt and ask, "Can we take that last part out where I slide through your legs?"

"You've always performed that part without a problem."

"Yes, but I think about it all through the dance and it's harder in this poodle skirt." I feel the need to stomp my foot like I'm some sort of diva. My Sandra Dee ponytail swings back and forth. "Maybe that's why I fall."

Rio pivots to face me and then takes both of my icy cold hands in his hot ones . . . or maybe they just feel hot because mine are freezing.

"Listen, Abby," he begins in a calm and soothing voice, "if you fall . . . well then, *you fall*, okay?"

"No, it's definitely not okay!" Have I caused Rio to lose his mind?

"Yes, it is. This is about who the audience likes, remember? And you are very likeable. If you fall the judges will ding you but the audience will eat it up."

"You're not telling me to fall, are you?"

He sighs. "No . . . Abby, just try to relax. Turn around and watch Mac Murphy the truck driver perform the paso doble. That should take your mind off falling."

"Okay," I say and take a deep breath, something I've been doing a lot of lately. My eyes widen as I watch Mac, dressed in a colorful red embroidered jacket . . . the tiny kind that bullfighters wear, tight black pants, and a black cummerbund. His partner is dressed all in red.

"He's supposed to be a bullfighter and she is the cape. Watch. This is an interesting dance."

One I hope we don't have to do, I think to myself. I don't relish the idea of being a cape. Although Rio would look amazing as a matador. He could cock that one eyebrow and all that.

After Ben announces them, "Pump It," by the Black Eyed Peas begins blasting over the sound system. I'm a bit surprised by the song selection but it works. At first I think Mac is going to be laughable in the little bullfighter jacket with the fringe on the back but he has this serious look on his face and is surprisingly believable. I'm starting to think that Rio was right. Mac Murphy is the dark horse in this contest. He's funny enough to please the audience and talented enough to please the judges.

"They're good," I whisper loudly in Rio's ear so as to be heard over the Black Eyed Peas.

"Yes, but you're still the underdog," he tells me with a wink and a smile and suddenly I begin to relax . . . a little anyway.

"If I fall, *I fall*," I whisper to myself.

Mac and his partner end the unusual dance with a twirling flourish and the crowd shows their appreciation with extended applause. Some of them even jump to their feet. Mac is grinning from ear to ear and I can't help but feel happy for him. This sure is different than being behind the wheel of a big rig . . . or cutting hair, plowing fields, or arranging flowers. All of those professions including mine are ones to be proud of but this . . . *this is a chance of a lifetime.* I look across the dance floor at Mac, who is beaming at the solid eights he and his partner have earned, and I have to smile even though he's going to be hard to beat.

Rio squeezes my hand as if reading my mind and I think that he's beginning to know me pretty darned well. Then I glance over at Mama and Jesse and think of my daddy watching over me and I refuse to let nerves ruin my performance. When Ben Sebastian announces our names I surprise Rio by giving him a big, steady smile. "Let's do this," I say and he knows by now to give me a double knuckle bump.

Although my heart is still pounding hard, I walk with Rio out onto the dance floor and we strike our beginning pose beneath the spotlight while waiting for Elvis's "He Ain't Nothin' but a Hound Dog" to begin.

When the music starts I let the steady beat and Rio's firm hands and sure lead guide me. In my head I hear "She Ain't Nothin' but an Underdog" and I smile. Rhythmical and swinging, fast and fun, the jive is a little bit boogie and a little bit rock and roll with the influence of American swing and deeply rooted in New

York Harlem. Yes, I did my homework, thank you very much.

Rio is smiling too and not just for the audience. He winks, letting me know that I'm dancing my ass off. We chassé to the left and right in a jaunty rock step and then Rio turns us to the audience and we flick, ball change. Yes, I remember to point my toes down! I do the really cool rolling-over-Rio's-back move and my frothy slip beneath my poodle skirt rolls with me in a cloud of lace.

In the background I hear the crowd go nuts and I do believe I pick out Jesse's whoop and Mama's whistle. Next comes the part where we hold opposite hands and dance in a circle with one hand over our heads. This makes my heart thud because it's been one of my falling-down parts mainly because we're leaning back with our weight and my hands get sweaty. Rio's eyes meet mine and his grip on my hand is like iron . . . but oh Lord, it slips a little so I'm only holding on to his fingertips and we still have half of the circle to finish. I start sweating bullets because my fingers are slipping and I just know I'm going to land on my ass and spin around just like I did in dress rehearsal.

My fingers slip from Rio's grip just before the circle ends, causing a little stumble on my part, but I hold it together with the smile frozen on my face and say a silent prayer because this is where we dance together for a moment while Elvis croons "You Ain't Nothin' but a Hound Dog" and then Rio leads me into a solo spin . . . another one of my falling-down parts.

"Cryin' all the time . . ." I'm spinning trying to remember to keep my eyes focused on one spot. One spin . . . yeah, I'm still standing. Two spins . . . wow, the world is beginning to look crazy, colors and music and . . . where the hell is Rio's hand?

Shit, I've spun too far away. Panic grips me because I have one more spin and he's supposed to reel me back in for the final slide between his legs. I do the spin anyway and by some miracle Rio manages to grab enough of my fingertips to swing me toward him, but I know that I need enough force to slide all the way under his legs and he really has to pull to do that. Thinking that I'm screwed, I propel myself through his legs and anticipate his next move. He's supposed to tug me back to my feet for our final hands-in-the-air pose.

The operative word here is *supposed*.

I soon know that I have overcompensated as I shoot through his legs like a cannonball. The floor is polished and very slick, so of course I'm now sliding like I'm on ice, totally out of control and not knowing where I'll land. I'm thinking maybe in the next county.

The world is rushing by me and I can hear the crowd roar and I'm hoping they think this was all planned. I manage to wonder if Rio is doing some sort of solo dance or standing there with his hands on his cheeks. I see the judges' table rapidly coming closer and I know that I'm going to crash smack dab into them. Their eyes are very big and their mouths are gaping open. I only know this because all this seems to be going in slow motion even though I know I'm traveling at the speed of sound . . . or is it the speed of light?

Whatever. I'm movin' like a bat outta hell.

I hope there is an ambulance sitting in the parking lot like at football games but I'm thinking *not* because ballroom dancing isn't supposed to be a contact sport. Knowing that the impact is going to hurt and maybe shatter a few bones, I bend my arms, put my hands near my face, and scrunch my legs up in a protective position, which sends me into a really, *really* fast spin, kind of like those street dancers do.

While I'm spinning like a top the crowd is roaring but I'm not sure if it's with laughter or approval. I somehow know even in my dizzy state, that I *have* to make this look planned, so when the spinning stops I lean one bent elbow on the floor and shoot my other hand up into the air in a finishing pose. My world is spinning, so there is no chance of me standing without Rio's assistance.

Where the hell is he?

While blinking I'm desperately swallowing the sudden icky feeling that's from either fear of my extreme state of dizziness or more likely both. Luckily the audience is on their feet, at least I think so since everything is spinning, but it's giving me time to recover.

But where the hell is Rio?

When the swirling in my head stops going so fast I spot Rio all the way at the other end of the floor and his arms are pointed at me in a showcase sort of pose like we planned this whole doggone thing and he's smiling. At least I think he's smiling. That might be a look of sheer terror on his face.

Thankfully, Rio starts coming my way because this is a live show and I'm sure we're using up more than our fair share of our time. He grasps my hand, the one still pointed in the air like I meant to do this, and tugs me to my feet. He's smart enough to know that he has to wrap his arm around my waist and let me lean against him or crumple into a room-spinning heap at his feet.

Ben Sebastian—and there are two of him since I'm still dizzy as all get out and seeing double—comes walking our way and sticks two microphones in my face. "That was . . . wow, amazing," he says like he's in shock. I'm not sure if he means this in a good way or not. Amazing, you know, can mean both. "How long did it take you to learn that spin, Abby? I've never seen any-thing like it."

I'm not sure which one is the real microphone so I sort of speak in the middle of them both. "I owe it all to Rio," I say even though I think it's the same thing I said last time. It shifts the attention to Rio, though, which is what I was going for since I'm not really seeing or thinking straight. I fear I may never do either one again.

Ben sticks one of the microphones near Rio's mouth. "Awesome choreography, Rio. Was this a move you've done before?"

"Um, no, actually. It's new."

Laughter gurgles up in my throat, either from the sheer hilarity of the question or from leftover terror from my near-death spin, but I squelch it.

"Well, let's see what the judges think of your innova-tive rendition of the jive. Myra, let's begin with you."

Myra gives us a wide grin and I let out the breath that I've been holding, because a grin is good, right? "That was . . ." she begins and then pauses as if she can't quite come up with a word to describe our performance. Can't say as I blame her. She squeezes her lips together and after making a popping sound throws her hands up and says, "Unbelievable!"

Again this can be good or bad.

"I was astounded."

Me too. God, good or bad, why doesn't she just say it!

"I give you a nine!"

"Peter, were you astounded too?" Ben asks.

"Most *certainly*!" He flips one hand back and forth and continues. "There were a few flaws, a few problems with the pointing of the toes"—he gives me a look and purses his lips—"but overall it was fantastic! I give you a nine!" He whips the card up so fast that it flies out of his hand and a cameraman has to go running after it.

I want to jump up and down but Rio is holding me fast and I'm still a bit dizzy, so it's just as well. Two nines!

"Carson?" Ben asks. "Give us your thoughts."

Carson laughs. Oh, that can't be good. He opens his mouth again but all that comes out is more laughter. "I . . ." he begins but has to pause to wipe a tear away from the corner of his eye. "Have never been so bloody entertained in my entire life. Abby, I realize that your fingers slipped but your ability to recover was perhaps the single most entertaining moment I've had in years. Hats off to you. Despite the obvious flaws you score bonus points. I give you a ten!"

The crowd goes crazy and, professionalism be damned, I turn and give Rio a big ole hug. Whether from surprise or relief, he breaks the rules and hugs me right back. Then after taking a bow where I almost topple over we hurry backstage so that Hank Dooley the construction worker and his partner can dance the rumba.

Julia, now that we've bonded and all, breaks the rules and gets out of the order we're supposed to keep and rushes over. "Mercy, Abby, are you okay? That was . . . was, well, I don't rightly know. How did you, you know, do that spin?"

I shake my head. "I can't tell you because it's all a blur."

"Back in line, please," says Jackie, the makeup girl who is also in charge of keeping us in the order that we dance. Julia wrinkles her nose at Jackie but dutifully gets back in line. Pursing her lips, Jackie rushes over and touches up Julia's makeup with a big fluffy brush like talking to me somehow messed it up.

Since Julia's my friend now I have to admit that she looks elegant in her long, sweeping dark green dress that glitters with embroidered sparkles. Her partner is dressed in a black suit with his hair slicked back and they look like ballroom dancers should look. Julia's hair is done up in a forties-style do, sort of puffed up on top and then pulled back into a bun at the nape of her neck. With her bright red lipstick she looks like an old-school movie star. The fox-trot might be boring but I'm sure that they will make up for it in drama, and from what I've read it is much more difficult than it looks, giving me my doubts that I'll be able to pull it off.

There are several dances left and I can tell you that it feels great to have ours over with. Since we no longer have to be in line Rio draws me to the side. "Are you *okay*?" he asks.

I shrug. "A bit shaken up but the dizziness has gone away. Mostly. I'm so sorry that I messed up, Rio."

He frowns. "Are you kidding? I've never seen such a recovery. Not even in real competition. How did you do it? I thought for sure you were going to crash into the judges' table."

"Me too," I admit and then start to tremble in an after-shock, I guess.

"Let's sit down," Rio says with an expression of concern. Taking my hand he leads me over to a couple of chairs near the back of the storage room that's now the greenroom that's still not green but Rio told me that it's a showbiz term. It's been cleared out and cleaned up so the stale beer smell is a bit better.

We can still see the television monitor from where we're sitting. Maybe it's because my accidental yet somehow amazing spin move is still fresh in the minds of the judges, but I think they are a bit harsh with the five and two sixes that they award Hank and his partner. Sure, he looked ridiculous doing the figure-eight hip rolls that the rumba is famous for and Hank looks a bit silly trying to be sensual but give the guy a break.

"Oh, come on, you know I'm right," Carson protests when the crowd boos his harsh criticism.

"He was just plain mean," I complain to Rio. "After all, Hank is a construction worker, not a professional dancer. And hey, the weave is danged difficult."

Rio looks impressed that I know all about the six quick steps in a row called the weave.

"I've been studying," I say a bit proudly.

"I see your point, Abby, but Jerry Rice is a football player. Jerry Springer is a talk show host. It's part of the entertainment factor of a reality show."

"I *know*. But still. Look at Hank hangin' his head!"

Rio pats my leg. "He'll be okay, Abby. Speaking of okay, how are you feeling?"

"Better."

Rio rubs a hand down his face and shakes his head.

"What?"

"I'm recalling thinking that you were going to . . . how do you say? . . . wipe out."

He looks so worried that it makes me want to kiss him. Of course everything makes me want to kiss him. Clearing my throat I say, "Yeah, who knew ballroom dancing was so dangerous? No wonder Mitchell Banks had me sign that paper that said if I hurt myself it's not his problem. Of course I've had my share of close calls waiting tables too."

"Close calls waiting tables?" Rio raises his eyebrows.

"You don't want to know. Just about everything I do involves an element of danger. Like walking for example."

He shakes his head. "You've hurt yourself walking?"

"I'm just pullin' your leg."

He glances down at his leg with a frown. "I'm having trouble translating that one."

I open my mouth to explain even though I don't

know where that expression came from but he holds his hand up. "No, let me guess. You were messin' with me," he says, trying to imitate my accent, and I have to laugh. Rio chuckles. "You're something else, you know that?"

I'm trying to decide if that is good or bad when he picks up my hand, brings it to his mouth, and kisses it. Now, I guess in Mexico this might be commonplace because it feels like a sexy-guy thing to do, but in Misty Creek having your hand kissed like that is enough to make a redneck like me, well, *melt*.

Rio frowns. "Abby, are you okay?"

Hell no, I'm melting but I don't let him know that. He's made it very clear this past week that we need to stick to our plan. Now that it looks like we will be moving on to the next round I realize that he's right. We need to stay focused, especially now that we're in the thick of the competition. "Sure, I'm fine." I turn my attention to the monitor to watch Daisy Potter the Piggly Wiggly cashier, who is doing the tango with her partner to "Whatever Lola Wants" by Sarah Vaughn.

I don't know if he realizes he's still holding my hand but I don't alert him to the fact since it feels so nice. Having someone care about me feels nice too. I know I have Jesse and Mama, but Rio's concern and protection seems so different and I know now that it's something I want in my life.

It feels good. It feels right.

With an effort I squelch my emotions and try to concentrate on the dances, but although I'm looking at the television screen, all I'm really thinking about is my hand tucked in Rio's.

Daisy Potter and her partner score some solid sevens and seem pleased. I notice that Travis the farmer is smiling as he watches the monitor and I think how cool it

would be if they ended up together. How many times has
he gone into the Piggly Wiggly and bought groceries and
never paid Daisy any mind except to tell her that he
wanted plastic over paper and smiled when she said to
have a nice day?

I'm contemplating how this show has changed our
lives already and have to wonder what kind of surprises
the next few weeks will bring. I sneak a peek up at Rio,
thinking that I'll find out soon enough.

17

Workin' Hard for the Money

Just when I think Rio can't work me any harder, I have to think again. This week's dance for us is the rumba (he pronounces it with a long *u*) and surprise, surprise, I'm having trouble with it. Now that Hank Dooley the construction worker and Brandon Walker the deputy sheriff were eliminated last night we are down to eight couples. Two more will go next Saturday and then two from there on out instead of one like we had first thought.

"No heels, Abby," Rio says with a sigh. "Roll the hips. Straight legs and plenty of swivel action with your feet are the keys to this dance."

"Right." I nod but rolling the hips makes me feel like giggling.

"This isn't funny, Abby." He gives me the raised eyebrow so I know I'm in trouble.

"Sorry."

After giving me a you-better-mean-it look, he says, "This dance tells the story of love and eroticism between a man and a woman. Not in the flirty, cheeky way like the cha-cha, but rather in a sensual, teasing fashion where you are trying to conquer me using your womanly charms."

My womanly charms . . . *right*. "'Kay." I nod again like I fully understand what he just said.

"In this dance the emphasis is on the body. The hip action is done by a controlled transfer of weight from one foot to the other," he explains and then demonstrates.

Mercy. I'm thinking again that this man must be double-jointed in his hips.

"The walks in the dance should be strong. Direct." He demonstrates for me but I'm still stuck on the hip action. Maybe I should ask him to demonstrate those again.

"Abby, are you paying attention?"

"Of course." I school my features into fierce concentration.

"The body never stops changing shape in the rumba. Sensuality is the key." He demonstrates with one of those figure-eight hip rolls that just about has me swallowing my tongue. "It's not that difficult," he tries to assure me, totally mistaking my wide-eyed look for fear instead of the lust that I'm fighting with all my might and coming very close to losing the battle with.

Just when I think I might just *have* to grab him and haul him in for a big ole kiss Rio abruptly turns around and walks away, leaving me with my wide eyes and pounding heart. It doesn't help matters that he's dressed in low-slung gray sweatpants that could be at his ankles with the tug of a string or that he's wearing a white muscle shirt that shows off his physique. No, it doesn't help a damned bit and I think I just might have to tell him so . . . I mean, if we are going to stick with the resistance plan, then there should surely be some rules, right?

Of course I don't tell him anything, or grab him for heaven's sake, but it suddenly hits me how hard it's going to be to perform this really sexy dance with Rio and not throw myself at him, sort of what I'm wanting to do right now, and we aren't even dancing yet, just moving our hips.

Rio grabs a bottle of water and chugs half of it while looking at his notes. Not knowing what to do I continue to blink over at him until he says, "You can begin stretching, Abby, while I read over some things here."

"Okay," I tell him and flop down onto the floor, spread my legs, and bend forward to stretch. His tone, I'm thinking, was a little short, making me wonder what I did to upset him. I think about this for a moment longer while sneaking a sideways peek. He's pursing his lips and has a deep frown on his face like something is really bothering him. I wonder if it has anything to do with Angelina. I saw her snag him last night after the live elimination show at the dance hall and engage him in what looked like a heated discussion but I never got to find out what transpired. Not that it's any of my business.

After I've stretched all that I possibly can, I look over at Rio expectantly but he's still frowning at his clipboard while tapping his cheek with his pencil. "Um, is everything all right?"

Rio raises his head and looks at me a bit blankly like he is still deep in thought. "What did you say?"

God, his accent is cute. "Is everything all right?" I ask slowly.

Rio gives me a look that sets my heart racing and for a minute I think he might say something really important like maybe that he's falling for me and that he can't stand another moment without kissing me . . . something earth-shattering like that . . . but then again maybe he's going to tell me that he just realized that he's still in love with Angelina. That would suck.

After giving me a long look he finally says, "I was making a few changes to the choreography. At a meeting this morning Mitchell told us that since there are only eight couples left we have another two minutes for each dance."

"Oh." I'm both relieved and disappointed at the same time, leaving me feeling a bit befuddled.

"We can go through the first sequence but then I have to make some adjustments. So we'll cut this morning's rehearsal short but stay a bit longer after lunch, okay?"

"Sure," I say and scramble to my feet. Rio seems so businesslike that I wonder if he ever thinks about the night we made love. With determination I shake off that depressing thought and tell myself to concentrate on the task at hand.

"The steps are slow, quick-quick, slow. Come over here and let's start in the closed position."

I clasp his hand and place my arm over his bent one and give him a nod that I'm ready.

"We'll begin with the basic rumba box and then add a walk and box combo. After that we'll add an eight-count underarm turn, okay?"

I must look like it's not okay because he says, "Just follow my lead. When you get used to the feel of the dance we'll add some music. This isn't a complicated dance but relies on the emotion. We have to showcase the romance, the interplay between us. This will sound silly but I want you to practice sultry expressions in the mirror back in your room, okay?"

I nod.

"But take it seriously. Don't just laugh at yourself."

I snicker. "You know me too well." I expect him to chuckle but he doesn't and I don't know quite what to make of that.

I catch on pretty quickly but then Rio is an excellent teacher. Dancing is becoming more second nature than I ever expected and I wonder how many other things I would enjoy given the chance to do them. Right in the middle of a box combo I vow to myself to start doing new and interesting things instead of the same old stuff. I'm not sure just what that might be but hey, if I can manage to do the rumba with a world-class dancer, then there must be other things I can master as well and I aim to try a few. Never again will I find myself in a rut.

Of course all of this contemplation on my life-altering ideas makes me lose my concentration and I stumble. Rio catches me around the waist and I grab his shoulders for balance. "Sorry," I say so close to his mouth that our lips brush . . . and I didn't mean to, I swear.

Rio's grip on my waist tightens and I'm about to say sorry again when suddenly we're kissing. I slip my fingers into his hair . . . God, I love his hair . . . and unable to stop myself, I lean against his warm, hard body. While I know that I'm no expert on kissing or anything, I can't imagine anyone kissing better than Rio Martin. His lips are soft yet firm and his kiss is demanding without being overbearing. His tongue teases, caresses, making me angle my head and slant my mouth across his for more.

And he gives it.

Deep and delicious, warm and tender, this kiss goes on and on, becoming increasingly hot and a little bit wild . . .

Then he pulls away. "Ah, Abby," he says, leaning his forehead against mine.

"You're gonna say that we shouldn't have done that, aren't you?"

"Yes. I make the rules and then I break them. I've always thought of myself as being disciplined but I lose my head where you're concerned. I'm sorry. It's just that—"

"Oh, my apologies, am I interrupting?"

Before I turn around I know who that Spanish accent belongs to. Rio stiffens and takes a step back. "Is there something you need, Angelina?"

"After last night you need to ask this particular question?" she purrs and arches an eyebrow. Damn, I wish I could do that . . . not the purr, the eyebrow.

I glance up at Rio, wondering what happened last night.

"We're rehearsing," Rio reminds her in an impatient voice. Ha, good for him.

The eyebrow arches higher, now looking stupid. "Right. Ah yes, *rehearsing*." She purses her full lips, giving Rio a knowing look while ignoring me. "I know that drill very well, Rio. I guess some things never change."

A muscle ticks in his jaw. "You overstep your bounds, Angelina, but then you always did, so yes, I suppose that you are right. *Some* things never change." His accent is thick, so I know that she is really upsetting him. "I also know your motives."

She gives him the pleading doe-eyed look. "Rio, you are so wrong in your assumption. I didn't even *know* what you had done with Starlight Dance Studio until I arrived here." She slices a dramatic hand through the air. "I've been abroad, dancing. How was I to know?"

Know what? Is she talking about how Rio came to the rescue of the studio and his daddy after she dumped him with his bum knee? I look at Rio, who folds his hands across his chest and gives her an I-don't-believe-you-for-a-moment stare. Good for him. I give her the same look even though I don't know what I'm not believing. I really want to know, though.

Angelina stabs a finger in my direction so hard that her boobies in her low-cut blouse jiggle like unset Jell-O. I glance at Rio to see if he notices her boobie jiggle and is impressed but he's frowning and his eyes are narrowed, so I guess not. "Phffft, and you think *she* is any different?"

"Yes, I do."

I give Angelina a *yeah, he does* look but her attention is all on Rio. She says something hard and biting in Spanish and I have the sneaking suspicion that it's directed at me since she tosses a terse nod in my direction and then flips her massive hair over her shoulder for good measure. I'm wondering what Rio ever saw in this woman other than the obvious big hooters and I guess the dancing part.

"*Pienso que usted tuvo va major,*" Rios says in a quiet but commanding tone. I make a mental note to tell Jesse to get an English-to-Spanish dictionary at the bookstore for me. I suppose Rio must have told her to leave, because Angelina raises her chin a haughty notch and then pivots on her high heels and sashays out the door. Yeah, *sashays.* That woman has some serious hip wiggle.

Rio sighs and turns to me. "*Perdon,* Abby."

I nod, thinking that he just said that he was sorry. I'm about to tell him that it wasn't his fault and maybe get up the nerve to ask what that little scene was all about especially the part about Angelina knowing something, but unfortunately, Angelina's little tirade alerted the camera crew. Suddenly we're being filmed so, of course, I don't ask my question.

The cameraman looks disappointed that he might have just missed a scoop for this week's teaser for the show. I guess my break-dancing, almost-wiping-out move is getting old.

Rio glances down at his watch. "It's almost time for your lunch break, Abby. Remember to watch the rumba tapes and come down to rehearse after that, okay? I need to add the extra minutes to our performance so we can begin to practice the entire dance this afternoon."

"Okay," I tell him but he looks rather upset, making me want to say more except those darned cameras are pointed our way just hoping for something juicy. "I'll see you at two o'clock, then."

He nods absently like his mind is elsewhere and I'm not sure if it's from the Angelina episode or thinking about the dance, but since I can't ask I simply take my leave and head to the cafeteria. When I get there I'm surprised with a box lunch. Since we're getting a taste of unseasonably warm springlike weather we're told that we have the option of getting out of the lodge and enjoying some fresh air instead of eating in the dining room.

Getting out of the lodge sounds heavenly to me, so I pick up my cute little basket, grab a bottle of juice iced down in a big tub, and head outdoors. I inhale a deep breath of fresh, pine-scented air and tilt my face up to the warm sunshine. It has to be pushing seventy degrees, which is warm for early spring. What is it about warm weather that lifts a person's spirits? Gives you energy and hope? It's a mystery to me but I just have to smile in the sunshine.

I'm thinking that I want to spend my free time alone to try and sort out the scene with Rio and Angelina but Julia spots me and gives me a wave and a smile.

"Hey there, y'all wanna come join me?" She pats the fat log she's sitting on.

Now, before, when I still had the chip on my shoulder plaguing me, I would have refused her company in the cutting-off-my-nose-to-spite-my-face way that my mama had warned me about, but today I walk on over to where she's perched on that big old moss-covered log and join her.

"Nice day, huh?" she asks and I nod in agreement, but she must have sensed a thoughtfulness about me because she says, "Hey, somethin' wrong?"

I unscrew my orange/pineapple juice and take a cold swig before answering. "I dunno."

"Tell me about it," Julia prompts while tugging open a bag of Baked Lay's.

I hesitate but then say, "You'll keep this on the down-low, right?" Now that there isn't any wine influencing me I'm a bit more cautious. I feel like I can trust her now that we're friends and all, but still . . .

"Of course," Julia says and then munches on a po-tato chip although I hesitate to call anything *baked* a potato chip. Just doesn't seem right. "I'm not gonna have to cross my heart and all that, am I?"

"No," I tell her with a grin. After taking a deep breath I say, "Try as I might I can't seem to keep my feelings for Rio at bay."

"Then don't." As she unwraps the plastic cover from her sandwich she says, "Take it from me. You don't want to miss the chance of being with the man you love. Don't let it pass you by, Abby. You'll regret it later."

I mull this over while I unwrap my own sandwich and peek between the slices of wheat bread to make sure it's edible and I'm relieved to see that it's turkey, lettuce, and tomato . . . good. I open the packet of mayo with my teeth, something that my mama would not approve of, and as I'm squirting it on my turkey slices I say, "Yeah, but I'm here to try and win this competition for Mama and Jesse. If chasing after Rio jeopardizes that I'll regret *that* as well. I feel like I'm between a rock and a hard place, ya know?"

Julia swallows a bite of sandwich and then leans to-ward me. "I'm of the opinion that you can have both. You know, Danny's football coach used to give them the whole speech about self-control and not having sex before a game but believe me . . . that was a bunch of hogwash."

"So you don't think that having a relationship with Rio would mess up my chances of winning?"

She chews thoughtfully for a minute and I'm glad that she's thinking this whole thing through so as to give me sound advice. "Well, unless of course things go south. Then it could seriously mess with your head."

"So then, you think I'm better off keeping things businesslike?"

"I might say yes to that except that you're already past that, Abby. So why not go after the whole enchilada instead of just the refried beans?"

I feel my face heat up.

"Oh, mercy, you've already had the whole enchilada?"

Now my face is surely flaming.

"I bet he was just amazing . . . my, my . . . *my.*" Julia fans her face and I should do the same since it feels ready to burst into flames and start a forest fire.

"I didn't say that we . . ." I lean over and whisper even though I don't think there are any cameras in the woods. "Do *you know*!"

"You didn't have to, but your secret is safe with me."

I start to deny it but her look says not to even go there, so I don't. "So you think I should go after him instead of sticking to the resistance rule that I agreed to?"

"Well, hell *yeah.*"

I take a spoonful of my fresh fruit cup. "Wow, there's watermelon in here," I comment and then ask, "How would I go about goin' after him?"

"You're dancing the rumba this week, right?"

"Yes . . . God, and those figure-eight hip rolls are hard to do."

Julia wags her eyebrows. "Well then, make smokin'-hot Rio sweat."

"He almost never sweats and I do think his hips are double-jointed if you ask me."

"I don't mean from exertion, although that hopefully will come later. I mean from . . . wantin' you. Oh, Abby, you can seduce him with the dance, girl. Easy as pie. He'll just think you're workin' it for the competition when you're really tryin' to get his boots . . . or make that his *dancin' shoes* . . . under your bed." She swallows a sip of her cranberry juice. "But actually you'd be killin' two birds with one stone if you think about it. Abby, you're not between a rock and a hard place, girl. You're in a win-win situation."

"You think?" I'm not so nearly convinced that this is a good plan or that I can pull it off. "Julia, I don't know . . ."

She shrugs. "It's up to you. Just don't let that Angelina chick have him, okay?"

"If you don't let her have Danny!"

A cloud of sadness passes over her face.

"Oh, don't give me that. You've got more fight in you than that, Julia. We can't let this woman come in here and take over like she owns the place, now, can we?"

"No damn way!" Julia says, sloshing a bit of juice. "Misty Creek is our turf." We tap our juice bottles together in a silent toast.

"Did we just bond again, Julia?"

"Yep, it's official now. The other night wasn't a fluke induced by the wine." She narrows her eyes at me. "You're gonna do this, right? Not wuss out on me?"

"Ye're damned tootin'," I say so loud that a squirrel scurries up a nearby tree. Of course I'm not really as confident as I let on. And I'm still wondering what the scene with Angelina was all about. "This is crazy, isn't it?"

"You mean leaving our regular jobs and doing this thing?"

While chewing on a bite of turkey sandwich I nod. "Do ya think sometimes you might just wake up and be cutting hair?"

"Yeah. And I keep wondering how it's all gonna turn out, don't you?"

Still chewing, I nod. The sandwich is pretty good.

Julia brushes the crumbs off her jeans and then polishes off her juice. "Well, I'd better get back. I'm doing the Viennese waltz."

"How pretty!"

Julia wrinkles her nose. "It's almost as boring as the fox-trot. And we're dancing to 'Chim-Chim Cheree' from *Mary Poppins*. James, my dance partner, is insisting that we dress up like Mary and Bert." She rolls her eyes. "Now, how corny is that?"

I shrug. "I think it will be cute."

"Maybe. I pitched a fit but he would have none of it. He pitched a fit right back. Every time I stomped my foot he stomped harder. It's a wonder we can dance at all."

"You like him, though, don't you?"

"Oh, he's amazing, so yeah."

"I think it'll be supercalifragilisticexpialidocious."

With a giggle Julia stands up and gives my shoulder a playful shove. "Hope you're right. Well, see you later."

I nod but opt to sit there for a while longer since I don't have to be back to rehearse for over an hour. I think about how different Julia is than what I always imagined. Then my thoughts shift to Mama and Jesse. I wonder if Mama is seeing Mitchell and I think about how her life has changed too. And how about Jesse having this hidden comedy writing talent? Who knew? I shake my head, thinking that none of us will ever be able to go back to who we were before this whole thing got started.

After a few minutes I realize that I had better get up to my room to study. After all, how am I going to seduce Rio with the rumba if I can't even do the darned dance?

I realize too that I'm coming to like ballroom dancing and that I'll really miss it once the show is over. It's really funny that something that I never even considered is now so important to me. Life sure is strange.

18

A Whole New Spin on Things

As I'm sitting here waiting my turn to get fitted for my costume for the dress rehearsal tonight I'm glumly realizing that my plans of seduction have fallen flat. No amount of sexy hip rolls, heated looks, pouting lips, near kisses, or lingering touches has gotten Rio into my bed. The best I've gotten is a pat on the back for dancing a hellava rumba. While that's nice and all I'm still not any closer to my goal.

I was lamenting this whole thing last night with Julia and she made me pinky-swear that I wouldn't give up. I'm wondering, though, just what else I can do without being totally obvious. Not that she has any room to talk since she isn't any closer to getting Danny's boots under her bed either. And he's been seen everywhere with Angelina. Julia says they're doing the tango this week. She knows this because she admits to peeking in on their rehearsals even though it's written in the packet that spying on other dancers is against the rules. She also said that Danny and Angelina are damned good.

I'm so deep in thought that I don't even hear Jackie the makeup and wardrobe chickie call my name until she shouts it very close to me, making me jump out of my seat. I would have gotten a bit peeved but the costumes arrived a day late so she's scrambling to get us all fitted and under a bit of stress. I follow her into the fitting room that's crammed full of racks of colorful stuff. Her assistants are buzzing around in a state of near hysteria . . . pinning, sewing, gluing like mad. I spot what looks like a Mary Poppins hat and grin.

"Maggie, bring me Abby Harper's costume," Jackie shouts.

Maggie tries to shout something back but she has straight pins between her lips so it sounds like she's humming. I think she said that she's coming but there might have been a hummed curse word or two in there. I really wish she would take the pins out before she swallows them or something. I'm about to give her that advice but my jaw drops when she comes over to me with my costume. "Wha . . ." is all that will come out of my mouth when I blink at the mere slip of purple sparkles and fringe.

"Let's try it on," Jackie says, obviously not seeing my distress over my costume or lack thereof.

"I . . . I." I swallow hard and finally manage, "Can't wear that."

"You can and will," she says without batting an eye. "Come on, Abby, I'm busy."

"No, really. I can't wear that in front of *my mama* and *the town*. And *mercy*, the *whole world*."

Jackie taps her foot. "You're dancing the rumba, right?"

I nod.

"Then this is your costume." She thrusts it into my hands.

"But can't I be Mary Poppins?" Oh, wait, that's been

taken. "Oh, how about Snow White? Rio can be the dashing prince. Whaddya think?"

Jackie takes a deep breath and gives me a long stare that doesn't seem to hold any sympathy whatsoever. "If you were dancing the waltz, then maybe. Abby, you're dancing the rumba, the sexiest of all the dances. This fits the bill. Go and put it on. Now."

I hold it up, thinking that maybe it's more substantial that way but, holy cow, it's cut out on the sides. Mama is going to have a fit.

"Abby, now!" Jackie says and I jump again. I would have glared at her this time, stress or not, but my eyes are too bugged out to narrow into a proper glare. Jackie shakes her head. "I don't know what you're wigging out about. You're going to look amazing in that costume. Your endless legs will stop traffic, Abby. Let's face it, you and Rio already sizzle on the dance floor. You should own this dance. Now go put on the skimpy outfit and have fun with it. I know I would."

I stand up, clutching the sparkly fabric to my chest. "So you think Rio will like it?"

"Seeing you in that costume is going to knock any guy for a loop, Abby. I'm sure that Rio won't be an exception. So you've fallen for him, huh?"

"No!" I lie, but not very well.

She arches a knowing eyebrow. Why can everybody arch an eyebrow but me? "Can't say as I blame you. That costume should catch his attention. You can thank me later."

Oh. Now, this puts a whole new spin on things. I'm just going to have to suck it up and wear the darned thing. Once it's on it might not be so bad . . . With that thought in mind I head over to the makeshift dressing room constructed from long red curtains hung from the ceiling on the other side of the room.

After slipping off my jeans and sweater I wiggle into the costume. It's tight and clingy but not terribly uncomfortable, and stretchy so as to dance in. Carefully avoiding the mirror I raise my hands to clasp the jeweled collar behind my neck and then slowly turn around.

Wow. I look . . . wow . . . sexy? Me? The sparkly purple material covers my chest but bares my arms halter-top style. From there it covers my breasts but has two cutouts on the sides revealing a generous slice of my torso. There is a cute little skirt cut up higher on one side and filled with layers of gold fringe. With a smile I give my hips a little Cuban motion. Sweet. The fringe sways with my hip action and I can picture how amazing it will look sparkling and swishing beneath the spotlight on the dance floor. I gasp when I take a peek at the back . . . or of my bare back. The gold fringe starts low on my spine at the top curve of my butt. With my hand over my mouth I give my butt a little shake and then giggle.

"Abby, let's see," Jackie shouts.

Holy cow. "Okay. Just a minute." Telling myself that there are bathing suits more revealing than this, I take a deep breath and then slowly come from behind the curtain. "What do you think?" I ask, trying to sound casual, but Rio's standing there and my voice trails off as I gauge his face for a reaction. I just know my face is flaming.

Jackie turns to Rio. "What do you think?"

My heart pounds while his gaze takes me in from head to toe.

"Sexy enough for the rumba?" Jackie asks but then her cell phone rings. She puts a finger up and turns away from us to take the call, leaving me feeling a bit awkward with Rio fully clothed and me in my skimpy outfit. I stand there wishing I had the nerve to ask him how I look and wishing he would say *amazing*.

"You look amazing, Abby."

Wait, did I just think that or did he just say it? "Really?"

"Didn't I tell you never to say that to me again?"

"I don't mind well."

He chuckles. "That costume is going to make some eyes pop open."

"My mama's gonna have a cow."

At the blank look on his face I'm about to explain but he holds up a hand. "No, wait, that means she is going to be upset, right?"

"You're catchin' on."

He grins. "Yes, I am, aren't I?" He runs his fingers through his loose hair that looks a bit damp as if he just showered. I lick my dry lips and he clears his throat.

"So, are you here to get fitted too?"

"Yes." He leans against a table and folds his arms over his chest, looking like he's about to tell me something, but then Jackie comes rushing back over to us.

"Rio, you need to hurry up and get dressed. Mitchell just called and wants you and Abby on the front page of the Web site. Looks like you two are the front-runners. He said that *People* magazine might be interested in doing a feature story too."

Rio gives me a grin. "Looks like you're no longer the underdog, Abby."

My heart starts pounding. *Wow.*

"Maggie, get Rio's costume!"

Maggie glares over the top of her glasses as she hems some pants. Muttering beneath her breath she tosses the pants down and scurries over to a long rack of costumes and grabs one. She's as sweet as sugar to Rio, though. He has that effect on women except for one and I don't want to think about *her.*

While Rio's changing, Jackie and Maggie fuss over my costume and then in a moment of inspiration Jackie tucks a big purple silk flower behind my ear. She steps back to take a look while nibbling on her inner cheek.

"She needs hair extension so her hair can flow down her back," Jackie finally says.

Peering at me over her funky reading glasses, Maggie nods in agreement. "I think we have something that will match her hair color."

Pursing her lips Jackie says, "Her makeup needs to be bold this week. Red lipstick and fake eyelashes."

They continue to discuss me like I'm a mannequin they're dressing up for a window display until Rio comes out from behind the red curtain. We all turn and stare.

He's wearing a black jumpsuit sort of thing belted at the waist with a high stiff collar in the same gold color as my fringe. Void of buttons, the shirt is open to his navel in a deep V, accented with shiny gold. The pants are tight and narrow but flair at the feet and have gold piping down the outside of each leg. His shoulder-length hair has dried in midnight waves and is tousled from tugging his turtleneck over his head.

"I look like Elvis," he says and for the first time I notice that he's scowling.

"But that's a good thing, Rio." My mama loves Elvis, as do most of the women in this town. We've been to Graceland three times and Mama bought a license plate, a key chain, a shot glass even though she doesn't drink, and an ashtray even though she doesn't smoke.

Rio shoots me a look to see if I'm kidding. He's never quite sure. In my opinion Elvis never looked so good, especially in the fried peanut butter and banana years, although Mama will argue that the King ever consumed such a thing. She also harbors a hope that he is still alive and living in peace in a quaint village in France.

"I think you look hot," Maggie gushes. "Don't you, Jackie?"

Jackie nods while tapping her cheek. "Oh yeah. We need to slick his hair back . . ."

"Are you wishing we had gone with the pirate theme? Rio could totally pull off Jack Sparrow."

"No way!" Jackie argues. "Rio is *totally* Will Turner."

"Ladies, may I remind you that I specified that Abby and I would not dress as characters? I think it takes away from the dance. So your argument is . . . how shall we say? . . . moot. I'm wondering, then, how I ended up as Elvis."

"You're not Elvis, Rio. It's just a sexy jumpsuit not so unlike other ones you've worn."

"I like to stick to a shirt and pants and forgo the jumpsuit. Can we do that?"

They both shake their heads. "Too late."

Rio sighs but is a good sport about his Elvis outfit. Personally I like it but decide not to voice my opinion. Plus, I might just like it because Rio is wearing it, so the pirate thing would have been pretty cool too.

"Okay, Mitchell has a limo waiting. Chop, chop."

"Wait, we're going into town now?" Rio asks.

Jackie nods. "Mitchell wants the pictures taken at the dance hall. I was told to tell you to bring a change of street clothes so you can dine in town and then head back to the dance hall for the dress rehearsal tonight."

"But we'll miss our rehearsal time this afternoon while taking pictures."

Jackie shrugs. "Don't shoot the messenger."

Rio looks at her for a minute as if trying to translate her comment but then shrugs and turns to me. "Maybe we can get some extra time at the dance hall to practice."

"Hey, your picture featured on the front of the Web site will get you votes, Rio," Jackie points out. "So I would be looking at this as a good thing. Hopefully the *People* spread will pan out for you too. This show is taking on a life of its own and you two are the sweethearts."

Rio nods. "Point taken." He turns to me. "I'll meet you at the limo in ten minutes, okay?"

"Sure." I'm acting all casual but I'm a bit stuck on being referred to as sweethearts.

"We'll meet you there to do your makeup," Jackie says and then calls for Travis to come for his fitting.

Wow, I think as I hurry to my room. A limo . . . a photo shoot, and a spread in *People*? What could possibly happen next?

19

Feeding Frenzy

There is just something so glamorous about a limo ride even in the light of day, and dressed in our costumes makes it more so even though we both have light coats on. Rio has on a black leather jacket and I wish I had something dressier than this raincoat but I didn't have anything better. If I win this competition Mama, Jesse, and I are going to the mall for some fancy clothes!

The tinted glass and soothing jazz as we cruise down the winding mountain road feel calm and relaxing after the frenzy of activity in the past week. Rio and I are sitting close but not touching in the very back seat and I don't think I've ever been so aware of a man in my life. I want to reach over and touch him, maybe just put a hand on his leg, so instead I lean my head against the cool, soft leather of the bench seat and close my eyes.

"Tired?" The low timbre of his voice is as soothing as the cool jazz.

"A little." But as I sit here I suddenly realize that I'm more exhausted than I thought.

"You can lean your head against my shoulder and rest

if you wish," Rio offers. "Today is going to be a long one, so catch a short nap. I don't mind."

"Thanks. I think I will." I can't hold back a sigh when my cheek slides against the butter-soft texture of his sleeve. He smells like leather and a hint of spicy cologne . . . not overpowering, just so damned sexy and sort of, I don't know . . . *intriguing.*

It feels so good snuggling against him like this that I fold my legs up onto the seat and smile just before closing my eyes. Since I want to savor leaning against him for the short ride into town I just pretend to sleep. But I don't want him to know that I'm savoring. I do have my pride even though it's so difficult to keep from tucking my arms through his.

Despite my effort to remain awake, the soothing music coupled with my fatigue has me dozing. But that's okay because when my head almost slips onto his lap, Rio wraps his arm around me and, while I know it's for safety's sake, it sure feels nice. Just when I'm feeling comfy and secure, the limo swerves sharply to the left, making me squish against Rio. My hand shoots out for support and comes into contact with the deep V of his Elvis outfit where his jacket is unbuttoned.

"What happened?" I ask in a sleepy voice even though I'm now wide-awake.

"We almost hit a deer," Rio explains.

"Oh." I scoot up like I'm interested and remove my hand like I didn't know it was poised on his bare chest.

"This is insane," Rio growls.

"Oh, this isn't unusual. There's deer up here everywhere and raccoons and . . ."

"I wasn't talking about the animals, Abby," he says in the same low growl that, by the way, is very sexy.

"Oh." I'm really wishing I had left my hand on his chest but I can't exactly put it back there for no apparent reason. While I'm trying to think of one, Rio leans over and kisses me.

Maybe it's from the surprise or maybe it's what I wanted to do but I suddenly find myself falling onto my back with my arms curled around Rio while kissing him right like it's my job. The hot kiss is deep and a bit wild, I'm guessing from pent-up desire . . . at least on my part anyway.

"I can't believe we're doing this," he says, pausing to nibble on my neck. Rio is an excellent neck nibbler . . . makes you tingle and shiver.

"It's a limo. . . . It was inevitable," I try to joke but it ends with a gasp when he sucks my earlobe into his mouth. I sink my fingers into his hair because I just *love* his hair and then we're kissing again.

"I can't keep my hands or my mouth off you," Rio says, pulling back to run a gentle fingertip down my cheek. I love it when he does that.

"Me too," I admit, swallowing hard. "Rio, why are we fighting this?"

He closes his eyes for a moment and then says, "Because I know how much the prize money means to your family. I'm your instructor and I should help you to win, not be the reason why you do not. I know from experience how important it is to stay focused. I could not forgive myself if I ruined your chances of winning."

"So you're doing this for me?"

Rio nods. "Of course. Winning this would be fun and I'm a fierce competitor, but in the long run it means nothing to me. Is that what you thought, Abby? That all I wanted was to win?"

I shrug. "I didn't know how much money, you know, a bonus or whatever that you got for coming in first."

"It doesn't matter to me."

"Couldn't you use the money for your studio in Mexico City?"

"That's not an issue," he tells me with a tender smile.

"But why? I mean surely—" I begin again but have to hold that thought when the limo stops.

"We'd better sit up," Rio warns, "because there are bound to be cameras. We'll finish this discussion tonight in the privacy of my room, okay?"

I nod and he's right because a moment later when the door swings open letting in bright sunshine, cameras from several news stations are there to film our every move. While this makes me feel important and everything I also realize how hard it must be for celebrities to deal with this all the time. It's enough to make a person nervous.

With his arm protectively around me Rio smiles, so I do the same thing.

"How do you feel about being the favorite?" a tall blond reporter asks while thrusting a microphone in Rio's face.

"Like we need to rehearse," Rio responds, widening his smile a bit.

"Think you can beat Danny Becker and the new threat, Angelina Perez?" she persists. "And weren't you and Angelina once partners?"

Rio's smile remains but he picks up the pace. "Yes to both questions," he tosses over his shoulder, and more questions are shouted at us but sometimes long legs come in quite handy.

We enter the dance hall a bit breathless. "Wow, I didn't know how popular this show is becoming," I comment.

"I have to admit that I'm surprised. I just bet that it will be a bit crazy as we approach the finals."

"Mama told me yesterday that business is great at the diner and the whole town is booming."

"That's good, Abby." His warm smile tells me that he really does care.

"So, are you happy that you're a part of this now? I mean, do you think this has helped or harmed your ballroom dance reputation?"

"I was wrong. Although unconventional, this has turned into a real competition and you should be proud of Misty Creek. I don't think that even Mitchell Banks anticipated this reaction."

"Oh, don't be so sure," says a cultured voice that has us turning around. Walking in the opposite door is Mitchell with my mama on his arm!

"Abby!" Mama shouts and rushes over to me. We hug like I've been away for years.

"I've missed you, Babycakes."

"I've missed you and Jesse too! And your cooking . . . *mercy*, I miss your meat loaf and mashed potatoes." We hug and sniff back tears so as not to make our mascara run. "How'd you get in here?" I ask in a stage whisper. "We were told that no one was allowed in except for us."

"Connections," she says with a pretty blush and a glance up at Mitchell. I swear he gives her an adoring look right back. I peer closely at Mama and I don't believe I've ever seen her this relaxed and . . . *glowing*. Ohmigod, they aren't . . . she *isn't* . . . holy cow; okay, I refuse to even go there. But still, it's so nice to see her happy. Not that she wasn't before but oh my, how wonderful it would be for her to find someone to share her life with. Mitchell Banks sure isn't whom I ever would have pictured her with but I'm finding that love happens when you least expect it. I remember Mama and Daddy being happy but she deserves another chance at love.

"Mama, are you missin' the lunch crowd?"

She grins behind her hand. "I'm playin' hooky. Mitchell *insisted* and we've hired two extra waitresses so he said that they could do without me for a couple of hours."

Well, I'll be . . . I never thought I'd see Mama leave the diner during regular hours.

"Abilene, are you tryin' to catch flies, child?" Mama asks with a girlish giggle.

I realize that my mouth is gaping open and snap it shut. "Well, I have to admit that I thought pigs would fly the day I saw you leave the diner in the middle of the day."

Mama giggles again. "I know, *I know!*"

I glance over at Rio, who has a perplexed expression on his face. "You're thinking about pigs flying, aren't you?"

He grins while nodding. "I have that expression figured out, I think."

Mama gives me a look that seems to be asking if there is something between Rio and me and I feel heat creep into my cheeks that I'm sure answers her question.

Mitchell clears his throat and says, "Well, Sadie, we had better get going. I'm sure they want you both in makeup for the photo shoot. I think Jackie just arrived."

I give Mama one last lingering hug and she says, "Good luck, Abby."

"Thanks, Mama. I'll do my very best."

"You always do."

"Good luck, Rio," Mama says quietly but then gives him a measuring look that says *you hurt my baby and there will be hell to pay*, but to his credit Rio remains unruffled.

"Thank you, Mrs. Harper," he says and adds a warm smile. "I am quite impressed with your daughter."

"As well you should be," she says, inclining her head. "But thank you just the same."

Just then Jackie comes rushing into the hall with Maggie in tow, lugging a big case of what I'm guessing is cosmetics. "Rio and Abby, hurry! We need to do hair and makeup," Jackie says as we're ushered over to two tall bar stools. "Maggie, take their coats."

"Okay," Maggie says a little irritably as she heaves the huge case down onto a table with a clunk that echoes in the hall.

"I'll do Rio and you do Abby," Jackie says.

"I want to do Rio," Maggie says defiantly.

I want to do Rio, too, I think and disguise my giggle with a cough. He glances my way and of course I blush.

"Ladies," Rio interjects smoothly, "I think you are hurting Abby's feelings."

All eyes turn to me, and my blush must have been interpreted as hurt feelings. Maggie glares at Jackie like it's all her fault and starts combing out my hair. It's all a moot point anyway because Rio is done in no time and both girls end up working on me. Finally, I'm handed a mirror.

"Wow . . . *wow!*" I blink at myself—at least I think it's my reflection—and I swallow hard. If I didn't know better I would have thought that the person in the mirror was somebody else. They've weaved extensions through my hair, making me have a blond tumble of curls piled high and then spilling down my back. My lips are tingling from some deep pink lip gloss that magically makes my mouth seem full and pouting and my eyes seem to have an exotic tilt to them and appear bluer than normal.

"Hot," Jackie says with a satisfied nod.

"Sexy," Maggie agrees and then turns to Rio and asks, "What do you think?"

My heart is pounding as I wait for his answer.

"I think she is going to steam up the camera lens," he says with a grin.

I would think that he's teasing except for the heat in his eyes, and for the first time in my life I feel confident and desirable . . . *and I like it.* Feeling sexy is fun. And I pretty much decide right then and there to quit squelching my feelings for Rio. Tonight in his room I'm going to let him know exactly how I feel about him and to quit pretending.

The photo shoot ends up being a blast. We do about a million poses, both campy and serious. Finally Rio says, "I'm sorry but we really must rehearse."

"One more," the cameraman insists. "I want this one to be a prelude to a kiss."

Rio nods. "Okay, *one* more."

"Abby, put your hand on his chest, right there in the center. That's right. Rio, place your hand low on her back and, Abby, lean back just a bit. Now, Abby, raise your left leg. That's right, now bend it up to graze his leg. Rio, now lean in very close and put your mouth almost but not quite on Abby's. Awesome, now hold that pose."

This is hard . . . not kissing him, I mean. I can feel the rapid beat of his heart beneath where my palm rests on his warm skin and I'm gratified to know that he must be feeling the same way. Oh, and with his mouth a hairbreadth away from mine, nearly touching, I can feel the heat, the cool tickle of his breathing on my cheek.

"Okay, perfect," I hear the cameraman say in a far-away voice because I'm caught up in the moment and I really want this to end with a doggone kiss. But just when I think I'm going to get my wish, Rio pulls back, leaving me standing there breathless and wanting.

I'm hoping to sneak a little smooch in during practice

but there are cameras and people milling around everywhere, so that is a no-go as well and, given the sensual nature of the rumba, I'm feeling quite revved up and nowhere to go by the end of the rehearsal.

Instead of heading back up the mountain we change into street clothes and then opt to eat dinner in town since we have to be back at the dance hall for the run-through that night before the live show on Saturday.

"How about eating at Mama's diner?" I ask Rio as we stroll through town.

"Definitely." He nods and gives me one of his smiles that make my heart beat faster. He doesn't smile often but when he does his face just lights up. Of course he has each and every female young and old turning to get a second look, making me want to slip my arm through his in a territorial way even though I have no real claim to him. Not that I can blame them. In his faded jeans, a black turtleneck, and aviator sunglasses, Rio deserves a second glance. His dark hair, untamed by a ponytail, is blowing in the cool breeze and he has his leather jacket flung over his shoulder in a nonchalant way and yet he oozes charisma.

We're stopped for pictures and autographs and I can tell you that I will never get over this as long as I live. I know that my fifteen minutes of fame will be over when the show ends, so I have fun with it but this is still so surreal, especially when I enter the diner to sit down and eat like a customer.

"Abby!" Of course Mama rushes over and there is hugging galore from her, the waitresses, and others who feel compelled to come over and hug me. Pete pokes his head out of the kitchen and gives me a wave but thank goodness he's too busy to come over for a hug. Jesse is in school so I miss getting to see him but Mama assures me that he will be at the show tomorrow.

We're ushered over to a booth and I feel really weird having Mama waiting on us. "What'll you have, Baby-cakes?" she asks me.

"Meat loaf, mashed potatoes with gravy, green beans, and corn bread." My mouth waters at the thought.

"Oh, we're out of meat loaf," Mama says.

"What? Say it ain't so!"

Rio chuckles. "I think she's . . . how do you say? . . . pulling your leg."

I look at Mama, and her mouth is twitching in an effort not to smile. "Mama, don't toy with me like that."

Rio laughs. "Good one, Mrs. Harper." He sticks out his fists for a knuckle bump. "Abby has been dying for your meat loaf. She can't stop talking about it. Please bring me the same."

"You won't be sorry," Mama says and winks at him. "Secret recipe." I've never seen Mama wink at anyone but I carefully keep my jaw from dropping. "I'll bring you two Cherry Cokes. The real thing, mind you, not from a bottle." She tucks her stubby pencil behind her ear and hurries off on her soft-soled shoes.

"Your mother is a very vibrant woman."

With a nod I say, "She's a hard worker and it's so nice to see a little kick in her step. She's always had energy to spare, bless her heart, but it's wonderful to see her so happy, you know?" I swallow sudden emotion. "It's not like her to wink or flirt. She's always had to be pretty much all business . . . pleasant and everything but not lighthearted. It makes me realize how much living she's given up for Jesse and me."

Rio reaches across the table and clasps my hand. "I wouldn't refer to it as *given up*, Abby. Don't feel guilt for something she has freely given." He gives my hand a gentle squeeze. "Life is unpredictable and rarely works out the way we think it will." He shrugs. "And perhaps that would be rather boring, no?" He says this seriously but has a hint of mischief in the depths of his brown eyes. "In fact," he begins but is interrupted by the arrival of our Cherry Cokes and meat loaf.

"Here you go," Mama says and sets our glasses and plates down with a flourish. "Enjoy."

"Oh, it looks wonderful! Mama, can you spare a few minutes to sit with us?"

"No, sorry. We're backed up. But hey, don't get me wrong. I'm not complaining! The competition has been a boon to this town. Good luck to you both. I can't wait to see you dancin' in your fancy outfits!"

I give Rio a look and he almost chokes on his Coke. Luckily I hadn't taken off my coat this morning, so Mama has no idea of the skimpiness of my costume. "Why, thank you, Mama."

When she is out of listening distance Rio says, "Think she's gonna have a . . . what was that you said?"

"A *cow*, and yes. A big one."

Angling his head, Rio says, "Then again, maybe not."

"You could be right. Mama has certainly loosened up."

I watch Rio take a bite of the meat loaf and for some reason it's important to me that he likes it . . . stupid really, but it somehow matters.

"Delicious," he says. "Onion, green pepper, a hint of garlic, and something else I can't place. What would that be?"

"If I told you, I'd have to kill you."

He laughs at that old one-liner and God help me, I'm falling harder and harder for him. "I won't tell, I promise," he says.

I point my fork at him. "Oh no, don't go crossing your heart and hopin' to die."

He gives me a confused look while buttering a slice of corn bread.

"Never mind. Just a joke I shared with Julia."

After a drink of his Cherry Coke, he says, "Interesting that you two have become friends."

I swallow a heavenly bite of fluffy mashed potatoes and say, "I guess it's all part of the unpredictability of life that you were talking about, but yes, I agree."

"This really is delicious," Rio says as he polishes off his meat loaf.

I flush with pride but I can't help it. "Yes, it's a shame that little diners like this are becoming more and more rare. Now it's all big chain restaurants and they're good and all, but there is just something about a greasy spoon that Americans will always love."

"Greasy spoon?"

I grin. "That's what we call little hole-in-the-wall diners like this one. Comfort food for the soul," I say with another bite. "The food at the lodge is good but this is where I come from." I wave my hand in an arc and realize how much I love this place. "So, is your mama a good cook?"

Rio hesitates. "I suppose."

"You suppose?"

"We have a cook so she doesn't prepare meals much."

"Oh." This surprises me but since two giggling girls wanting pictures and autographs interrupt us I can't ask how they could have afforded a cook.

The two girls seem to have been a cue for just about everyone else to approach us but we're more than happy to oblige. After all, these are potential voters. But after a few minutes Rio announces that we have to go back to the dance hall for dress rehearsal and the fans moan but understand. I hunt Mama down for a quick hug and we're out the door. Rio calls the limo driver and in no time we're back to Bluegrass Dance Hall.

Rio hasn't mentioned me coming up to his room

again but it seems to hang in the air between us, causing this sexual electricity that has my heart pounding hard even while I'm sitting here getting my makeup touched up.

"You look amazing, Abby," Maggie gushes after fluffing and tinkering with my hair extensions.

"I have you to thank for transforming me from geek to gorgeous. I swear you're a miracle worker."

Maggie clicks her tongue in a tsk-tsk way. "Abby, you were gorgeous to begin with! All I did was add a touch of glamour."

I find this compliment from spunky little Maggie heartwarming and I'm about to tell her so when she gives me one of her scowls and says, "God, I hate it when tall, gorgeous girls like you act like they need to put a bag over their head. Okay, so you have a bit of that redneck thing going on, but damn, girl, you're *hot*. No wonder Rio can't keep his eyes off you."

"Really?"

While touching up my eyeliner she rolls her eyes and then says, "*Really*. Now, stop with the aw, shucks attitude and go strut your stuff."

"'Kay." Now, maybe it's because of our heightened sexual tension or due to the confidence boost Maggie gave me or the long flowing hair attached to my head or the fringe on my outfit . . . *whatever*. But when Rio and I dance our rumba the scurrying around by the staff ceases and everyone stops to watch us dance.

After we take a bow Rio says in my ear, "That was amazing. If we dance like that tomorrow night we'll . . ."

"Knock their socks off?" I supply when he can't seem to find the right words.

With a laugh he leads me off the dance floor and says, "Yes, we'll knock their socks off. Listen, I have to go back up to the lodge to do some paperwork. I will see you later, though, no?"

I nod and whisper, "I'll be there as soon as I can."

With a smile he leans in and gives me a brief kiss on the cheek. "Excellent. I will be waiting."

20

Dancing in the Dark

Never in my life have I worried about the color of my underwear and now I wish I had something other than white Hanes Her Way. Don't get me wrong, Hanes Her Way is nice and comfortable and all, but high-cut cotton briefs aren't the sexiest panties in the world, and of course it's all I have. If I win this thing I'm going to get me some very nice Victoria's Secret underpants . . . I mean lingerie.

"Maybe I just won't wear underwear," I defiantly say to my reflection in the bathroom mirror where I've been standing for the past fifteen minutes. Knowing that will never fly I shake my head at myself. "Right." Finally I tug on my jeans and soft blue sweater and decide I will just have to do. Now if only I can get my heart rate down to a not so nervous state of mind I'll be fine. "He's just a guy and I'm just a girl about to do what comes naturally. No big deal."

But it is a big deal to me. Sure, we already made love in the back of his car but that was different. This time it's planned . . . clearly thought out, something we both need and want, so it's like taking a giant step forward in our relationship . . . a relationship that I hope will last longer than this show.

I take a deep breath and let it out, thinking that I'm about to put my heart on a platter for Rio Martin. Then I think about how my daddy's life was cut short in the prime of his life and I just know my mama would do it all again just for the time she had with him. In other words, you really don't know what's around the corner so you might as well live life to the fullest.

Okay, pep talk over, I spray on a hint of White Shoulders, fluff my extended hair, apply a bit of nude lip gloss, and head out the door. Rio's room is in the other wing of the lodge, much bigger suites where the counselors used to stay when I was a kid. I'm halfway there when, as I pass one of the doors to the outside, I spot the red-tipped glow of a cigarette. Curious, I peek out the window and I see that it's Julia sitting on a fieldstone wall puffing away. Even though I'm in a hurry to get to Rio I can't help but stop to see if she is okay. Pushing open the heavy wooden door I say, "Julia?"

She jumps as if she's deep in thought and I guess I startled her. "Oh . . . Abby." Her voice is husky either from the smoke or because she's been crying. I suspect a bit of both.

I step out into the cool night air. "You okay?"

"Sure," she says but not convincingly.

"I didn't know you smoked."

"I don't," she says and takes another long drag. "Well, okay, I don't anymore. Gave it up five years ago but I suddenly felt the need."

I know this is kind of nervy of me but I pluck the cigarette from her fingers and grind it beneath my shoe. To my surprise she doesn't protest. "Does this sudden need for a smoke have anything to do with Danny?"

She snorts. "Am I pathetic or what?" She juts out her chin and says, "Smack some sense into me, please."

The whoosh of the door opening has us both turning our heads.

"Julia!" Danny growls. "Damn it, I've been looking all over for you. Why'd you run off like that?"

"Because you were with Ange-*li*-na. Sure looked damned cozy sittin' by the fire in the dining room."

"She's my dance partner, Julia. We were discussing our dance."

"Sure you were."

His eyes narrow. "Have you been smoking?"

"What's it to ya?" she says hotly but ruins the effect when her voice cracks.

"*Everything*, damn you."

"Wh-what?"

"You heard me. You mean everything to me. Always have and always will, *damn it all to hell.*"

I'm thinking Danny needs to soften his word choice as I watch the exchange like a tennis match. And maybe not growl.

Julia pushes away from the stone wall. "What are you sayin'?"

Taking a step closer to her, Danny says, "I'm saying that I've been working overtime with Angelina to win this competition so I can add a body shop to my business." He takes another step closer to Julia.

"What's that got to do with me? My car's in fine shape," she says in a sassy tone and gives him a lift of her chin but her lips tremble.

"Well then, let me spell it out for you."

"You do that."

"I love you, Julia. I've loved you since I was fifteen and I'm never gonna stop even though I've tried. I want the body shop to make more money to give you a better life than I can now."

Julia closes the gap between them and grabs a fistful of flannel shirt. "Why have you tried to stop loving me, Danny? If it's because of that bullshit that you think you're not good enough for me, then just give it up, darn it. I don't need fancy things. Can't you get it into your thick skull that all I need is you?"

I watch her pull his head down for a kiss and although I feel like applauding and cheering I decide to give them their privacy. Plus, they've totally forgotten about me anyway. As I walk away I have to brush away a stray tear. Although it wasn't a flowery speech, what Danny said was heartfelt and honest and has me all choked up and ready to laugh at the same time. I do hate the idea, though, that if I win, Danny won't have the money for his body shop. Not that I'm going to throw the dance competition or anything but God, I hate competing against friends.

It occurs to me again how this whole thing has changed us in ways we never suspected. This really hits home when I reach Rio's door. I stand there for a good minute or two with my heart beating wildly. My poor old regular-beating heart must be wondering what in the world is up with all this excitement. Finally, I take a deep breath, blow it out in a soft whoosh, and then lightly rap on the door. When there's no answer I get a little panicky thinking that I've got this all wrong or he's changed his mind. I start to pivot on my heel to save myself some extreme embarrassment but then something tells me to try the door handle. Sure enough, it's open.

My heart of course does the beating-hard thing again as I push the door open slowly, because this is like something out of a movie and what if something creepy happens? I mean, life has been a bit off-kilter lately. I swallow hard, which is really silly because what could I possibly find on the other side of the door? To make matters worse, the door actually creeks as I push it open. I shiver, push the door open wider, and *oh my God* . . .

The door on the far side of the room opens, letting out a wave of fragrant steam. Rio emerges through the mist while drying his hair with a small towel that covers the top half of his face. Another towel is knotted and slung low on his hips. I follow the path of water that's beaded up on his chest and running south in little rivers until being soaked up by the towel that I imagine yanking away with one small tug. His biceps bunch and flex and ab muscles ripple as he vigorously rubs his head.

Holy cow.

I know I should announce my presence but my throat has suddenly gone dry. Finally I clear my throat. Rio immediately stops drying his hair and our eyes meet.

"Viene aquí."

I don't know what he said but I sure hope he's talking dirty to me.

"Wh-what?" *Oh, that was smooth.* I feel a blush heat my cheeks.

Rio gives me that slow, sexy smile that got me from day one. "I said, come here."

Okay, close enough, I think as I move in his direction on my wobbly legs. Needless to say my heart is slamming in my chest and I'm wondering if it would be too forward of me to just yank the towel away in one fluid motion and then sort of circle around him like we're dancing the paso doble.

Of course I don't because I've already used up all my nerve just coming here but I do manage to place one hand on his damp chest wishing I could dip my head and lick away a bead of water.

"Whatever you are thinking about doing, Abby . . . *do it.*"

I swallow, torn between the yanking and the licking. Perhaps I should do both?

Rio chuckles, low in his throat. "I love the play of emotion on your face." He reaches over and runs a fingertip down my cheek and then over my bottom lip, making me shiver. Then with a tender smile he takes my hand in his. "Come over here and have a glass of wine. I took the liberty of pouring one for you."

I recall my strawberry wine incident and hesitate.

"It will . . . how do you say? . . . take the edge off." He picks up the goblet from the nightstand and hands it to me. "I could only find one glass, so will you share?"

I want to say something sexy or flirty but the best I can do is nod. Tilting the glass to my lips, I take a small sip. The red wine is tart and rich with a dark cherry, slightly smoky flavor.

"You like it?"

I nod again like a complete ninny and take a bigger swallow.

"May I?"

My head bobs again. When I hand him the glass our fingers brush and I know this sounds silly as all get out but I feel a jolt of heat that starts at my fingers and slowly sinks lower like sweet, thick sorghum on a warm slice of corn bread. I watch him take a swallow and then he hands the glass back to me. I sit down on the bed since my legs are trembling a bit and he joins me. The tart wine tastes better with each sip and I slowly feel mellow and a bit more relaxed.

Rio drains the last bit and places the glass back onto

the nightstand. "I hope you don't mind leaving the light on, because I love looking at you."

"Not at all," I assure him but then think of my Hanes For Her and wish for something more seductive.

"Good. I've been thinking about this all day long and I want it to be right. I want to go slow," he tells me while cupping my chin, "and easy . . . savoring each kiss." His mouth is so very close to mine . . . almost touching but not quite. He hesitates a fraction longer, heightening my senses until just when I think I can't stand not kissing any longer his soft lips capture mine.

My eyes flutter shut when Rio's mouth melts into my own, tasting of fine wine and hot male. His freshly showered scent invades my senses and I cling to his smooth shoulders while he lowers me to the soft mound of pillows at my back. His damp hair feels cool against my cheek and I thread my fingers through the damp tresses while I open my mouth for the kiss to go deeper, hotter.

Passion takes over and I frantically begin to shed my sweater and jeans. Rio makes quick work of my Hanes Her Way and then tosses his towel to the floor. I moan into his mouth when his warm skin slides against mine and he kisses me again while caressing my skin. His smooth, long fingers cup my breast, gently kneading while circling my sensitive nipple with his thumb until I arch up with the pleasure of it all.

"*Mi Dios, que yo le quiere tan,*" he whispers hotly into my ear and then begins a moist trail of kisses down my neck that makes me sigh. Then his mouth plays and teases my breasts, going from one to the other, driving me wild. When he sucks my nipple into his mouth, laving in a circular motion, I feel like I'm sinking into the pillows drowning in sensation and desperate to have him buried deep inside me.

"Rio . . ." I plead but he continues his sensual assault with his hot, hungry mouth. As if that isn't enough, he slides his hand up my thigh, caressing, *teasing* so very close to where I want him to touch. While I arch my hips in open invitation his teeth graze sharply over my nipple, sending a white-hot stab of desire to my groin just as he slips a long finger deep inside me. "God . . ." I drench his finger with wet need and he eases it out to circle my clit, bringing me to near orgasm. "Rio!" My eyes open when the weight and the heat of his body are suddenly gone but I'm relieved to see that he is rolling on protection.

"Abby," he moans as he threads his fingers with mine and takes me with a long, deep stroke that fills me and streals my breath. He moves slowly, easing in and back out, making my pleasure climb even higher. When I want *more* he holds back until I'm aching for release. He rocks gently while kissing me deeply until I wrap my legs around him and arch up, driving him deeper. He quickens the pace . . . harder while his kiss becomes wild. My breasts slide against his chest, teasing my nipples while sending tingles of pleasure higher and higher that seem to spread and finger out until a sharp climax bursts upon me with such intensity that I cling to Rio's shoulders. He thrusts hard and deep, joining me for sweet release. I feel the pulsing power of him buried deep and he cries out hoarsely while arching his back for a long muscle-straining moment before dipping his head for a tender kiss.

Our fingers are entwined while our bodies remain as one and I *swear* I never knew that lovemaking could be so beautiful.

"Stay with me tonight, Abby," he says with a warm smile that goes straight to my heart.

Not trusting my voice I can only nod.

"I want to wake up with you in my arms."

I look into his brown eyes and see sincerity and I know that no matter what happens from this day forward I will always have this . . .

21

Walking on Sunshine

I just know I have this goofy smile on my face but I can't make it go away. Not wanting to look silly, especially since those doggone cameras are everywhere, I try to put on my Saturday evening game face but the smile keeps popping right back in place. Julia, of course, immediately has me all figured out.

"Somebody got lucky," she says as we're walking back to our rooms after a huge buffet lunch. Very soon we have to head into town for the competition but we have a little downtime to rest.

"Talkin' about yourself?" I ask, wishing I could crook my eyebrow.

"I'm talkin' about you, girlfriend. Spill."

"I don't kiss and tell," I say primly.

"Oh, so you admit that you did at least *kiss.* Come on, Abby, give me some juicy details. I promise I won't tell. Plus, I would love to have something to think about other than the doggone competition tonight. I'm a nervous wreck. The Viennese waltz is just too slow and I'm wondering if the Mary Poppins and Bert costumes are way over the top. What if everybody laughs their asses off?"

"They *won't* and if they do it will likely get you votes. Julia, you're talking to the person who did a wild break-dancing move in an effort not to take out the judges' table."

"I can only do what I can do, right?" she says with a sigh. "So I guess details of you and Rio are not forth-coming?"

I shake my head but then give her a hug. "I'm so happy that you and Danny are back together. He's a nice guy and you're a nice girl even though you were prom queen and all that."

She gives me a playful shove. "Yeah, and to think I was worried about Angelina sinking her claws into him. Truth is, Danny thinks she's a bitch even though she *is* an amazing dancer. Abby, watch yourself. Danny hinted that Angelina is out to get Rio one way or the other and you mark my words, she will try to mess things up for you if you let her."

"I'm not worried." Not much anyway.

"Well, I got yer back. You remember that, 'kay?"

"Thanks, Julia. And good luck tonight."

"You too even though you and Rio are the favorites." She wrinkles her nose good-naturedly at me.

"I can't really believe that a klutz like me could learn to dance but Rio is a good teacher, I guess."

"I'll just bet he is."

"Oh, stop!"

"What fun would that be?" she tosses over her shoulder as she walks away.

I have to chuckle as I continue down the hallway to my room. I push the threat of Angelina to the far corner of my brain and refuse to let this walking-on-sunshine feeling disappear because it just feels so doggone good.

I lie down in bed hoping to catch a catnap but I'm too keyed up to sleep. Before I know it, though, it's time to head to the Bluegrass Dance Hall for the competition. We were given instructions to change into our costumes at the dance hall after Mac Murphy had an unfortunate ketchup stain incident last week. So I grab my costume from the closet, my duffel bag with my shoes, and hurry down to the limo.

Although we all smile and greet each other with hugs and well-wishes, there is an air of nervousness about us that is almost tangible. We're coming down to the wire in this competition and we could all use the cash. Before this I don't think any of us thought we would be so far along without being voted off and now the prize is within reach. Rio and I are the favorites but that somehow puts extra pressure on the expectation to be excellent. In some ways it sure is better to be the underdog. If you win, great, and if you don't, well, no one expected you to. Not that I'm complaining! I totally would have bet against myself.

Mac Murphy, as Rio said from the beginning, is the dark horse in this competition and his sheer size, his good sense of humor, and the total surprise that this trucker can really get his groove on make him a fan favorite. Both Danny and Julia are definite contenders but I think that everyone else is a total guess. I suppose we'll soon find out and because of the nature of the show anything can happen.

Once again the streets of Misty Creek are lined with cheering crowds holding huge homemade signs saying things like MAC, KEEP ON TRUCKIN' and DANNY, MARRY ME and WHAT'S COOKIN', BETTY? Oh, and there's one for me that says WE LOVE YOU, ABBY! I get a little excited to have some fans until I see that it's Mama holding up the sign.

Because only a couple of hundred people can fit into the dance hall, we were told that a huge television screen has been set up at Misty Creek High School where the town can gather as one big group to make it a more festive atmosphere. Mitchell also announced at lunch today that there will be a live camera feed to the television viewing audience just like they would do on *American Idol* . . . except of course we're all from the same hometown.

After hair and makeup we're once again lined up in the greenroom. Rio and I are smack dab in the middle of the competition.

"It's neither an advantage nor a disadvantage," he tells me as we sit and wait our turn. He holds my hand as if he's keeping me calm but what no one can see is that his thumb is rubbing little circles on my palm. "You look sexy as hell," he whispers in my ear.

"You look like Elvis," I tease. "But a very sexy Elvis."

"Thank you . . . thank you very much," he says, curling his lip while trying to imitate the King. I have to giggle at his accent. I know he's trying to keep my nerves under control but the truth is that I'm way more relaxed than I have been. I guess amazing sex will do that to ya.

"You okay?" Rio asks.

"Never better."

"Stop looking at me like that," he says in my ear, "or I'm going to embarrass myself in my tight Elvis pants."

It takes me a second to get it and then I giggle a little too loud for Jackie's liking. She puts her index finger to her lips. With an elbow to Rio's ribs I say, "You're getting me in trouble."

"Okay, put on your . . . what do you call it?"

"Game face?"

"Yes, that." He points to the monitor just as Ben Sebastian announces that Travis Tucker the farmer will be dancing the paso doble with his partner, Sasha Travinski. Now, whereas Mac the trucker somehow pulled off the whole matador thing, well, Travis just cannot. He looks ridiculous in the tiny jacket and he knows it. Bless his heart, he can't keep from smiling when he's supposed to be serious. At one point he misses reeling his partner back in and poor Sasha flaps around aimlessly on the dance floor like a red cape without purpose. When Travis realizes his mistake he puts a hand over his mouth and blinks in confusion. Sasha, the cape, tries to ad-lib by twirling around him in a cloud of red silk but the audience is on to the mistake and titters with laughter. To Travis's credit he manages to end the dance, whipping one hand across his chest and one up in the air, but Sasha the swirling cape gets clipped on the chin by Travis's hand and goes twirling and staggering backward, landing on her ass.

The crowd collectively gasps and, bless the hearts of Misty Creek, most of them refrain from laughing . . . except for a few, and I prefer to think they are out-of-towners. The camera pans over the judges' table and all three of them are bug-eyed and silent. Even smooth Ben Sebastian has his mouth hanging open.

Travis helps Sasha to her feet while apologizing profusely. She flexes her jaw but nods that she's okay and gives a wave to the crowd and they begin cheering wildly.

Rio leans over and says, "They are going to get slammed by the judges but they have the crowd in their corner."

I nod and feel both sorry for and proud of Travis at the same time. Poor guy probably wishes he were plowing a field about now. As predicted, the judges' scores are low, fives and one four, but enough votes from the viewers could keep them in the competition.

Next up is Jimmy Joe Porter, the plumber, who is totally inept but endearingly cute, dancing the tango. He gets solid sixes from the judges and a fine round of applause from the audience. Rio predicts that they will advance as well.

Julia and her partner are next. She's right in that the Viennese waltz is a bit on the boring side but the Mary Poppins and Bert costumes as they glide across the dance floor to "Chim Chim Cheree" seem to charm the audience. The judges are generous with technical phrase.

"Julia," Peter Kelly says, "there is a softness about you that was missing before and your execution was almost flawless. I give you a nine!"

Carson and Myra are almost as generous, both of them awarding Julia with eights. Julia gives them a radiant smile and a deep bow. I sneak a peek over at Danny and he's grinning from ear to ear.

My heart rate rises when Daisy Potter and her partner take the floor, because Rio and I are next. Jackie ushers us to the wings to wait our turn.

"You still okay?" Rio asks in my ear.

I nod. "Pretty much."

"The rumba is our dance, Abby. We can hammer this one."

I frown. "You mean nail this one?"

"Yes . . . that." He holds his fists out for our knuckle bump and then we stand and watch Daisy Potter the Piggly Wiggly cashier dance the quickstep. A faster version of the Charleston, the quickstep is sporty and springy and with the basic feel being *slow,* quick, quick, *slow*, quick, quick. Daisy does fine at first but the dance depends upon total synchronization and they suddenly run into some problems during one of the runs near the end of the dance. They are dinged hard by the judges. Daisy looks close to tears and I feel like marching over there and slugging Carson Sage right smack in the nose.

Then we're up. Ben announces our names and is it my imagination or did I just hear my mama gasp at my tiny costume? I refuse to think about it and smile for the audience even though I avoid looking in the direction where Mama and Jesse are sitting. We begin dancing while Pavarotti and Celine Dion belt out "I Hate You, Then I Love You" over the speakers that Mitchell had replaced since the other ones popped and cracked. As we dance, the crowd and the cameras seem to fade into the background. I sink into the song . . . feeling the heat, the passion without really thinking about the steps. The hip rolls seem to come naturally while I tease Rio and then withdraw. My feet swivel and I remain on the balls of my feet and my body never stops changing shape. I know that my gold fringe is shaking like no other but I'm not really concentrating on any of this . . . because all I can think about is Rio. I want him and I aim to have him.

Our rumba ends with my hand on Rio's chest and a near kiss. When the crowd roars and I smile into Rio's eyes he breaks his own rule and hugs me. "We hammered it, Abby," he says in my ear and then leads me over to the judges' table where we wait breathless but smiling.

"That was quite a performance," Ben says. "Congratulations. Judges, what do you think? Myra, you're up first."

Her huge hair flops and bobs as she shakes her head. "First of all, you totally got it that the rumba is danced for each other and not for the audience. I was blown away. Ten!" She flips up her paddle and the crowd cheers her on. I look over to Mama and Jesse and they are jumping up and down.

"Carson?" Ben asks. "Your thoughts?"

"Well," he begins in his clipped accent, "some of the dance was a bit unconventional . . ." When the audience boos he holds up his hand. "I wasn't finished, people. Although some of the rumba was a bit *unconventional* almost as if the dance was unrehearsed . . ." The audience boos again and he gets a bit peeved. "Hold your horses. I don't mean that in a bad way. It was as if the dance was a natural seduction of a man and a woman happening before our very eyes and not a practiced number . . . Now do you see what I'm saying?"

The crowd roars in approval and I see my mama put her fingers in her mouth and whistle.

"Sensual, charismatic . . . if there were flaws in the execution I was too caught up in the seduction to notice." He flips up his paddle. "Ten!"

My heart is racing and I smile at Rio. I can barely keep from jumping up and down.

"Peter, your turn," Ben says.

"Oh . . ." Peter says with a dramatic sigh. "Does anyone have a cigarette? Because I think I need one and I don't even smoke! Abby and Rio, you are too hot to handle!" He gets up out of his chair and peers down at the floor.

"What are you doing?" Ben asks and shrugs his shoulders at the crowd.

"Looking for scorch marks. That was amazing. I give you a perfect ten!"

Okay, I can't help it. I jump up and down. This moment just calls for it. Rio doesn't join me in my jumping but he smiles and draws me in for another hug and then swings me in a complete circle, making my hair extensions whip around and my fringe stand on end. After the applause dies down we float off the dance floor and head back to the greenroom where we are given hugs and high fives until Jackie makes us sit down.

The rest of the competition is a blur. Later, while trying in vain to fall asleep, I remember bits and pieces of the performances . . . Betty Cook tried hard but her moon-pie face couldn't pull off the cheeky cha-cha. Mac Murphy was solid and entertaining dancing an updated

fox-trot. Danny and Angelina rocked the house with their
sultry samba, scoring a ten and two nines, ahead of Mac
but trailing Rio and me.

Unless the home viewers disagree with the judges Rio
and I are once again the front-runners. As I slip my hands
beneath the cool side of my pillow and snuggle my head
into the squishy feather softness I have to smile. Who
would have thought that any of this was possible? Mama
has a beau . . . a sophisticated silver fox who Jesse tells
me treats her like she's made of spun glass. For Mama,
who has had to be so strong and work so hard, this is truly
wonderful. Julia Mayer and I are friends. How about
that? Jesse has a flock of girls mooning over him and has
a hidden talent for writing comedy. I'm competing in a
ballroom dance competition on national television for
fifty thousand dollars! I mean, come on . . .

And I have Rio. That's the cherry on my sundae.

My smile gets a bit dreamier as my eyes flutter shut.
Even though my brain is still racing, my body is too danged
tired to stay awake much longer. But as I sink into sleepi-
ness I'm thinking that, to top it all off, if Rio and I can
pull off the next dance, which is the freestyle, we will
have only one more dance before the finals.

I could win.

My eyes open wide at the exciting thought. For a long
while I stare at the far wall watching the shadowy play of
moonlight filtering in through the gap in the drapes. Jesse
might get to go to a college that he deserves after all. We
can spruce up the diner and maybe, just *maybe* I can go
to baking school and add coffee and desserts to the diner,
a dream that I told to Rio and no one else.

Rio. How will he fit in? Will he stay and be a part of
my life? Or will I just be a pleasant, perhaps amusing
memory once he is back giving dance instructions at his
studio in Mexico City?

I push the thought of him leaving to the back of my mind, telling myself not to ruin the magical evening with worries. Surely it will all work out in the end, right?

My brain is too tired to ponder such a complicated question, or maybe I don't want to face the possibility of failure or disappointment after coming this far, because I find myself once again drifting off to slumberland. Good thing because I just know that tomorrow Rio is going to rehearse without mercy . . .

22

A Kiss for Luck

"Okay, Rio, where's my Kibbles 'n' Bits?"

"Excuse me?" He gives me a confused glance up from mopping the sweat from his brow. Yes, *he* is even sweating.

"Well, since you're working me like a dog I thought I might as well eat like one too."

His eyebrows draw together. "You want to win this, right?"

"Rio, I was just kiddin'. What's happened to your sense of humor? You leave it at the door?"

Rio tosses his towel to the floor. "Abby, with the elimination of Daisy and Travis last night we are down to the final six." He puts his hands on my shoulders. "You have a real shot at first place. We have to get serious. Stay focused," he says in his firm instructor voice.

Although he doesn't say it I'm reading between the lines that we won't be making love again any time soon but I feel compelled to ask. "So . . . you're sayin' that we shouldn't *be* together?" I will myself not to blush but I feel heat creep into my cheeks.

He gives me a tender smile. "I don't think it's wise."

"It didn't hurt us when getting a perfect score with the rumba."

Rio rubs a hand down his face. "I know. Believe me, Abby, I *want* to."

"I don't understand. Then why can't we?"

He takes a deep breath and blows it out. "Because, you see, we're talking about it right now. I've been doing this for a long time and my gut is telling me that we need to keep on task. There is just too much at stake."

I would argue but maybe he's right. I owe it to Jesse and Mama to listen to his expert advice. But then a thought occurs to me and I say in a small voice, "You're not letting me down easy, are you? Because if you are, just say so and—"

In a flash he snakes his arm around me and reels me in for a hot, breath-stealing kiss. "I want to push you up against that wall and make crazy love to you until our legs give out. Does that answer your question?"

"Um . . . yeah."

"But we must save the passion for the dance floor until this thing is done. I think it will make our chemistry even more palpable, you know?"

"Do you think we can . . . ?"

"Keep our hands off each other?" He leans his forehead against mine. "Not really. But I owe it to you to try . . . *again.*"

"Don't do me any favors."

He laughs. "Ah . . . Abby, what am I going to do with you?"

"Uh, I think you just mentioned something about that wall . . ." I jerk my thumb over my shoulder.

He gives me a swift kiss on the forehead. "All in due time." He flicks a glance at the wall and moans. *"Ayuda de Dios mío."*

I don't ask but I think he was throwing a prayer up to God. Smart man. We're going to need it.

You would think that freestyle would be easier than one of the actual ballroom dances but in fact it's harder since the sky is the limit and yet we have to incorporate classic ballroom dance steps with new and inventive moves. Rio has decided that after my little break-dancing episode we would incorporate a bit of hip-hop and floor spinning into our routine.

And then there's the music. After listening to about a million songs we finally agreed upon "Here for the Party" by country sensation Gretchen Wilson to play up to the hometown—okay, I'll just say it, *redneck crowd*.

Finally we have to choose our costumes. Jackie and Maggie are technically in charge of this but Rio has strong opinions about what we will and won't wear. Jackie did her best pleading to us to do a character theme, but Rio resisted although he did give in somewhat by agreeing to wear cowboy attire with me in Daisy Duke shorts and a red-and-white-checkered shirt tied beneath my breasts. I suppose after my costume *last* week it will appear tame.

"Okay, Abby, let's get back to work," Rio says after I chug the better part of a bottle of water.

Rio might have said back to work but what he really meant was back to dancing until you want to weep. I do believe my butt has a blister on the left cheek from our hopefully crowd-pleasing, song-ending, break-dancing spin that we have done about a million times in the last hour. I have to admit, though, if I pull it off it's going to be sweet. *If.* It's sort of a redo of my near disaster. I slide through Rio's legs and then go into the spin except this time it's planned. Rio is hoping the irony won't be lost on the judges or the audience. The problem is that most of the time I go off all cock-eyed instead of the tight and controlled nifty little move.

"Had enough?" Rio asks with a tired grin.

"No, just one more time, *please.*" I put my palms together as if praying.

"You're pulling my . . . uh?"

"Leg?" I supply the correct limb with a grin.

"Yes, *leg.* I'm never quite sure although I'm getting better."

"Yes," I confess.

"Thought so. Hey, you're being a trooper, you know. If you don't win it's not for lack of trying."

"Thank you. What I lack in talent I make up for in moxie."

"You're more talented than you give yourself credit for." He looks at me tenderly as if he wants to kiss me and I stand there letting him know that I want him to but after a long, heated moment he says, "Well, I suppose we should call it a night."

"Okay," I agree with a nod but Rio remains standing there as if waiting for me to argue or plead with him about the no-sex rule being reinstated. I've decided that I'm prepared to do a little bit of both because this is dog-gone stupid. My pleading argument is going to be that being together won't hurt our dancing one bit as we've already proven. He will argue that there is more at stake now that we've come this far and I'm racking my brain for a rebuttal when Angelina comes bursting into the room like a little tornado . . . or maybe the Tasmanian Devil. Yeah, that's it. The Tasmanian Devil.

Angelina slides a glance over to me and gives me a curt nod before returning all of her attention to Rio. "Because there are only six couples left in the competition," she says in her heavy accent, "Mitchell Banks wants us to perform a dance to fill in the gap. I told him that our specialty is the tango."

"It *was* our specialty. *Was.* You danced your last dance with me a long time ago."

"But Mitchell said—"

"There's nothing in my contract that mentions dancing with you, Angelina. Find someone else."

She narrows her eyes but Rio doesn't see it since he's already turned his back on her. She turns the glare on me and I try not to flinch. She has some serious eye venom going on there. Not knowing what to say I simply shrug and this seems to annoy her.

"Pah," she says to me and I wonder if it's a Spanish cussword. Jesse has a dictionary that has cusswords in eight different languages and used to say them and Mama thought some of them were cute. Little did she know. I'll have to ask him what *pah* means.

"Right back at ya," I say and wrinkle my nose even though I know it's childish. Hey, I'm tired and cranky and can't have sex with Rio, so I can't help myself. But she just frowns like she doesn't know I tossed her maybe cussword back at her. With a little flip of her hand over her head she exits as quickly as she blew in here, letting the door close with a thud that seems to echo in the room.

I'm waiting for Rio to comment, hopefully with something like "that little bitch" even though I haven't heard him curse since he dropped the F-bomb the very first day unless he's been doing it in Spanish but he seems a little preoccupied with gathering up his things and my heart sinks a bit. "Does she still have the power to get to you, Rio?"

He turns around with raised eyebrows. "Is that what you think?"

I shrug. "I don't want to appear petty or jealous. But

I'm just a small-town girl and I want to know where I stand."

He comes over and gently tucks a damp lock of hair behind my ear. "Abby, the simple truth is that I don't want to dance with her. Angelina trampled on my young love and tossed me aside when I was no longer of value to her. But believe me, what I once thought was love I now realize was just infatuation. She only wants me back now because . . ."

"Because what? Because your knee is better?"

Rio hesitates a fraction but then shakes his head. "It doesn't matter. What matters is winning this competition. Now go get some dinner and a good night's rest, okay? Forget about Angelina. She doesn't deserve your time or energy."

I want to ask more but he has a closed, weary expression on his face, so I don't have the heart. "Okay." It's so hard, though, not to slide my arms around him and kiss the lines of worry away. He puts on this tough guy act but there's a vulnerable edge to him that shows in his eyes and squeezes my heart.

But as I walk back to my room I can't help feeling as if Rio is holding something back from me although, for the life of me, I can't put my finger on how or why.

Instead of going down for dinner I decide to have a tray sent up. I'm simply too tired to smile and make conversation. I kick off my shoes and wiggle my weary toes and then flop down onto the bed to call for some dinner. I hope it's real honest-to-goodness food and not some fancy stuff drowning in sauce. That done, I ponder calling Mama for no other reason than just to hear her voice but in my tired emotional state I might end up in tears, so I don't make the call. I ease back against the pillows and point the remote at the television for a little connection to the outside world.

After a few minutes of Katie Couric letting me know that the world hasn't changed much my food arrives. When I remove the domed silver cover I'm relieved to see that it's lasagna, garlic bread, and a nice regular tossed salad with mostly normal stuff except for the black olives that I pick out and put to the side. The aroma makes my mouth water and it tastes heavenly. Now if I can only stay awake long enough to eat it . . .

Rio is just as relentless the rest of the week and every night I fall into bed with my body feeling as limp as a wet noodle. When I attempt to fall asleep sometimes I feel as if I'm still spinning, sort of like when you spend a day boating and then feel like you're still floating in the water when you close your eyes. Yeah, I'm beginning to wonder if my equilibrium is permanently damaged when it really wasn't all that good to begin with.

So, now here I am standing in the wings at the dance hall in my Daisy Duke jeans and the bouncy pigtails that Rio fought against but Jackie insisted upon. He also battled against wearing a black cowboy hat but Jackie and Maggie tag-teamed him on this issue. I tend to get ignored in these situations but I finally butted in and suggested that Rio wear the hat for our beginning pose but then toss it into the audience as soon as the music begins. He agreed with a bit of a scowl and something muttered in Spanish.

Rio makes a really hot cowboy but, then again, he would make a really hot mailman. Not that there has been anything steamy going on between us other than dancing . . . Rio has stuck to the no-sex plan like Krazy Glue.

"Are you okay, Abby? You look tense."

"We should have had . . . you know . . . *sex*," I whisper. "That's why I was so loose and relaxed last week." I roll my shoulders and gripe, "Your plan is stupid."

He looks at me like I'm one wrench short of a toolbox. "This is not the time to get upset, Abby. You're going to lose focus."

"A little hanky-panky wouldn't have hurt," I say but no one wants to listen to Abby.

"Abby . . ."

Rio looks at me like the pressure has finally made me crack and maybe it has because I persist with, "A little roll in the hay wouldn't have done a bit of harm and I wouldn't have been lying awake at night wishing I was making love to you." I throw my arms up and say, "Now look at me. I'm as stiff as a board and I have to do that doggone spin and—"

Rio shocks me but effectively shuts me up by pulling me into his cowboy arms and kissing me senseless. Mercy, it's like giving water to a wilted plant. I lean into the kiss, not caring that my carefully applied lipstick is getting smeared, and forget about the fact that in just about thirty seconds Betty Cook will be finished dancing her wild and wacky freestyle dance to "The Time Warp" from the *Rocky Horror Picture Show*.

When Rio pulls back, leaving me a bit dazed he says, "That help?"

I nod but then hear a little squeal. Jackie and Maggie come running forward with their little touch-up kits. "What were you thinking?" Jackie hisses and frantically starts reapplying my lipstick. "Are you *crazy*?"

Maggie swipes at Rio's mouth with a tissue. "Put your hat on." He obeys but she adjusts the angle.

"I can't see."

"But it looks cool that way. Like Tim McGraw."

"Shh!" Jackie hisses even though we're whispering.

While we're getting touched up Betty Cook and her

partner are getting their scores. The judges were not impressed with their "Time Warp." Carson is especially cruel. "I found it inventive but a bit creepy," he says. "I give you a five." The crowd boos but Myra and Peter aren't much more generous with sixes.

"Next up are Rio Martin and Abby Harper dancing to Gretchen Wilson's 'Here for the Party.'"

Rio and I hurry to our spots and strike a pose while waiting for the music to begin. When Rio tosses his hat the crowd cheers. Because of the distracting, bone-melting kiss I'm relaxed and have a smile on my face. Although it's freestyle Rio incorporated a lot of cha-cha moves into the dance that fit the sexy, sassy song. The audience knows the words and chants along, giving us an extra kick. Knowing we have them in the palm of our hands, I put some extra Cuban motion into my Daisy Dukes and I'm rewarded with cheers and catcalls.

But the spin is coming up and my heart starts to race. *You can do this*, I tell my scared little self, and the look in Rio's eyes tells me the same thing. After a crossover break and a walk-around turn Rio releases me and tugs hard, propelling me through his open stance. I give myself an extra heave and zing through his legs and begin a brain-scrambling spin while Gretchen belts out "here for the . . ." and hangs on to the word "par-teeee . . ." When she sings the final word, "Yeah!" Rio grabs my hand, stopping my mad spin, and hauls me to my feet in one fluid motion.

The audience is on their feet . . . Some of them, my mama included, are jumping up and down . . . or maybe it's the dizziness but they're screaming, whistling, shouting, clapping, basically going nuts.

"Amazing! Simply amazing!" Ben's toothy smile seems to take up his entire face as he points the microphone at Rio, who probably knows that I'm dizzy as hell.

"Thank you. Abby worked nonstop on that spin. It was a risk since it's so difficult to control but we knew that with the competition winding down we had to pull out all the stops."

"The audience certainly was entertained. Let's see what our esteemed judges have to say. Carson?"

"Well, I have to say that I was leery when the song began but boy oh boy you certainly changed my mind in a hurry. You had some cha-cha with a touch of old-school disco and modern hip-hop. Excellent choreography, Rio. My hat goes off to you if you don't mind the pun. And, Abby . . . oh, Abby. Let me tell you that you can dance!" He whips up a nine.

"Myra?" Ben asks.

She waves a hand over her head and smiles. "I haven't been this entertained in a long time. *Dancing with the Rednecks* might have begun as a big joke but I am totally impressed. Abby, girl, you rock. Those legs were meant for dancing and I hope you never stop! Rio, you have taken this little waitress and turned her into one hot mama. I give y'all a ten!"

The crowd cheers so loudly that Ben has to wait for them to calm down before asking Peter his opinion. "Peter?" he finally shouts in order to be heard. The audience hushes in order to hear him.

Peter shakes his head and my heart pounds because I'm thinking that he's going to slam us. Of course the audience gets restless when he hesitates for drama. Peter is all about drama.

"Peter," Ben warns, "this is a live show. We have three more couples to dance."

"Sorry, but I was speechless there for a moment." He

smiles at Rio and me. "Do you know the last time I was speechless?"

I shake my head.

"Never. I do believe this was a first."

The audience collectively laughs and cheers.

"Rio." Peter kisses his fingers up to his mouth. "Excellent! But then again you are a champion and an esteemed instructor. It's to be expected."

He turns his attention to me. "Oh, but, Abby . . ." He pauses to put his hands to his cheeks. While shaking his head he says, "To see you blossom and burst forth with such passion! I'm moved! I'm astounded!"

"Peter . . ." Ben warns.

"Let me finish! I know I'm over the top but this dance deserves it. Abby, as Myra reminded us, this reality show is supposed to be a joke . . . something to laugh about and not take seriously. But the joke is on Comedy Corner because *you might be a redneck* . . . Oh, wait a minute, that line is taken." He taps his cheek while the audience laughs.

He stands up and shouts over the cheers, "You might be a redneck if *you can dance.* I give you a ten!" He whips his paddle from behind his back and I think I'm going to cry.

Rio must sense my oncoming tears because he whisks me off the dance floor, which is no easy feat since I'm still a little dizzy. We're supposed to go back to the greenroom but Rio breaks the rules and takes me outside where the cool night air clears my dizziness a bit.

He pulls me into his warm embrace in the shadowy parking lot away from cameras and prying eyes. I bury my face in his western-cut shirt. "Are you okay?"

"Yes," I bravely tell him but then floodgates open.

"Abby, are these . . . how do you say . . ."

"H-h-h-happy tears?"

"Yes, those. Are they?" He has that panicky what-should-I-do edge to his voice that guys get when women cry.

I nod. Man, he smells good. Feels so warm . . . "N-nobody ever gave me a standing ovation before."

"Not even for your mama's meat loaf?"

My laughter comes out gurgled from my tears. "You're developing quite a sense of humor. Guess you had to in order to put up with me."

"Ah, Abby," he says and rubs his hand up and down my back. "I might have taught you to dance but you showed me how to laugh . . . how to feel again."

I tip my head back to look at him. "We're quite a pair, you and I."

"That we are," he agrees and dips his head down to give me a quick but tender kiss.

This might not be the right moment but I decide that I have to tell him how I feel about him. "You know, after my daddy died everything I knew about my life changed in an instant. You must have felt the same way when your daddy got sick."

Rio nods. "It made me value my family."

"And you had to jump in and save your family business. We have much more in common than I originally thought." I'm about to muster up the courage to tell him that I'm falling in love with him but he interrupts my train of thought.

"Abby, about that. There's something that I want to—"

"There you two are!" Jackie shouts and raises her hands skyward. She angles her head and talks into her headset. "Found them, Maggie." She glances at me. "Yes, we need a touch-up.

"Have you forgotten that you need to go back out for the final recap?"

"Sorry," Rio says, trying to soothe Jackie's ruffled

feathers. "We only meant to step out here for a breath of fresh air. Guess we lost track of time."

"Well, you about gave me a heart attack! Get your butts back in there!"

When Rio leads the way to open the door for us Jackie leans over and says in my ear, "You *go*, girl."

23

Winner Take All

"Who invented this dance, anyway?" I ask while taking one of our few breaks.

Rio pats a small white towel to his forehead. I try not to notice how his sweat-dampened white muscle shirt molds to his chest but of course I do and I disguise my sigh as a yawn. The tender kiss in the parking lot is as close as I've gotten to anything intimate and we never did get to finish our conversation, not that we've had any free time anyway.

When we're not dancing, we've been doing photo shoots, one for *TV Guide* and one for *People* magazine. Yeah, I know! It's hard to wrap my brain around this sudden fame. Realistically I know that celebrity status will be fleeting but still . . . Mac, Danny, Julia, and I were all featured with a small bio in both publications and it will be something to tell our grandchildren, that's for sure. Jesse called yesterday to tell me that *Dancing with the Rednecks* was mentioned on *Entertainment Tonight* and that Jay Leno told a redneck joke about us on *The Tonight Show* and showed a clip of Betty Cook doing her creepy "Time Warp" dance dressed as Magenta the maid and her partner equally scary as Riff Raff the butler.

"You want to know who invented the quickstep?" Rio asks after taking a slug of water.

"Yes, so I can send them hate mail."

Rio chuckles for the first time that morning. "During the 1920s the big bands were playing the traditional quickstep too fast, making it difficult for couples to keep up. After a while a faster version was invented using some extra elements of ragtime such as the Charleston where we get the up-and-down swinging motion."

"Oh."

"More than you wanted to know?"

"Not at all. I think it's fascinating how these dances have evolved from all over the world . . . Cuba, Africa. It's pretty interesting stuff. I want ballroom dancing to stay a part of my life even after this competition is over. Jesse told me that there are already people in Misty Creek who want to learn."

Rio seems pleased by my answer and nods as he screws the cap back onto his water bottle. "I think Mitchell Banks had an inkling all along that this show was going to end up being much more than a spoof on reality television. He's drawing a much bigger audience than teenagers looking for a laugh on the Comedy Corner Network."

"He's a smart man."

"And I hear that he likes your mother."

"I know! They are such an unlikely pair and I'm not sure where it's going since he lives so far away and all, but if it's meant to be I suppose they will work it out."

"And you're okay with it?"

"You mean because of my daddy?" I ask softly. "I know Daddy would want Mama to be happy, so yes, I'm okay with it."

Rio sets the water bottle down. "Are you aware of how wealthy Mitchell Banks is, Abby?" He asks this sort of carefully.

"Oh, I guess I never really thought of that. Should it matter?" I ask, wondering just what he's getting at. "Are you saying that Mama isn't good enough for Mitchell?"

"Not at all!" He looks so taken aback that I believe him. "I was just . . . curious." Something tells me that there's more to it but he motions for us to get back to work. "Okay, time to learn the trick steps."

I gasp. "You mean we haven't done that yet?"

"Nope. And we have to work on our leg tension and the use of our ankles. Remember that it is slow, quick, quick, slow, quick, quick. The majority of the slow is on the heel and the quick on the toe."

"Right," I say and I realize with a smile that he makes perfect sense.

"Why the smile?"

"A month ago I would have been shaking my head in wonder but now I—"

"Catch my drift? I'm learning too, Abby. More than you know."

I wonder what he means by that but he points the remote at the CD player and "Dueling Banjos" starts playing.

"Wait. . . . That's what we're dancing to?"

Rio grins. "A bit of a risk, I know, but it fits my choreography and at this point we have to think outside the square."

"The box."

"What?"

"Never mind."

"I think the crowd will . . . how do you say? . . . *get into it.*"

"But 'Dueling Banjos' is so fast and gets even faster!"

"They don't call it the quickstep for nothing."

I'm still not sold on the "Dueling Banjos" theme. "What will our costumes be like?"

He clicks the music off. "Jackie and Maggie think we should dress in overalls so we look like . . . what did she say?"

"Rednecks?" I ask dryly.

"No."

"Hillbillies?"

He snaps his fingers. "Yes, that. She said we would look like Jethro and Ellie May and seemed to think that was clever. Does that make any sense to you?"

I nod. "They are characters from the television show *The Beverly Hillbillies*. It was a classic comedy from back in the early 1960s but can still be seen in reruns. The show was about country folk, or *hillbillies*, if you will, who struck oil on their property and moved to a mansion in Beverly Hills, placing them totally out of their element. It was silly, campy fun and the audience will get the joke. We'll be sort of spoofing the spoof. You'll be a character, Rio," I warn him.

He shrugs. "Sometimes you have to bend, I suppose. The trick will be to make the dancing amazing, to prove a point that rednecks, or hillbillies, as you say, can dance. Think we can pull it off? We can change it and go with something more traditional."

"I'm flattered that you're asking my opinion."

Rio takes a step closer. "I value your opinion."

"Thank you, Rio," I tell him with a little hitch in my voice. I'm used to doing what's asked of me and I've been happy to do it for my family. But I have to say that it sure feels nice to have someone interested in what I think.

Rio puts his hands on my shoulders. "Abby, not only are you beautiful but you're smart as well. You need to speak up. For instance, tell your mother that you wish to go to baking school. Let her know your aspirations and dreams about the coffee and pastries for the diner."

"You make me feel as if I can do anything," I tell him softly. "You really do."

He gives me a slow smile and for a heart-pounding moment I think he's going to kiss me. But instead he says, "I'm going to hold you to that. This routine is difficult."

With a lift of my chin I say, "Bring it on, buster."

Rio points the remote at the boom box and the banjos once again start dueling.

"Dueling Banjos" is one of those songs that once it's in your head you absolutely can't shake it. When we're not rehearsing, and granted that's not often, the song is bouncing around in my brain. I hum it at dinner without even realizing it. It annoys everyone including mild-mannered Mac Murphy, although I think it's really the pressure that's getting to the group. With only four couples left we know that this next dance has to be perfect. So instead of the usual banter that we've shared over the last few weeks, we all have our game faces on and pretty much eat our dinner in silence.

Finally I can't stand it any longer. I put down the forkful of sea bass and say, "I hate this."

"I know," Mac says, shaking his head. "I want a greasy cheeseburger and onion rings."

I shake my head. "Not the food, although that cheeseburger sounds heavenly."

"What, then?" Julia asks.

"I hate that we *all* can't win. That I'm in competition against y'all." I feel tears well up, and I clear my throat. "I'm sorry, I'm just a wreck."

Mac reaches over and pats my hand. "I promise to

harbor no hard feelings against you if you kick my butt, Abby."

Julia gives me a warm smile and then tucks her arm through Danny's. "What I've gotten from this competition is already priceless."

"Oh . . ." Okay, now I can't stop the tears from flowing. Julia dabs at her eyes with her linen napkin and the men are looking like they need to do something but don't know exactly what.

"How 'bout this?" Mac says with a bighearted trucker grin. "No matter who wins I'm gonna have a big ole pig roast out on my grandpappy's farm. How's that sound? We'll invite all the dancers and their families."

"That sounds wonderful," I tell him.

"The winner can provide the pig," Danny says.

"It will all work out one way or another," Julia assures me and by her expression I know that she is referring to Rio.

I nod, hoping that she's right.

As the tiring week wears on I begin to wish that the banjo and the quickstep had never been invented. During our Friday afternoon rehearsal at the dance hall the fatigue is getting to me both physically and mentally.

"Abby, you have to remember to smile. This dance is bright and happy. Your delivery has to be twinkling."

"Sorry, Rio. I'm trying but it's doggone hard to twinkle when my feet are killing me."

"I know," he says gently and draws me in for an unexpected hug. His strong arms and warm embrace are like a comfort zone that for a moment shields me from all of the stress and worry of the semifinals. Rubbing his hands up and down my back, Rio says, "I'm sorry to push you so hard but it's because I believe in you."

With my head resting on his shoulder I say, "I'm just so afraid of letting everyone down."

"Abby, that's impossible. Win or lose, you won't be letting anyone down. You know that, right?"

I lift my head up to look at him. "It means college for Jesse. Updating the diner . . ."

"Don't worry so much. It will all work out. *Trust* me."

"Rio, I appreciate your faith in me but I'm not so sure."

"Just trust me," he says and then dips his head and captures my mouth in a sweet and tender kiss. I think it was meant to be brief but when our lips meet we both lose our heads and suddenly we're kissing like I've been dying to be kissed all week long.

"Um, so sorry to interrupt your little . . . *interlude*," says the biting voice of Angelina. "But your time is up. Danny and I have the floor."

Rio pulls back but keeps one arm looped around my waist.

"Whoa there." Danny slides Angelina a don't-be-a-bitch look.

"Oh, how sweet. You have both the rich man and the poor man coming to your little redneck rescue."

"Angelina, that's enough."

I feel Rio stiffen in anger.

Wait a minute . . . I give Rio a questioning look. "Rich man? What is she talking about?"

"Oh, did I let out a little secret?" she says in a singsong voice and puts a hand over her mouth in mock horror. "You didn't know that Rio is a multimillionaire? He owns Starlight Dance Studios."

"I know." I frown at Rio. "In Mexico City, right?"

Angelina laughs. "Yes, and franchised all over the United States. My, *my*, seems like you are suddenly out of your league, little hometown girl."

I give Rio another questioning look, and his expression says it all. A cold knot forms in my stomach but I don't give Angelina the satisfaction of seeing my discomfort.

"You're a bitch," Danny snaps at her.

My eyes widen but he doesn't apologize.

"If I wasn't under contract I'd quit."

"Oh, right." She snickers. "And give up your shot at the money? I don't think so. Consider yourself lucky, Danny the mechanic. I'm the only one who can beat Rio."

Danny shakes his head. "Yeah, well, *you're* lucky you're a woman or you'd be picking yourself up off the floor."

"How very redneck of you," she purrs. "I find your crudeness rather sexy." She slides her hand suggestively down his chest.

"Lady, I wouldn't touch you with a ten-foot pole."

With a hiss she snatches her hands away. "Your loss, then," she snaps but looks a bit disappointed.

"Danny, don't let her get to you," I tell him, feeling responsible for this little scene.

Danny manages to grin. "Don't worry. We're doing the tango so I'm supposed to glare at her and believe me, it's not a stretch to do that."

"Enough!" Angelina says and gives Rio and me a shooing motion with her hands. "Off with you."

Rio looks like he's going to give her a piece of his mind, so I tug on his hand. "Come on. She's not worth it."

"You're right," Rio says and we remove our dancing shoes and quickly gather up our duffel bags to exit the dance hall.

Once outside in the sunny parking lot I turn to Rio. Trying to sound casual I say, "So, you own a chain of dance studios, not just one?"

He nods and has the grace to look a tad embarrassed. "When I took over for my father I felt so guilty that the studio was going under that I threw myself into the business. When it was back to flourishing it was just about when ballroom dancing was becoming popular again in the United States. I decided to franchise Starlight Dance Studios and hit the market at just the right time. I agreed to do this show to give the newest studios a boost. That's why I was so angry when I thought this was nothing but a joke. But, Abby, it's become so much more than that to me. Please believe me when I say that."

"Why didn't you tell me?"

"I didn't think it mattered."

I shake my head. "Rio, that's not true or you would have told me. Were you afraid I'd try to sink my claws into you like Angelina?"

"Of course not," he answers hotly. He runs his fingers through his hair. "You've got it all wrong."

"Yes, you're right, I do." I swallow the moisture clogging my throat. "See, I thought I could trust you, Rio. Just like you asked me to do. I thought I knew who you were but now I don't."

"I didn't really lie to you, Abby."

"You just conveniently let me think you were part of a small family business like me. I thought we had so much in common and now I realize that's so far from the truth. Angelina's right about one thing. I'm out of my league." I turn away from him and start walking, which is silly since he's the one with the car, but I have to get away.

"Abby, *wait*," he pleads and gently tugs on my arm. "I didn't tell you because I was afraid you'd overreact like this."

"You should have been honest. I'm reacting to your dishonesty, not your money."

"Really? Are you so sure about that?"

I think about this for a second. "No, you're right. This changes everything."

He pulls me in close. "It changes how you feel about

me, Abby?" A cool breeze blows my hair across my face and he gently brushes it away. "Surely you must know that I'm falling for you. Don't let this come between us. So I own some studios. So what?"

"Oh, Rio, I feel like a huge gulf has just opened up between us. I'm already having a hard time coping with the competition. This is just too much to digest." It hurts to tell him this but I'm feeling overwhelmed.

Rio nods. "I understand. You have to keep focused on the dance."

"Yes, I do. I'm going to head back up to the lodge to rest instead of having lunch in town."

"Do you want me to drive you back?"

"No. I'll catch a limo. I'll see you at the dress rehearsal."

He nods but doesn't let go just yet. "I'm *sorry*. You have to believe that. There were so many times when I wanted to tell you, and to have you find out this way was the last thing I wanted to happen. But it really doesn't matter." His eyes are so stormy that I hug him before heading over to the waiting limo.

But once I'm back up in my room I flop onto my bed and stare at the ceiling. I want to believe that it doesn't matter that Rio is wealthy. I mean, am I crazy or what? He's handsome and rich and he's made it clear that he's falling in love with me.

So why do I suddenly feel like the rug has been pulled out from under me?

24

Down to the Wire

"We can do this, Abby." Rio gives my hand a squeeze as we wait in the wings to perform the quickstep for the live performance. We're last to perform, which he reminds me is a good thing. The dance hall is packed to the gills and there is an air of excitement rippling through the audience. Jesse told me last night that tickets for tonight and the finals are selling for hundreds of dollars on eBay and that there isn't a room left in town.

I give Rio a nod even though my hands are trembling and my knees feel weak. I don't voice that I'm having second thoughts about our Jethro and Ellie May getup, especially when we're following Danny and Angelina, who are sexy as hell in more traditional ballroom dance attire as they perform the tango to "Roxanne" from the *Moulin Rouge* soundtrack. It makes me feel dorky in my tight jeans cinched at the waist with a frayed rope. I feel as if we should be doing a barn dance instead of ballroom. What were we thinking?

"Our attire is going to be unexpected and original, Abby," Rio says as if reading my mind. He's getting good at doing that.

While Danny and Angelina might be rocking the house, Julia, bless her heart, fumbled a bit while dancing the rumba and the chemistry with her partner just wasn't there. Mac and his partner danced to "Beauty and the Beast" dressed as Belle and the Beast. But while his partner was a vision in her yellow gown, Mac looked ridiculous in a curly mullet Beast wig, and titters from the crowd took away from the otherwise lovely waltz. I'm thinking that Jackie and Maggie were overdoing the costumes. I make a mental note to request something stunning for next week . . . if we make it. Danny and Angelina are sizzling and are going to be a tough act to follow.

When the song ends the crowd roars in approval. After deep bows Danny and Angelina spin closer to the judges' table and breathlessly wait for their scores.

"That was hot," Ben says and fans his face. "How do you feel about your performance?" Ben asks Angelina.

"Confident," she says with a lift of her chin. "We worked hard on our technique."

"Let's see what the judges have to say. Peter?"

"Yes, the technique was definitely there . . . the staccato movement, the emphasis on the head and torso. But I found the chemistry to be more angry than sexy. But perhaps it was just me." He flips up his paddle. "I give you a nine."

Angelina smiles up at Danny but he doesn't return the smile.

"Carson?" Ben asks.

In his clipped British accent Carson says, "I have to agree with Peter but to me the tango is an angry dance. I think they were perfect. Ten!" The crowd cheers in approval.

Ben turns his attention to Myra and she shakes her head, making her big hair bob. "Yes, it was *angry* almost to the point of danger. I felt it sitting here like a hot wind blowing in my face. Angry but smokin'-hot sexy. I give you a ten!"

"There you have it, folks," Ben says with his wide MC smile. "Now to a commercial break before we see your final couple in this very exciting semifinal of *Dancing with the Rednecks*!"

Rio and I hurry to our opening spot in the middle of the dance floor. The three minutes we have to wait seems like forever but then the spotlight snaps on and "Dueling Banjos" begins. I hear a collective gasp from the audience and a bit of laughter and I'm thinking that this can't be good but then again perhaps they're getting the irony of the whole thing. Pushing that thought to the back of my mind, I concentrate on the trick steps, trying to keep it light and twinkling . . . slow, quick, quick, slow, quick, quick . . . slow on the heel and quick on the toe. My Ellie May pigtails bounce and I try to keep a smile on my face but it feels a bit forced. Our synchronization and leg tension are working, though, and Rio's lead is strong and powerful, yet he's light on his feet . . .

Oh God, here comes the really fast part where the banjos play together and we do a complicated run across the floor. The crowd roars in approval and the smile on my face finally relaxes when I realize that we are nailing the hard part. We end with me perched on Rio's knee. My left leg shoots out and my right arm reaches skyward for our big finish.

The audience is once again on its feet. People are waving huge cardboard signs. Rio swings me to my feet and we take a bow and then spin in a circle, milking the moment for all it's worth. The disco ball spins, sending confettilike light spinning everywhere.

After the applause dies down . . . and I have a sneak-

ing suspicion that the last loud clap and whistle belong to
my mama . . . we head over to stand before the judges.

"Interesting choice of song and costumes," Ben comments. "Were you trying to make a statement?" he asks
and thankfully thrusts the microphone in front of Rio, because I'm still trying to catch my breath.

"As a matter of fact," Rio says while trying to slow
down his breathing, "yes." After another deep breath he
continues. "I have to admit that I was leery when I began
this competition. When I first saw the contestants, I
shook my head, thinking that this was going to be impossible. But as our costumes suggest, anyone can learn to
dance. Ballroom dancing is all about romance, love, and
strength of character. The people of Misty Creek have all
of that and more." He waves to the crowd and they cheer
like mad.

"Well said," Ben says with a nod and for once I think
his toothy smile is sincere and not just for the camera.
"Let's go to our esteemed judges. Carson?"

"First of all, I want to say that I'm in agreement with
Mr. Rio Martin. I too was leery and, while there have admittedly been some painful and hilarious moments, by
and large this show has proven that dancing is to be enjoyed by all. I began with my tongue in my cheek but I
was proven wrong."

"Okay, now down to business," Ben warns. "We're
live."

Carson nods. "Sorry to have gotten on my soap-
box. Rio and Abby, this performance was unique and
entertaining."

My heart starts pounding when he hesitates. That can't
be good. I hear a big but coming.

"The technique was there but there was something . . .
lacking. Abby, you seemed a bit on edge, making your
normal bubbly nature feel a little forced. While I under-

stand that we are coming down to the wire, this is where it all counts. I give you an eight."

The audience gasps. Rio slips his hand in mine and gives me a reassuring squeeze.

"Myra?" Ben asks.

"First of all," she says and comes to her feet. "I have to say that rednecks rock!" She raises her hands over her head and the crowd goes nuts for so long that Ben holds up his hands.

"I agree but we are live!" He gives Myra a look of warning.

Myra dutifully sits back down. "I've made no bones about the fact the you two are my favorites."

Oh no, another *but*! Rio feels it too, because he squeezes my hand harder.

"But this wasn't my favorite performance. While I liked the dance itself and even the cheesy costumes I too felt a lack of your usual zing. Granted, it's a difficult dance but as Carson says these are the semifinals. I also give you an eight."

Boos erupt from the audience. Out of the corner of my eye I see my mama on her feet with her hands cupped around her mouth. I don't know what she's hollering but Jesse pulls her back into her seat. He leans in and says something to her and she wags her finger in his face and then points at the judges' table. In other circumstances I would have found my mother's behavior amusing.

Ben raises his hands for silence. "Peter? Make it short because we're running out of time."

"Abby, you know I *love* . . . you." He draws out the word *love* while giving me an apologetic smile that lodges my heart in my throat. "But I *hated* . . ." He draws out *hated*. "The costumes. *Hated* the song."

"Peter . . ." Ben warns.

"Oh, *all right* already. I deserve my turn. Anyway,

beyond that the dancing was superb if a little lacking in emotion. You and Rio usually have that special something that heats up the dance floor but tonight, Abby, I felt you holding back. I hope that you do the very sexy rumba next week if you make it to the finals, because it is your chemistry that sets you apart from the others. Tonight, at least for me, you didn't have it."

"Peter, your score!"

My heart skips a beat as he whips up his paddle. "I also give you an eight."

The booing and disgruntled yelling from the crowd is cut short when they show clips of our dances for the home audience.

"Remember to vote online or call one-eight-hundred REDNECK with your votes. Combined with the judges' scores your votes will determine who will go on to the finals next Saturday night. Tune in Monday for the results. Until then this is Ben Sebastian . . . see ya!"

I'm shaking like a leaf and want nothing more than to hightail it out of there but Mama and Jesse are waiting to speak to us. Rio leads me through the boisterous crowd. Mama throws herself at me for a huge hug. "Those judges stink!" she says in my ear. "You and Rio were amazing and I personally think that your outfits are cute."

She pulls back for Jesse to give me a hug. "You're still solidly in second place, Abby. Keep your chin up. Next week is the week that counts."

"If we get there."

"You've been the favorites all along. You'll make it."

"Hang in there, Babycakes," Mama says and gives another hug so hard that my head threatens to pop right off. For a little thing she sure is strong. She backs away when others are pushing forward for pictures and autographs. I smile and pose until I think my face might crack. Finally it's announced that our limo is waiting and we are whisked out the door surrounded by big beefy guys talking into headsets. Overkill, but looks impressive.

Except for Danny none of us performed the way we wanted to, making for a mostly silent ride back up to the lodge.

"Whew, that was brutal," Julia finally mutters, shaking her head. Danny puts his arm around her and draws her in close.

"Tell me about it," Mac agrees. "Damn, that was scarier than a hairpin turn on a slick mountain road."

Danny chuckles and that sort of lightens the mood just a bit. When we reach Rabbit Run Lodge Julia pulls me aside. "Come on up to my room and we'll have a glass of wine. I know I could use one."

"Okay. Just let me change into some sweats."

I drag myself up to my room, peel off my tight jeans, and tug on some comfy sweatpants and a hoody. I slip on some flip-flops and head to Julia's room.

"Hey, girl, you doin' okay?" she asks and hands me a glass of white wine.

I shrug but feel a definite slump in my shoulders.

"Tell me."

"Rio's rich."

Julia almost chokes on her sip of wine and sits down on the bed. "Really? Like how rich?"

"I dunno. Millions, I think."

"And why aren't you grinning from ear to ear like this?" Pointing to her mouth she gives me a big silly grin.

I flop down into a fake leather chair. "Because it changes everything."

"I'll say. I'd be turning a cartwheel."

"I never could do one of those."

"Tell me again why this is a bad thing."

I let a swallow of cold wine trickle down my throat. "I thought he was like me . . . had a struggling family business! Instead he's this big tycoon with dance studios all over the danged place! And the worst part is that he never let on. He knew I thought he was a regular guy . . . well, aside from the champions dancing thing, but not loaded! He's not the same person I thought he was. It changes everything. I'm totally out of my league."

"Says who?"

"Angelina."

"Fuck her."

"Julia!" I burst out laughing in spite of myself.

"No, seriously. Say it."

"I *can't*!"

"Okay, then say *screw Angelina*."

I hesitate and then say in a rush, "Screw Angelina."

"Feel better?"

"No . . . well, a little. Seriously, though, she's right. I'm out of my league."

"That's a bunch of bull and you know it."

I shake my head sadly. "It was hard enough that he's from another country . . . sophisticated and all that . . . but wealthy?" I shake my head harder. "No way."

"Look, this week has been stressful. Learning that Rio is well off was a shock and yes, he should have been up front with you. But, Abby, he probably realized that it would scare you off and it seems like he was right. Take it from me, the longer you let something stupid go on, the harder it is to fix and it will get even stupider. . . . Wait. . . . Is that a word? More stupid . . . whatever. Maybe you should cut him some slack."

I sip my wine thoughtfully. "I'm just a small-town girl with simple dreams. I just can't see myself with someone so . . ."

"Filthy rich? Yeah, *that's* a problem."

"It is," I protest but it suddenly sounds stupid to complain about someone being successful.

Julia scoots up into a cross-legged sitting position on the bed. "Come on, give me the real scoop. Yeah, he sort of misled you, but *hey*, it's not like he was hiding a prison term or something. So he's a Spanish hottie . . . not so very different from us when you really think about it, and the accent is so danged sexy. Confess, Abby. What's the real problem?"

I take a sip of wine to avoid her question.

"Abby . . ."

"Okay! Not that those other things don't matter, because they do, but . . . *I'm scared.* I've really fallen for Rio and I keep thinking that when the competition is over and all of the hoopla and everything has died down, you know, when our fifteen minutes of fame is over? I'm afraid that he'll see that I'm just a small-town waitress and nothing more."

"Like that isn't enough?" Julia sits up straight and plunks her wineglass down so hard that I think it might break. "Danny thought he wasn't good enough for me once he wasn't the big football star. It's stupid. Do you hear me?"

I grin. "Loud and clear."

"Sorry. I get a little loud when I get riled up." She makes an effort to lower her voice. "Abby, don't *do* this. Rio is so into you. Can't you see that?"

"You think?"

"I know."

"It's damned scary giving your heart to someone." I play with the stem of my wineglass. "I guess it has something to do with my daddy's death. I never wanted to suffer the heartbreak that my mama did, and putting your heart out there does that."

"Oh, Abby . . ."

"I know. I'm going to tell him how I feel."

"When?"

"Soon."

"Promise?"

I cross my heart.

"I know, I know . . . you're not doin' the hopin' to die part."

I giggle and then polish off my wine. "I'd better get going. Thanks for everything."

"Hey, we're gonna stay friends after this is over, right?"

"You betcha."

25

A New Attitude

"I can't believe you got kicked off," I tell Julia while riding back up the mountain in the limo. We're hugging and blubbering while Mac and Danny say silly things to try and get us to stop. But when you get two southern women in hysterics you might as well give it up.

"Mac, I can't believe you got kicked off either!" I pause in my wailing to tell him this and then go back to hugging Julia.

"Hey, I'm not complaining. To tell ya the truth I've been missin' my rig anyway. And I've got women from all over the country wantin' to meet me . . . some even want to marry me," he says with a good-natured chuckle. "Since startin' this thing I've lost almost forty pounds. With my fame and new svelte figure I'm itching to get back on the road."

"Can't say as I blame ya," Danny says and gets an elbow from Julia.

When we pull up to the lodge we all hug since Julia and Mac will be leaving the lodge in the morning, although Mitchell announced that the entire cast of contestants would be at the final show next Monday.

"Good luck to you both," Mac says.

"You keep your promise," Julia whispers in my ear. "And good luck."

"You'll be rooting for Danny," I tease.

"Yeah, but it sucks that Angelina is his partner. And if you win that's cool too. The money would be nice but we'll be fine without it. Let Rio know how you feel, okay?"

"I will."

Letting Rio know how I feel is easier said than done since he's become all business once again and I become increasingly frustrated as the week progresses. By Friday I'm at my wits' end.

"Rio, we need to talk," I plead during a water break.

"I know, but we need to stay on task. We're so close to winning. The rumba is our dance, Abby. Let's stay focused."

"I didn't know that winning meant so much to you."

"Of course it does . . . for you, I mean."

My heart sinks. "Really? For me or do you want to beat Angelina?"

He tosses his plastic bottle in the trash harder than necessary. "How can you say that?"

"Is it true?"

"Of course not, Abby," he says gently. "We can talk tomorrow after the competition. For now we need to get back to our rehearsal. Let's start at the crossover break and underarm turn."

"Okay," I tell him, "but I really want to talk soon."

Rio nods and gives me a swift kiss on the forehead before we start dancing again.

I never do get my chance to talk to him, though, since right after rehearsal we have an interview with the local news. From there we're taken back to the lodge to rest up before the dress rehearsal that evening.

"Wow," I breathe as Danny and I enter the Bluegrass Dance Hall. The rustic bar tables and stools have been covered in white linen. Bud Light beer signs, the big moose head, the bass fish that talks, and even the dartboards have been covered in silky silver material that's been draped over the walls. "It's elegant!"

"I'll say." Like me, Danny is craning his head to take it all in.

"Come here, you two," Jackie says and hauls us back to the greenroom to do our hair and makeup.

"Where's Rio?" I ask.

"He and all of the other instructors came in early. They have a big group dance number to open the show. Mitchell wants to add glamour and of course keep the viewers waiting for the final dances from you two."

"So," says Maggie, "are you excited?"

"More like nervous as hell!" Danny says.

I nod my agreement. "Yes, tomorrow is *it*."

Jackie weaves my extensions back into my hair. "Has Rio seen your costume yet? *Very sexy.* I do believe I've outdone myself."

I feel a blush heat my cheeks. "No, I haven't seen much of him except for rehearsals and some of them have been cut short for photo shoots and interviews. Luckily we already know this dance, so it's just review."

"Well, the instructors have been working hard on this big dance number. It's going to be amazing."

I nod, a little relieved that he hasn't been trying to avoid me . . . at least I hope not. There's been something secretive about him lately that has me on edge. He's been on his cell phone a lot and even let it ring during our last few rehearsals . . . and took the calls! I finally had the nerve to ask him about it and he just shrugged and said that it was business.

I try not to let it bother me but I feel like he's pulling further and further away. It doesn't help to watch him dance with the other instructors and see how amazing he really is. In six weeks we've come a long way, but to watch the professionals dancing in a circular kaleidoscope of color is breathtaking. Because of my knowledge of ballroom dancing I realize that they are doing a small sampling of each of the dances, changing partners as they progress. When Angelina twirls into Rio's arms I feel a twinge of jealousy that she moves so gracefully . . . something I will never be able to do. As if reading my mind, Angelina looks my way and raises one eyebrow, hammering my thoughts home, and I suddenly have that awful awkward feeling I used to get at high school dances as I stood on the sidelines.

Insecurity washes over me like a cold splash in the face and I get a panicky feeling that I'm way out of my element. "What am I doing here?" I whisper. My hands get clammy and icy fingers of dread claw at my stomach. For a horrifying moment I think I might throw up. Hoping that some fresh air will help, I slip outside and take big gulps of cool night air. Feeling weak I start to lean against the wall but I'm afraid that the rough brick will snag my beaded costume, so I prop one hand against the building and pray for the feeling to pass.

"There you are."

I look up to see Rio approaching me.

"Are you okay?" His brows are drawn together in concern.

"No . . . my stomach is . . . *upset.*"

"Do you feel queasy?"

Ew, I hate that word. Just hearing it makes my stomach lurch. I nod.

"Was it something you ate, do you think?"

"Could be." Okay, that wasn't exactly a lie but better than telling him I'm never dancing again, at least in front of millions of people. No, make that never.

"What did you have for dinner?"

My hands are shaking and my mind is blank but I feel compelled to answer. "A meatball hoagie." Of course I don't really remember what I ate, if anything.

"A hoagie?" He shakes his head in confusion like a hoagie is a foreign object or something.

"It's like a sub sandwich," I explain even though I didn't eat one and I don't have food poisoning but I think it's better not to let him know that I'm having a panic attack or a nervous breakdown or that he's going to be dancing the rumba solo.

"So you think you can dance? We're next."

"No," I answer in a small pathetic voice. Not now, not ever, but I leave that part out.

"You should go back up to the lodge."

I nod. "I think so."

"I'll go with you."

"No! You stay. I'll be fine." Someday.

"You're shaking. Abby, I'll go with you." His look of concern is almost my undoing.

"No . . . just help me over to the limo."

He doesn't look convinced but nods and slips his arm about my waist. The limo driver is leaning against the hood of the car but straightens up when he sees Rio helping me.

"Everything okay, Abby?"

"She's not feeling well," Rio says, answering for me. "Can you take her up to the lodge?"

"Sure thing."

He opens the door for me but I hesitate before getting

in. "Will Mitchell be angry with me? Missing this rehearsal is a big deal."

"I'll take care of it," Rio assures me.

"Okay, thanks."

"Just get some rest. Do you want me to call a doctor?"

"No. I'll be fine."

He looks uncertain but I fold myself into the backseat. To my credit I hold it together during the ride up to Rabbit Run Lodge and long enough to take off my costume and carefully hang it in the closet. But then I dissolve into a quivering puddle onto the bed.

I really want my mother. I need her strength, her wisdom.

"My God, they're counting on me," I whisper into the darkness. "They believe in me and I'm letting them down!" I think of my mother, who at a young age was left with two children and a pile of debt. She was able to scrape together a decent living for us and here I am with the opportunity of a lifetime and I'm screwing it up.

Hot tears slide down my cheeks and soak onto the pillowcase. Ticked off at my sorry self, I flip the pillow over and finally drift off to sleep . . . and dream that I'm dancing. I know it's a dream because I'm me but a little girl and I'm not on the ballroom dance floor but dancing in a field of wildflowers . . . with my daddy. He spins me around and around and I'm laughing without a care in the world.

"Spin me again, Daddy," I plead in my little girl voice.

"You'll get dizzy."

"I don't care. I love to dance. Spin me again."

He does because he's my daddy and I'm laughing and twirling . . . with my eyes closed. I can smell the clover and feel the sun on my face and I'm so happy . . . but when I open my eyes my daddy is gone and I'm dancing alone.

When I wake up the next morning I remember the strange dream. I wonder if there is any truth to dreams having meaning. Try as I might I can't think of what the dream might be telling me. Life is short? Happiness is fleeting?

What?

My phone vibrating on the nightstand distracts me. I pick it up and look at the text message from Julia: YOU CAN DO THIS, YOU BIG CHICKENSHIT.

I toss my hair extensions over my shoulder and laugh. Danny must have told her that I skipped out of the dress rehearsal. With a squeal of determination I toss back the covers, swing my legs over the side of the bed, and sink my toes into the shag carpet. I wish I had some inspirational music to go with my sudden change of kick-ass attitude. Like the theme from *Rocky*, but for some reason the theme song from the movie *Nine to Five* starts playing in my head. I hum along with Dolly Parton, refusing to let my old insecurity rear its ugly head.

26

A Day Without Dancing?

I'm hanging on to my kick-ass attitude by the skin of my teeth while Rio and I wait in the wings to perform for the last time. It doesn't help that Danny and Angelina are nailing their reprise of the tango to "Roxanne" from the *Moulin Rouge* soundtrack and the packed house loves it.

When their dance ends Ben has a difficult time shushing the fans so that the judges can speak. I don't blame them . . . the dance was amazing and Danny was once the hometown football hero, so I guess I'm back to my underdog status.

"Terrific," Ben gushes to Angelina. There has been rumor that they hooked up last night. "I was spellbound."

Spellbound? I groan. "Give me a break," I say in Rio's ear. He grins and it's obvious that he is happy to see my old self back. "Yeah, that's right. I'm ready to kick some serious Angelina butt."

"Carson, what do you think?" Ben asks . . . and did he just wink at Angelina?

"Stunning! Ten!"

"Whoohoo!" Ben says and I wish he could see me glaring at him. "Myra?"

"Sexy! Danny, you nailed the rock turns this time. And your links . . . the sharp staccato movements were spot-on! A ten!"

"Pah," I say and I so hope it's a cussword. I never really did find out even though I've been using it. My heart sinks but Rio leans over and says in my ear, "We can get a perfect score too, Abby. We've done it before with this dance and you're even better now." He holds out his hands for our traditional knuckle bump and it hits me that this is the last dance for us. My throat clogs with emotion but I determinedly swallow it and lift my chin. "Let's do this!"

Because of the special night the lights dim to nearly complete darkness while we wait in the center of the dance floor for the commercial break to end. The candles flicker on the elegant tables and overhead the disco ball sends shimmering light over the silver walls.

"Now for their final dance in the *Dancing with the Rednecks* competition," Ben says with high drama, "I give you Rio Martin and Abby Harper dancing the rumba!" He rolls the *r* and it echoes in the room and then in an instant the spotlight illuminates our pose in the dark room. A hush falls over the crowd and then the beautiful Celine Dion and Pavarotti duet "I Hate You, Then I Love You" begins . . .

My heart is pounding but I look into Rio's eyes and let the beauty of the music fill my head. Soon the crowd and the cameras fade into the background. I let the sensual Latin dance take over my body. *Slow*, quick, quick, *slow*. I roll my hips, tease, and then withdraw while Celine croons . . . "I hate you and then I love you . . ." Rio draws me in for a near kiss as the duet crescendos with the powerful voices blending but then I spin away, making Rio chase me . . . wanting me more.

My feet swivel, causing the silver fringe on my costume

to shimmer. Rolling my hips I let Rio lead me into a walk and box combo and into an eight-count underarm turn, but my feet do this from memory while my body charms and retreats, teases and taunts until I give in to the love that I so strongly feel, letting Rio pull me in while Celine's and Pavarotti's voices blend together in the final few notes, singing "Anyone but you . . . but you . . ."

We're supposed to end in a near kiss but instead Rio captures my mouth with his while the spotlight fades to black with the final notes of the amazing song.

The lights flash back on and Rio spins me around to the crowd. There is a hush that has my heart pounding. *Why isn't anyone clapping?* Rio's hand tightens on mine and I start to tremble. But when we take a deep bow the audience erupts in thunderous applause. Rio spins me again and we smile and then dance closer to the judges. So I guess we were good after all?

Ben, who usually has a big MC grin on his face, is standing there holding the microphone blinking at us. Finally he says, "Wow."

I'm hoping that it was a good wow because wow can go either way.

Ben finally manages to give us a big grin. "Sorry. I was speechless and that's difficult to do. At the risk of sounding cheesy, I have to say that your rumba was beautiful. Abby, any comments?"

"I just let the music, the emotion take over."

Rio looks like he wants to comment but Ben turns to the judges, I suppose in the interest of time. "Carson? How do you feel about Rio and Abby's final dance?"

"Well, I have to say that I was amazed at the emotion. Technically there were a few glitches but the beauty of the dance overcame any flaws. I was so moved that I have to give you a ten!"

The audience cheers in approval as Ben shouts over them, "Myra?"

"Rio and Abby, if there were glitches in the technique I missed them because I too was caught up in the emotion. The first time you performed the rumba it was all about the sex, the sizzle. Oh, but this time there was something deeper and I was moved by your performance. I too give you a ten."

Rio smiles at me and squeezes my hand.

"Peter?" Ben asks over the applause.

"Danny and Angelina brought the heat, the sizzle, but Abby and Rio brought the love, the emotion. Both dances were a joy to watch. I give Rio and Abby a ten! I suppose the audience will have to break the tie."

"You heard it, folks," Ben booms over the roar of the crowd as confetti falls from the ceiling. "America, you must choose, so pick up your phones and dial one-eight-hundred-REDNECK or go online and break this tie. We'll be back for one last love show where the winner will be crowned and take home fifty thousand dollars! Until then . . . see ya!"

"I want to find Mama and Jesse," I shout into Rio's ear since the noise is deafening.

"I'll try," he says and we begin to weave through the massive crowd. Somehow, though, my hand slips from his and the crush of the people has the big bodyguards suddenly surrounding me. They part the way and take me outside to the limo where Danny is already waiting. Fans rush toward the car and the driver says something in his headset and starts the engine.

"We've got to get out of here before we're blocked in," he says over the speaker.

Danny shakes his head. "Crazy, huh?"

"Yeah." I look out the window and there are actually people trying to follow the limo. "This is unreal."

"You rocked tonight," Danny comments with a grin.

"You too! I wish we both could win, doggone it."

Danny shrugs. "I won't lie. I'd love to win the cash but I've already gotten something worth more than the money."

"Oh, Danny, I'm so happy for you and Julia."

He angles his head. "Thanks. But it looks to me like you've fallen in love too, Abby. Am I right?"

Catching my bottom lip between my teeth, I nod.

"I hope things work out for you two. Rio seems like a nice guy."

"Thank you. There are obvious complications but I hope we can overcome them."

"If you really love him don't let anything stand in your way."

I nod and then we both fall silent for the rest of the ride, both of us lost in our own thoughts.

Mitchell Banks declares Sunday a day of rest even though he advises us not to go into town for church services because it would just be a media circus. Not wanting to deal with that, I spend a quiet day in my room watching movies and trying not to be nervous about tomorrow night. After trying to contact Rio several times I finally realize that the little red light is blinking on my room phone and I hurry over to retrieve the message.

"Hey there, Abby," he says in that low sexy voice that sends a shiver down my spine. "I was called out of town for business, so I won't see you until late in the afternoon on Monday or even just right before the show if I get hung up. I tried your cell but it must have been turned off."

Damn!

"So just get some rest and enjoy a day without dancing."

"A day without dancing," I say with a bit of wonder

and I realize that although there were days over the past six weeks that I wished for that, I no longer do . . . especially if it means dancing with Rio. I might not ever be as talented as Angelina but like Carson said I make up for it with emotion.

Of course after the message I can't go back to watching *Ghostbusters* even though it's almost to the Stay-Puft Marshmallow Man part that never ceases to make me laugh. This makes me think of Jesse since this is also one of his all-time favorite movies, but I've already talked to him and Mama twice and I don't think I can take them telling me not to worry about winning one more time, bless their hearts.

So instead I lie on the bed and think about Rio and contemplate just what kind of business he's up to. Of course all kinds of things run through my head like he's seeing his secret girlfriend or has gone home never to return. After going through a million and one scenarios, none of them good except for the one where I daydream that he's buying an engagement ring for me, I drift off to sleep and dream that I'm doing the tango with the Stay-Puft Marshmallow Man . . . so I guess my day wasn't without dancing after all.

27

Sweep Me off My Feet

"The moment we've been waiting for has finally arrived," Ben announces from the center of the dance floor. The crowd cheers but then he says, "But first we have a special treat for you. On the big screen we have clips from the highlights of the past six weeks of *Dancing with the Rednecks*!"

I turn my attention to the huge television screen along with all of the contestants who are sitting here with me. After a big dinner together up at the lodge we were brought here via limos and of course the streets were packed with cheering fans both from Misty Creek and from all over who traveled here for the final show.

Donna Summer belts out "Last Dance" while we watch bloopers and crazy moments like Mary Lou Laker's out-of-control spin, Betty Cook's creepy "Time Warp" dance, and of course my break-dancing, saving-me-from-crashing move. There are arguments caught on film, weary-end-of-the-day moments . . . how'd they get Rio rubbing my feet? And tender tears when contestants get voted off.

Ben teases the audience again when the instructors

come out and dance . . . all of them except for Rio, who has failed to show up yet. I've gone back and forth from anger to worry and back again. Right now I'm ticked. How dare he not be here for this! And then I picture him lying in a ditch somewhere . . .

Damn him! God, I hope he's okay!

When the dance ends, the instructors twirl over to sit in chairs on the opposite side of the dance floor from where we're sitting. Finally, just as Ben announces that he is going to reveal the winner of the contest, I see Rio slip into his empty chair. He's dressed in a tuxedo like the other male instructors, so at least he got *that* memo . . . but what about the eight o'clock starting time? I'm going to kill him for this! But then relief washes over me. He's here. He's safe. Thank God.

"Now we're going to announce the winner of *Dancing with the Rednecks* . . . right after the commercial break."

"Oh, come on!" Julia hisses in my ear. "The suspense is killing me!"

"Me too," I whisper back.

After making us squirm a few more minutes, Ben raises the micophone to his mouth. "Now I'm going to announce the winner of the fifty thousand dollars!" Ben says and is given a slip of paper. "Wait a minute," he says, raising his hand, and the crowd gets restless. "Mitchell Banks, the producer of the show, wants to have the honors. Mitchell, come on up here and end this suspense."

Mitchell, also dressed in a tux with his silver hair slicked back, walks up and takes the microphone from Ben. "Thank you, Ben." He turns and gestures toward the judges' table. "And a very big thank-you to Carson Sage, Myra Jones, and Peter Kelly!" The audience politely applauds but there is a feeling of restless anticipation in the air.

Mitchell clears his throat and begins. "The margin

between Danny Becker and his partner, Angelina Perez, and Abby Harper and her partner, Rio Martin, was so slim that I didn't feel right awarding the prize money to either contestant, so after careful deliberation, I decided to split the prize money between Abby Harper and Danny Becker! So we don't have one winner but two!"

The audience hesitates, clearly wanting a winner and a loser, but one person begins clapping and suddenly everyone is cheering and whistling.

"Danny and Abby, come on down here!"

My heart is beating so hard and my legs are shaky but Danny comes over and assists me to my feet. I have to walk carefully in my long emerald green evening gown so as not to trip and end up as the watercooler clip of the day. My hair is piled high thanks to Jackie and Maggie, who both insisted on working on me, and a teardrop diamond that I get to *keep* makes me feel elegant.

Mitchell hands us each a big fake check to hold up to the crowd. Cameras, even though they were not supposed to be allowed, flash like strobe lights. I'm smiling from ear to ear, thinking that this tie's not as good as winning but not as bad as losing. I'm glad that Danny will have half of the money but there is a bit of disappointment that twenty-five thousand can't spread nearly as far as fifty grand.

"I have another announcement to make!" Mitchell says when the cheers die down enough for him to be heard. "There is a talented young man sitting in the audience. This young man is responsible for Misty Creek being chosen as the host of *Dancing with the Rednecks*. Jesse Harper, come on up here and take a bow!"

My heart just about bursts with pride as tall, handsome Jesse comes walking out onto the dance floor. He's wearing a nice blue suit and looks so grown up!

"In fact, I was so impressed with Jesse's comedic

essay that I've created a scholarship in his honor. I'm awarding him a full ride to the college of his choice in the first annual Jesse Harper Comedy Corner writing scholarship!" Mitchell turns to shake Jesse's hand.

I look over at Mama, who is beaming and dabbing at the corner of her eyes with a hankie, and I'm dabbing at my own eyes while itching to hug Jesse, but Mitchell says he has another announcement.

"Rio Martin, I believe that you have something to tell the residents of Misty Creek. Come on up here!"

Rio gets up from his chair and takes the microphone from Mitchell. Is it my imagination or did the women in the audience collectively sigh? Oh, maybe that was me . . .

Rio gives me a warm smile and my nerves relax a fraction even though my heart rate must be in the danger zone.

"Thank you, Mitchell. I have to admit that I wasn't happy to be a part of what I thought was going to be nothing more than a joke." He waves a hand toward the contestants and continues. "But I was wrong. In fact, I'm so impressed with this town that I've purchased the Rabbit Run Lodge and I plan on turning it into a ballroom dancing retreat so that people from all over the country can come to Misty Creek to learn ballroom dancing and to enjoy the other fine attractions in your wonderful town. One that comes to mind is Sadie Harper's meat loaf."

There's a collective gasp and then wild cheering goes on for a few minutes until Rio holds his hand up for silence. Since he has single-handedly given Misty Creek hope for a prosperous future, they give him his silence.

"Something else happened to me while I stayed here for the past few weeks. I might be a ballroom dance instructor but it seems that I was the one swept off my feet . . .

"Abby Harper, may I have this dance?"

I nod and walk into the now familiar closed position.

"Wait a minute!" Julia Mayer comes out onto the dance floor holding a sparkling tiara in her hands. Rio grins, so I know he's in on this.

Julia takes the microphone and says, "Abby Harper was never prom queen but I now crown her Redneck Dancing Queen!" She places the tiara on my head and gives me a hug while the crowd cheers.

A hush falls over the room, however, when the music begins and Rio and I glide over the dance floor like we're floating on air. I pass my mama and she's smiling with her arm linked through Mitchell's.

Ben announces that all of the contestants and their partners should come onto the floor and join us.

"Te quiero," Rio says in my ear.

I look into his deep brown eyes and needing no translation I say, "I love you, too."

Can't wait for LuAnn McLane's
next sexy and hilarious hoedown?
Read on for a sneak peek of

TRICK MY TRUCK BUT
DON'T MESS WITH MY HEART

Coming from Signet Eclipse in January 2008

"Oh, shut up," Sarah says as she shifts the Jeep into reverse. "I never should have told you about Ben." After looking both ways, she eases out into traffic. "Okay, your turn. Surely you had a Coyote Ugly night in the Windy City. Spill. We're twin sisters, Candie. You *have* to share."

"Yeah right, I would have been hard pressed to find someone ugly in the fancy martini bars downtown. It was the land of designer clothes and perfect teeth. Truth is, I never really fit in."

Sarah gives me a sideways glance but remains silent.

"What?"

"You sure look like you could fit in, with your sophisticated hair and polished ways. What the hell happened to your natural curls?"

"I tame them with a flatiron and a little bit of product." I reach up and touch my pencil-straight, chin-length bob. "Don't you like my hair?"

Sarah shrugs. "I always thought your curls were cute. The highlights are pretty, though. And I like how it's stacked in the back and angles toward your face."

"I hear a but."

"Okay, *but* you're a Southern chick and you should have big hair. You need your accent back, too. It's only right."

Sarah says this so seriously that I have to laugh. "My hair will get big on rainy days, no matter how flat I iron it, and I've already said y'all twice today."

"Humph," Sarah grumbles and reaches up to fluff her own big tresses. She suddenly snaps her fingers. "Hey, I know what'll put the redneck back in ya."

"A moon pie?" I ask hopefully.

"A longneck and a game of pool over at Pete's Pub. Whadaya say? I'll let you choose the first song on the jukebox. Come on, let's blow off a little steam and have some fun."

When she gives me her hopeful pout, I can't resist. "Oh okay. *One* beer," I warn, holding up my index finger. "I want to get up early tomorrow and visit Daddy before heading over to the car dealership."

"Sweet!" When we stop for a red light, Sarah looks my way. "Say, are you okay livin' in that four-family? I know it's kind of a dump. Daddy had planned on doing some renovations to the property, but that was before his health problems started. You're welcome to move in with me."

"It's a little rough around the edges," I admit, "but I promised Daddy to do some painting and gardening to spiff up the place a bit in exchange for the rent. Plus, it's so close to the car lot that I could walk if I wanted to."

"Well, the offer stands. If you're wondering if I'm still a slob the answer is no . . . well, not as bad as I used to be anyway. My cooking has improved since I *thought* I was going to have to cook for Nick until he dumped me. I'm a big Rachael Ray fan."

"Thirty-minute quick-and-easy meals?"

"You're a fan, too?"

"Yep. I love the Food Network."

"Cooking is something you and Mama had in common," Sarah comments as she pulls the Jeep into the graveled parking lot shared by Pete's Pub and Gayle's Glamorous Nails. "I still pretty much suck but I'm improving."

"Instead of cookin', I'd like to have the Take-Home Chef, Curtis Stone, whip me up a fancy meal," I comment as we pick our way over the lumpy parking lot. I'm wishing that I had on tennis shoes or boots instead of these dressy mules. My khaki slacks and pale blue oxford shirt aren't exactly Pete's Pub attire either, but since we're only popping in, I'm not too concerned about how I look. Sarah is a bit more casual in Dockers and a pink golf shirt, but in Pete's, you really need boots, jeans, and a tight T-shirt.

"I'd like that spiky-haired chef to do more than cook for me," Sarah says with a grin. "Like *be* the dessert. Might require a little whipped cream . . ."

"Sarah!"

"Hey, I'm just sayin'—"

"His Aussie accent is kind of a turn-on," I admit.

"And those eyes!" Sarah gushes as she opens the door to the pub.

"Oh I know!" I reply loudly so as to be heard over the music.

"Are we hard up and horny or what?" Sarah asks just as loudly, and as luck would have it, the music stops, making her comment heard loud and clear to a couple guys standing near the door.

"There's a cure for that," says a long-haired guy in a cowboy hat and Wrangler jeans.

"Oh shut up, Tommy," Sarah shoots back. "We're not *that* hard up."

Tommy chuckles, flashing white teeth. "Let me know if y'all change your mind."

"Don't go holdin' your breath," Sarah says but smiles back at him.

"That goes for you, too." While tipping his hat, Tommy winks at me with a good-natured grin.

I might have been offended if he hadn't been so young and cute. Besides, I remind myself we're in a honky-tonk, where the world isn't always politically correct, not to mention that Sarah just shouted that we're hard up and horny.

"Bud Light?" Sarah asks.

"Make mine a Heineken."

Sarah's mouth drops open. "I don't think Pete has those here."

"Just kiddin'. A Bud Light sounds good."

"Lord, for a minute there, I thought we had lost you to Yuppieville. Don't scare me like that. Be right back."

While Sarah goes up to the bartender for our drinks, I look around and acknowledge that except for a couple flat-screen TVs suspended from the wall, Pete's Pub hasn't changed one bit. Battered round tables with equally worn chairs flank one side of the room, and the long wooden bar runs the length of the other. There are a couple ancient pinball machines in one corner and a dartboard in another. To the rear of the bar is a separate room with three pool tables, which always have a wait.

I'm still glancing around when Sarah presses a cold, wet bottle into my hand. "Thanks." I tip the beer back and almost sputter when through the doorway to the back room, I watch a tall, jean-clad guy bend over to shoot some pool. "My . . . *my*, that is quite simply the nicest butt I've ever laid eyes on."

"Yeah, well that amazing butt belongs to a big ass."

"Okay, that didn't make a lick of sense." I flick a

glance at Sarah before my gaze is drawn back to the butt. Angling my head, I suddenly notice that the jeans are sporting a designer label. Guys from around here wear Wranglers or Levi's. "Don't tell me."

"Yep. That's none other than Carson Campbell, who is too high and mighty to do business with our little old used-car lot." Sarah spits his name out like it's something vile, yet I notice that her eyes are glued to his fine form as well.

Carson straightens up and turns so I can view his profile. "Wow." He's handsome in a Rob Lowe, almost too perfect way, and although he's dazzling to look at, I prefer men who are a little rougher around the edges. Someone a bit more . . . "Holy crap." My heart kicks it up a notch when Nick Anderson walks into our line of vision.

I shoot Sarah a look. Her eyes narrow and her lips thin before she tips her beer bottle up and takes a long drag.

Nick is standing there with one hand casually wrapped around his cue stick while Carson takes his shot. Nick is tall like Carson but more muscular, and there's nothing pretty boy about him. Not that he's not handsome, because he sure is . . . but in a "rugged, should be chopping wood, fixing a truck or tossing a football" kinda way.

Once I manage to pull my gaze from Nick, I turn to Sarah. The look on her face has me saying, "Let's get outta here."

"Not before I finish my beer."

"Forget the beer!"

"It's almost full!"

"Well, then, chugalug!"

"I can't chug a beer."

"Wuss. Bet I can finish mine before you."

Sarah rolls her eyes. "You're just trying to get me outta here without a scene."

"Uh, *yeah*. Unless you think you can stay without creating one."

"Does throwing my drink in Nick's face qualify?"

"Yes."

"Okay then. Go!" Sarah tips her bottle back and starts some pretty impressive chugging. I watch openmouthed for a second before tipping my own bottle up to my lips. I guzzle the beer, ignoring the brain freeze and the bubble in my tummy, which threatens to send the beer back up. I'm an athlete, and while this isn't exactly a sport, except maybe on college campuses, the competitor in me has me winning, even though Sarah had a head start. I thump the bottle down on a nearby table while Sarah is still choking her beer down. To her credit, she finishes without coming up for air.

"I win. Now let's go before they see us," I say while blinking from the brain freeze coupled with the sudden blast of alcohol to my system. I notice that Sarah is blinking, too.

"Give me a minute," she pleads with a discreet little burp behind her hand.

"No! Let's go!" I grab her by the hand and tug, but as we sort of wobble out of Pete's Pub, I can't resist a look back, which is a mistake because at that same moment Nick looks my way. Our gazes lock for just an instant but my pulse races, and it hits me hard that I'm not nearly over loving him.

When we're outside I pause to take a deep breath of warm summer air.

"Hey, are you okay?" Sarah asks with a look of concern.

"Yeah, I guess. I'm just not used to chugging a beer."

Sarah nods and I'm relieved that she buys my explanation, which is much better than telling her that it was seeing her ex-fiancé that set my stomach churning. When we reach the Jeep, she says, "Thanks for getting me outta there, Candie. I didn't want to cause a scene by dumping my drink on Nick. I've already given this town enough to gossip about."

"It's no biggie."

She looks at me from across the hood of the Jeep. "You know, Candie, I never really did understand your need to leave Pinewood but I'm glad that you're back. I'd never be able to save Daddy's car dealership without you."

"I'm glad to be back," I assure her with a smile. In that moment, I realize that it's not going to be easy whipping Daddy's used-car lot back in shape or dealing with my feelings for Nick but running away was never the answer to begin with. It's about time that I let go of my silly girl-hood crush on Nick Anderson anyway. While I'm sorry that it was Daddy's ill health that brought me back to Pinewood, it feels good to finally be home.

DARK ROOTS AND COWBOY BOOTS

LuAnn McLane

Not just another small-town babe...
Teetering on the Tennessee border, Hootertown,
Kentucky, suits beautician Jamie Lee Carter just fine.
She's the kind of gal who prefers longneck beers to
cosmos, bare feet to high heels, and Daisy Dukes to
Prada, but a bit of flash might still win out over another
pool-hall line dance. That's where Parker Carrington, a
hunky Hollywood producer, comes in...

Not just another Saturday night fling...
He's pegged Hootertown as an ideal movie site—and
Jamie as more than a sexy extra. He's adding sizzle to
Jamie's romantic slump and firing up something called
jealousy in Griff Sheldon, Jamie's brother's best friend
and her longtime crush. Now two hot-blooded rivals are
going head-to-head. One's got a Jaguar. One's got a
pickup. And only one's got what it takes to give Jamie
the ride of her life.

0-451-21892-2

LuAnn McLane

"An author to watch!"
—Lori Foster

LOVE, LUST AND PIXIE DUST
0-451-21950-3

Three new entrancing, erotic stories that are a little
bit country—and a little bit out of this world.

HOT SUMMER NIGHTS
0-451-21907-4

When the sun sets, temperatures rise. So turn up the
air-conditioning, pour a cool drink, and let LuAnn McLane make
your summer nights hotter than you've ever imagined...

WILD RIDE
0-451-21762-4

McLane takes readers to the Wild Ride Resort and theme park,
where the thrilling rides will have everyone screaming for more...